Praise for

Blessed Is the Busybody

"A well-crafted story with both humor and mystery. Emilie Richards has a writing style that reels the reader in with her first words. Aggie is a fun character . . . Any of Emilie Richards's books are keepers on my shelf!"

—*Romance Junkies*

"A delightful cozy that stars an amateur sleuth who feels as if she swims upstream against the tide . . . All comes together in this fine 'Ministry Is Murder' thriller."

—*Midwest Book Review* (five-star review)

"An absolutely delightful mystery that fans of Emilie Richards and anyone who enjoys light mystery will adore . . . This novel takes a clever and unexpected turn at its conclusion. It also marks the beginning of a new mystery series involving Emerald Springs. I think Aggie is just getting started with her sleuthing and if future adventures are as well-written as this one, we are in for a treat."

—*The Romance Reader's Connection*

"An enjoyable read . . . Any new book by this gifted author is cause for celebration."

—*The Mystery Reader*

"A cozy mystery with style. Aggie is adorable and her sleuthing efforts will fill the reader with admiration—as well as chuckles . . . Ms. Richards's characters are particularly vivid and all have interesting little twists that make them memorable and very real . . . A lighthearted and endearing read with a great deal of flavor and wit."

—*Roundtable Reviews*

"Fun and suspenseful."

—*Fresh Fiction*

W9-ASI-788

continued . . .

Let There Be Suspects

Emilie Richards

BERKLEY PRIME CRIME, NEW YORK

THE BERKLEY PUBLISHING GROUP
Published by the Penguin Group
Penguin Group (USA) Inc.
375 Hudson Street, New York, New York 10014, USA

Penguin Group (Canada), 90 Eglinton Avenue East, Suite 700, Toronto, Ontario M4P 2Y3, Canada
(a division of Pearson Penguin Canada Inc.)
Penguin Books Ltd., 80 Strand, London WC2R 0RL, England
Penguin Group Ireland, 25 St. Stephen's Green, Dublin 2, Ireland (a division of Penguin Books Ltd.)
Penguin Group (Australia), 250 Camberwell Road, Camberwell, Victoria 3124, Australia
(a division of Pearson Australia Group Pty. Ltd.)
Penguin Books India Pvt. Ltd., 11 Community Centre, Panchsheel Park, New Delhi—110 017, India
Penguin Group (NZ), Cnr. Airborne and Rosedale Roads, Albany, Auckland 1310, New Zealand
(a division of Pearson New Zealand Ltd.)
Penguin Books (South Africa) (Pty.) Ltd., 24 Sturdee Avenue, Rosebank, Johannesburg 2196,
South Africa

Penguin Books Ltd., Registered Offices: 80 Strand, London WC2R 0RL, England

LET THERE BE SUSPECTS

A Berkley Prime Crime Book / published by arrangement with the author

PRINTING HISTORY
Berkley Prime Crime mass-market edition / December 2006

Copyright © 2006 by Emilie McGee.
Excerpt from *Beware False Profits* © 2007 by Emilie McGee.
Cover art by Griesbach/Martucci.
Cover design by Annette Fiore.
Interior text design by Stacy Irwin.

BERKLEY® PRIME CRIME
Berkley Prime Crime Books are published by The Berkley Publishing Group,
a division of Penguin Group (USA) Inc.,
375 Hudson Street, New York, New York 10014.
The name BERKLEY PRIME CRIME and the BERKLEY PRIME CRIME design are trademarks be-
longing to Penguin Group (USA) Inc.

PRINTED IN THE UNITED STATES OF AMERICA

10 9 8 7 6 5 4 3 2 1

1

Given a chance to make a Christmas wish, most people ask for peace on Earth. This year, peace is high on my list, but maybe not quite at the top. In addition to the really important stuff, I'm also wishing for a personal miracle. I, Agate Sloan-Wilcox, the wife of a minister and theoretically something of a role model, am praying that Junie, my mother, will arrive in the middle of our parsonage open house wearing something, *anything*, straight off the rack of a Dillard's department store.

In a moment of contrition, I confessed this to my oldest sister Vel. An extraordinary cook, Vel knows instinctively how to season or spice anything and improve it doublefold. She had been blending cloves and nutmeg to make a mulled wine punch, but now she reached for a cinnamon stick and pointed it at me.

"Junie? You're kidding, right? Last December when she visited me in Manhattan I gave a quiet little holiday dinner. She wore a royal blue sari studded with rhinestones and embroidered with shepherds and Magi."

I had no trouble picturing this. Junie is short, pale, and Polish, but this has never stopped her from dressing like a maharani or geisha. To Junie, clothing is theater.

Of Junie's three daughters, Vel, with her ash blonde hair and gray blue eyes, actually looks the most like our mother, although she's a head taller and her features are sharper and stronger. But Vel is as cautious as Junie is reckless, as conventional as Junie is free-spirited. While Junie might show up at *my* party dressed as the ghost of Christmas past, Vel, an accountant for a Fortune 500 corporation, was already dressed in the ubiquitous uniform of her profession. Dark power suit, pale silk blouse, a simple string of pearls.

Vel shook the cinnamon stick in emphasis. "Junie claimed the sari was her personal rendition of Christmas night in the Holy Land. The Magi looked like the Grateful Dead."

Teddy, my youngest daughter, looked up from the platter of Christmas cookies she was decorating with colored icing. A green spot at one side of her mouth told me where some of the icing had gone.

"How can somebody wear a sorry? What was Junie sorry for?" Teddy is a first grader at Grant Elementary School and a collector of words. It's possible she's getting a head start on the SATs.

"Not spelled the same way. S-A-R-I," Vel said, always happy to instruct. "It's a length of cloth, usually silk, that women in India drape around them like a dress."

Since both Vel and Teddy are precise, logical creatures I knew a discussion of culture and clothing was on its way. As it picked up speed without me, I thought about the past weeks.

Accompanied by our youngest sister, Sid, Vel arrived two days ago for a family reunion. The reunion was Junie's idea. Unfortunately, she forgot to mention it to me until three weeks ago. By the time she remembered, everyone had their airline tickets, everyone except Junie herself, who twenty years ago envisioned her death in a midair crash and hasn't boarded an airplane since.

Even less fortunately, by the time Sid and Vel called to tell me their flight times, my plans for an all-church open house to spread Christmas cheer to our congregation were already carved in stone.

The open house is a necessity. My husband Ed is barely into his second year as minister at the Consolidated Community Church in Emerald Springs, Ohio. Last Christmas we were just settling in, and entertaining was out of the question. Things quickly went from bad to worse. This past September when I should have entertained the church board at a traditional Labor Day party, the chalk outline of a body was gracing our front porch.

Now it was time to make up to our parishioners both for my lapses as a hostess and our front porch drama. It was time to erase memories of bodies and near-death experiences. It was time to take back the parsonage.

I just hadn't expected to take it back with my screwball family on the premises.

Vel and Teddy had exhausted the topic of historic Asian dress, and I quickly routed the subject back to Teddy's grandmother. "Don't you think just this once Junie will realize that blending in is its own form of creativity?"

"Who's blending what?" Sid stumbled in from my living room where she had been busily adorning everything that didn't move. At least I was fairly certain this was Sid hiding behind the brush pile nestled in human arms. I glimpsed a green angora sweater and heather-toned wool pants. From what I could tell she had stripped the branches from every evergreen in a ten-block radius.

"We're talking about Junie," Vel said. "Aggie thinks Junie will have the good sense to try and blend in today, since a minister lives here and his entire congregation has been invited to the open house."

I love to hear my sisters' laughter. Sometimes.

After the noise died down Sid deposited her assortment of limbs by the kitchen door and stood back to survey the space above my cabinets, a showcase only she and Martha Stewart would consider embellishing.

"I thought I'd drape these along the tops. Maybe here and there I'll add those satin balls we tied in clusters last night. I still have some left."

I tried to picture this. Until now my cabinet tops have housed only dust balls, spiderwebs, and a collection of toothpick holders. My mother-in-law Nan started the collection for me and gives me another each Christmas as payback for marrying her only son. Fragile bits of china are the perfect gift for a mother with young children and a cat. I was pretty sure the latest addition was wrapped and waiting under the majestic blue spruce in my living room.

As she planned where to place the garlands lying at her feet, Sid wound her brown hair into a knot on top of her head. With only a twinge of jealousy I can say that Sid is the prettiest of Junie's daughters. She has the delicate features both Vel and I lack, a slender model's figure, and posture so perfect people invariably ask if she's a dancer. Sid, short for Obsidian, has eyes as black as the stone she was named for and a rose-tinted complexion inherited from her Irish father.

Men see Sid and they register the entire perfect package. Men see me and register my ample breasts and little else. I have Sid's dark hair and Vel's dimples, but no stranger who sees us together suspects we are sisters.

"You're going to need a stepladder," I warned. "We only have a rickety one, and it's going to take a lot of effort to haul it in here. You're afraid of heights."

Sid wasn't swayed. "You just don't want to clean up the needles."

"I'll only consent if you promise to accidentally destroy Nan's collection."

"Deal," Sid said. But of course we both knew she

wouldn't. The toothpick holders are antiques, and Sid is a great admirer of all things pedigreed and dignified.

Take Bix Minard, for instance. Bix is Sid's latest conquest and a reluctant addition to our family reunion. Boyfriend Bix wasn't in my house more than ten minutes before I'd been treated to a rundown of the many branches of his family tree, heavy with the fruit of Revolutionary War heroes and latter-day diplomats. As an encore I'd been gifted with a description of the family home in the Hamptons, where he was pining to spend the holidays with folks more notable than we.

We—the progeny of Junie Bluebird and her assortment of husbands—are definitely not notable. My sisters and I were raised at craft festivals and Renaissance fairs, wintering in campgrounds, ersatz artist colonies, and dumpy city apartments. Traveling back and forth from coast to coast we gained and discarded fathers, banded together to thwart our craftswoman mother, and developed the ironclad bond a more normal childhood would not have encouraged.

We know each other far too well. Vel and I have already predicted that Bix Minard will not be the last of the men Sid latches onto in her endless quest to feel settled and respectable. As if to prove our case, Bix went for a walk several hours ago and hasn't been seen since.

Finished with her preparations, Vel backed away from the stove. "Okay, I've combined the spices and cranberry juice, and I'm putting it on to simmer. All we have to do when people arrive is add the burgundy and keep it away from anyone under twenty-one."

"Shall we card everybody who walks through the door?" I thought this might be a new high mark in my approval rating with the church Women's Society. For the most part the Women's Society is made up of older women who meet during the day in what is mostly a historical reenactment of Women's Society meetings of a century before. Most of those who attend are warmhearted and generous, able to overlook my failings and those of my children. A few thrive on the details. I hope the open house will convince them to find a new calling.

"I'm done." Teddy slid back her chair, pale amber pigtails flapping. "I only decorated the ones that are real."

She abandoned the room before her aunts could question her. I walked over to peer down at the platter of cookies and saw that although the trees and stars were fully adorned, the cutouts of angels were as naked of frosting as the moment they'd emerged from my oven. I was left to explain this newest wrinkle in Teddy's pursuit of a workable theology.

"Remember when I told you that somebody on the school playground told Teddy there's no Santa Claus? Well, now she's skeptical about *everything*. Over the holidays she's supposed to write a story about angels, but last night she told me that since angels aren't real, there's no point. I guess she's extended the angel ban to cookies."

Sid slipped her arm through mine. "There's not much of Junie in Teddy, is there?"

She was right. Our mother is a great champion of angels. Of course Junie is a great champion of a lot of things: leprechauns, unicorns, anything that goes bump in the night. She's not a believer exactly; she's just eternally optimistic.

Sid disappeared to find the stepladder so she could plunk pine boughs and clustered ornaments among the cobwebs. By the time Vel and I had cleaned up our messes, the ladder had come and gone, and the kitchen was transformed.

Technically Vel, Sid, and I are only half sisters because each of us has a different father, but a childhood shared is more important than genetic code. Having survived together, we are closer than identical triplets. Now I felt a wave of warmth as I realized how much they had helped me today.

Warmth wasn't the first thing I felt when I realized this

family reunion and open house were going to overlap. I very nearly panicked. But now that the shock is over, I'm beginning to think it might be a lucky accident. My sisters have an issue or two to settle in their personal lives, but they are lovely, talented, and approachable. Sid has decorated the parsonage until it looks like a Christmas fairyland. Vel has spent the last two days cooking her generous heart out.

So what if our mother is a little unorthodox? If Junie comes in the midst of the merriment wearing nothing but a reindeer skin, there's still one chance in a thousand nobody will notice.

As she is prone to do, Vel took charge. "I think we ought to set out Sid's fruitcake and everything that won't spoil."

Although Vel is our gourmet cook, Junie made sure Sid and I know our way around a kitchen, too. The moment Junie announced this reunion, Sid baked a fruitcake, and it's a masterpiece. Her recipe is loaded with dried fruits, nuts, and butter, and for weeks the finished product has been aging in her Atlanta kitchen wrapped in a whiskey-soaked cloth. In the true spirit of Christmas, she agreed to donate it to the open house. This is one fruitcake guaranteed not to be recycled for years to come.

As Sid retrieved the cake I made my way to the dining room laden with dishes. Only a small portion of the food had been prepared by my hands, but as Vel and I heaped the table with spreads and dips, home-baked brownies and cookies, platters of tea sandwiches, and slices of fruit, I pictured my stock rising with the congregation.

I know it's not my mission to make everybody at Tri-C love me, but at least one afternoon a year, I don't mind making them blissfully happy.

The fruitcake arrived on a crystal platter I had borrowed from a locked closet in the parish house. Sid set the platter in the center of the dining room table and everyone in attendance applauded. Sid had studded the glazed top of the cake with fruit and nuts in the shape of holly boughs. If

Junie got here in time to see the cake before it was demolished, she would be proud.

Sid stepped back to be sure the platter was in the center of the table. "Did Junie tell the rest of you she's bringing a surprise with her?"

To appear as if I was involved in the preparations, I rearranged two of the dips so they were on opposite sides of a platter of vegetables. "She forgot to tell me there *was* a reunion, remember? What kind of surprise?"

"Vel? Did she say anything to you?" Sid asked.

"Nothing concrete."

Sid stopped fooling with the fruitcake and moved on to a platter of brownies, building a perfect pyramid. I expected to see Aman-Ra poking his head between crumbs.

"If Junie's bringing a surprise, it could be just about anything," Sid said. "Maybe we have a new father."

"Maybe she's delivering a herd of alpacas. Junie's version of a college fund for Deena and Teddy." Vel brought in the last of the dips and set them near the middle before gesturing to an empty space at the edge. "Have I left enough room for the sacred punch bowl?"

The bowl that matches the crystal platter is still safely packed in a box in the hallway, because it, too, belongs to the Women's Society. In the fall I destroyed its predecessor trying to thwart a murderer. The Women's Society claims to have forgiven me, but the subject still comes up now and then. It *was* an unlikely choice for a weapon.

Since I wasn't fooling anyone, I stopped playing with dips and vegetables and tried to sound prim. "The punch bowl is not sacred. Not in the same way a cow is sacred to Hindus or a tree is sacred to a Druid." I paused. "Of course Ed will need a new church immediately if anything happens to this one and I'm remotely involved."

Even a mere mention of the world's religions will pull my husband from the unlikeliest places. Ed, looking scruffy and sleepy-eyed, wandered in from installing the Christmas lights on the porch and pondering—I'm sure—which version of the New Testament to use for his Christmas Eve readings. Last year he used the Cotton Patch Version, in which Jesus is born in Gainesville, Georgia. He still gets questions about this.

Ed was wearing his favorite green sweater, which is older than our firstborn Deena. The corduroy coat he'd thrown over it is an orphan from the church's lost and found. His blond hair stuck out like the straw in the living manger scene at the local Catholic church.

He dropped a kiss on my cheek, tickling me with the beard I'd expected to disappear months ago, then stopped to peer over Vel's shoulder and give his approval. "I might need a new church if we don't get busy and finish the Christmas tree. We've just got an hour and a half before everybody arrives."

Since we had done everything we could in the dining room, we let him lure us into the living room. The room was so different after Sid's hard work that I hardly recognized it. All of Junie's girls are talented at making something out of nothing. These days I do it professionally, renovating and flipping houses with my realtor friend Lucy Jacobs. But Sid is the one who really inherited our mother's artistic talents. Professionally, she uses them as an event planner at an Atlanta-area country club.

Once again I admired glass bowls of polished fruit, willowware platters of pinecones and evergreen tips, red and green bows tucked in among books and family photos. Candles of every shape and size nestled in odd little spaces with rocks and shells, and discount store poinsettias communed in corners. Quilts and afghans Junie had made were folded over sofa backs, and plump bed pillows were wrapped in red and green calico and tied with ribbon like the gifts under the Christmas tree.

"It really is perfect," I told Sid. "But you've set a standard I'll never meet again."

Sid is not particularly sentimental, but at the praise, she slipped her arm around my waist. "No prob. I'll always be on call."

Despite Ed's fears, the tree was well on its way. Our garage sale bubble lights were in place, and Sid had tucked and wired tiny bouquets of red and green, silver and blue silk flowers deep inside the branches. Christmas trees were a big deal during our childhood. My sisters and I could never be sure where we'd spend Christmas, but we could always depend on a tree and a party to decorate it. I had passed on the tradition to my own children.

The moment the girls had waited for all day had arrived. I went to the stairs and called them to come down. Deena showed up first. My eleven-year-old daughter is poised on the brink of adolescence, although most of the time I'm in denial. Her skin is still clear, her figure is more American Girl than Barbie doll, but day by day, disdain for the adults in her life is growing. Luckily that disdain hasn't yet extended to her aunts. In the past two days she has spent copious amounts of time with each, sharing thoughts and feelings, bonding, and pumping them for information she can use against me.

Today Deena was wearing flared jeans and a red and black T-shirt with a scooped neck and too much spandex. Sid had brought her the T-shirt as a pre-Christmas present, but Sid and I are destined to have a little talk. I don't need reminders of what's ahead. Deena, with her strawberry blonde hair and adventurous spirit, is going to need as lengthy a childhood as we can muster.

Teddy arrived with Moonpie, our silver tabby, under one arm, so that he could supervise. She dropped him on the couch, where he immediately took cover behind one of Sid's gift-wrapped pillows. Pushing her glasses up the bridge of her freckled nose, Teddy came to rest in front of the tree. She's a hard kid to excite, our Teddy, but the thought of decorating the tree had done it. Her blue eyes were sparkling.

For a moment I found it hard to breathe. I adored every single person in the room. And how often can anybody say that?

An hour later I still loved them, although possibly a tad less. The girls had squabbled over where to place every ornament. Vel and Sid had dug out every memory of childhood Christmases including the one when our motor home broke down on an isolated gravel road in Arizona, and Junie made us decorate the tallest cactus in the vicinity. As he installed his childhood train set under the tree, Ed had regaled us with tales of the ancient Romans, who decorated with evergreens during the pagan celebration of Saturnalia.

But the blue spruce was stunning nonetheless.

I looked at my watch and officially started the countdown. "Thirty minutes until they begin to arrive."

"Haven't we forgotten something?" Sid pointed to the bare top of the tree. "Don't you have Junie's angel?"

Every year of our childhood, each member of the family made one ornament to add to our Christmas tree. Since I'm the only daughter with children, I was given most of Junie's ornaments along with my own. Add to these the ones my girls make each year, and our tree is one of a kind.

But each year the highlight of our tree is another Junie heirloom, a porcelain angel clad in ethereal lace, satin, and tulle, with gossamer wings laced with gold filigree. The year she crafted our tree topper Junie made hundreds and sold them at astronomical prices, though none of the others were as lovely. Every Christmas as a finale to the tree decorating party, the youngest child in attendance was lifted high to place the angel on the highest branch. My own family has continued the tradition.

"Teddy?" I turned to find Teddy squinting at the top branch where the angel should be. "You're the youngest today. Are you ready?"

Teddy folded her arms over her red corduroy jumper. "There's supposed to be a Christmas party."

"This *is* a party. Everybody's together to decorate the tree."

"No, the party is later. You said the youngest child at the *party*. When you told the story."

Last night I had reminded Teddy about our Christmas tradition as a bedtime story. I was sorry now I had been so precise.

"It's okay," I assured her. "This is close enough."

"No. It has to be a party."

"Then we'll put the angel on the tree at the open house." Ed lifted her into his arms for a hug. "But you might not be the youngest."

"Hillary has a star on her tree. Stars are real."

I thought it was too bad Teddy had chosen Christmas as a time for logic. Now that Santa Claus had gone permanently up the chimney, he'd taken an awful lot of childhood fun without leaving so much as a ho-ho-ho.

We were saved another go-round in the angel wars by someone hammering on the front door. Suspecting Bix had finally returned, I made it to the hallway just in time to see the door open with a bang and my mother appear in the doorway. Junie's short body was smothered by a gorgeous gold caftan with a pair of jeweled Aladdin-style slippers curling out from under them. The caftan wasn't from any rack at Dillard's, but I was so relieved to see Junie merely looked exotic, I wanted to weep with gratitude.

Then I heard Sid gasp. At the same moment she grabbed my arm.

"Oh, my God. Keep her away from me."

Before I could ask what she meant, Sid tugged harder. "I mean it!"

I realized Sid wasn't referring to our mother. Junie had stepped to one side and with a flourish, she had ushered in someone who had been hidden behind her.

Years had passed since I last glimpsed Ginger Newton, but there was no mistaking the young woman who was now standing beside my mother. I stared at cinnamon red hair, porcelain skin, and a smile so sweet my blood sugar launched into orbit. Ginger Newton, an all too frequent guest at our childhood dinner table.

Ginger Newton, the poster child for Sociopaths Anonymous.

"I mean it. Keep her away from me, Aggie," Sid whispered as her fingers dug ditches in my arm. "Or I swear I won't be responsible for the consequences."

2

Ginger Newton became a part of our lives when she was only four years old. That was the year Ginger's mother, "Fig," a stained glass artist, started traveling the craft show circuit, a circuit that ended twelve years later when Fig drove off a mountain pass in a Colorado snowstorm. The alcohol level in her blood hadn't been quite high enough to serve as antifreeze.

I'm not sure if Fig took one look at Junie and saw a soft touch, or if Junie took one look at ragged, undernourished Ginger and knew she had to intervene. Whichever way it happened, that first summer Ginger moved into our travel trailer while Fig tried unsuccessfully to piece her life back together. Fig created the most stunningly original windows I have ever seen, but her life was a sorry collage of broken promises.

Ginger, who had never had regular meals, bedtimes, or unqualified love, thrived on Junie's steady diet of all three. But Ginger had already learned that manipulation was the key to survival. Ginger looked at Sid, who had also turned four that year, and saw a spoiled youngest child who was not happy to share her exalted place in our family. Sid looked at Ginger and saw the most serious competition of her young life. Junie, who puts Pollyanna to shame, looked at the two little girls and envisioned a lifelong friendship.

How wrong can one woman be?

Now even as my sister's expensive French manicure made deeper inroads into my protesting flesh, I glimpsed a mental slide show of the problems Ginger had caused poor Sid, who is seven years younger than me. The mysteriously broken toys; the baiting that always ended just moments before Junie walked into the room; Ginger's pathetic tears when my desperate sister resorted to shouting. Then later, as Ginger repeatedly left and rejoined our family, the lies Ginger told Sid's girlfriends; the rumor about Sid that she started with the football team; the teachers who punished Sid for crimes Ginger had committed.

And *almost* the most memorable of all, the high school heartthrob Ginger stole right out from under Sid's nose. Just in time for the prom.

I'm as much a fan of forgiveness as I am of world peace. But I'm also aware of the odds. Maybe we're all technically grown-ups, but at times like this, I'm afraid we are, at heart, still the same outraged little girls.

Junie has a high, lilting voice that carries a hundred yards farther than necessary. Today it probably carried to Columbus. "Isn't this terrific? Ginger and Cliff live just outside Indianapolis. It was so easy for me to stop by on my way and guide them here. Cliff?" Junie turned and motioned, and a man appeared. "Girls, Ed, meet Cliff Grable. Cliff and Ginger were married last year."

A man in his mid- to late thirties stepped up from the porch. He was tall and thin, with a hesitant smile and ordinary features embellished with wire-rimmed glasses. I watched a prominent Adam's apple bounce as he swallowed convulsively. Cliff Grable, who was already going gray, was as average to look at as Ginger was extraordinary. Our pathetic, ragged four-year-old was now a voluptuous red-head of the Julianne Moore variety. Cliff was more Richard Benjamin than Brad Pitt.

Cliff stepped forward and extended his hand to no one in particular. I was closest and knew I had to be first. I wrenched my arm from Sid's grasp and stepped forward to shake his hand. "I'm Aggie, Cliff. Welcome to our house." Then, before my slide show could progress any further, I turned to my ersatz foster sister and took her hand. "And Ginger. It's been a long time, hasn't it?"

Ginger was dewy-eyed and breathless with emotion, but if it serves a purpose, Ginger can have a good cry over her grocery list. "Agate, you've hardly changed at all."

Junie clapped her plump little hands, all fingers of which were glittering with rings. "I just knew you would be so surprised. But how could we have a reunion without our darling Ginger?"

Let me count the ways.

I struggled to find something to say, but Ed, who has occasionally thrown himself between warring factions at weddings and wakes, stepped up to the plate. He introduced himself to Cliff, kissed Junie's cheek, then Ginger's. I remembered the last time Ginger and Ed were in the same room. Junie had invited Ginger to our wedding. Ginger had taken a fancy to one of the wedding gifts. Ed had quietly taken it back.

I motioned Deena and Teddy forward to meet Cliff and Ginger, but I didn't fall into the trap of introducing Ginger as their aunt. Since Sid is a healthy twenty-eight, there are a lot of years ahead when I don't want every sisterly phone conversation to begin with "I can't believe you . . .!"

The girls were polite to Ginger and Cliff and ecstatic to see their grandmother. With one at each arm they tugged Junie into the living room to view our Christmas tree. That left Vel, Sid, Ed, and me to face the Grables alone.

Vel, who always does her duty, stepped forward. There were no dimples with this smile, and her eyes were the color of sleet. But she put out her hand and murmured a greeting. Then she stepped back and waited.

Ginger's smile was cotton candy cloying. She held her hand out to Sid. "And Cliff, this is Sid. We grew up together. Just like twins. Sid, it seems like forever."

Sid's eyes blazed, but the manners Junie had drilled into us took control and she, too, extended her hand. The two brushed fingertips. I swear an electrical charge passed between them. Then Sid shook more naturally with Cliff.

"I'm afraid we're just about to have an influx of guests," Ed said. "In fact we have to change before they get here."

"Oh, Junie told us about the open house," Ginger said. "I hope you don't mind, but I whipped up a little something to add to your table. I've been working on recipes for my next cookbook. Have you had the opportunity to try Kobe beef?"

Even after a year of Emerald Springs, I'm not such a rube that I don't know what this means. I saw dollar signs piling on dollar signs. Kobe is the most expensive premium beef on the market, a product of a prime breed of Japanese cattle. I suspected that if Ginger was telling the truth, this might be the first Kobe beef to cross our city limits.

As for the cookbook? For once I can be fairly sure Ginger is telling the truth. For years Junie has told us about Ginger's success as an author and cooking show host. In the fall during my short career as a bookseller, I had ordered Ginger's first cookbook for a customer, although I had been afraid to try any of the recipes myself. Old habits.

Before I could reply Junie twinkled back into the room. "Oh, just wait until you see what Ginger brought you. I swear, she's made me a carnivore again. I've never in my life eaten anything so marvelous." Junie put an arm around Vel and another around Sid and pulled them to her. Then she released them and grabbed me.

It's hard not to love my mother. She's Glinda the Good,
Joan of Arc, and Georgia O'Keefe all rolled into one. Attila
the Hun would fall captive under Junie's spell. She has
never drawn a breath, uttered a word, taken a step that was
not 100 percent from her heart. She may look flighty. Like
many creative people her mind is a delicate butterfly that
won't light for more than a moment. But Junie's affections
are deep and genuine. Although she found she couldn't live
with any of the five men she married, she adored them all
and probably does to this day.

I hugged her hard, then let her go. "You'll be in Deena's
room. But I don't know where . . ." I glanced up at Ginger
and Cliff.

"Don't worry about us," Ginger purred. "Cliff and I are
staying at the Emerald Springs Hotel." She took his arm,
the first time she had touched him since their arrival. "We
don't want to intrude."

Nor did I want them to, but I'll admit I felt a twinge.
Had Ginger been my real sister I would gladly have found
room for her somewhere.

Let the guilt begin.

"Cliff and I will bring in our little delicacy," Ginger
said. "You scoot now and change your clothes."

I glanced at Sid, noted again the fury in her eyes, and
knew what the immediate problem was. "Junie," I said too
loudly, "let Sid show you her incredible fruitcake before
you go upstairs. I don't know if there'll be a bite left once
everybody arrives."

"My little Sid? A gourmet cook? Just like Ginger." Junie looked thrilled. I was afraid to look at Sid. Junie left for
the dining room with Vel and Sid in tow, and Ed and I
scrambled up the stairs to don our party clothes.

Once we were in our bedroom Ed tried hard not to
smile. I punched him once in the arm, just because he was
there and enjoying himself.

He held up his hands in surrender. "Okay, I was a

disadvantaged only child. Nobody ever wanted to kill anybody in my house."

"Disadvantaged my eyebrow! You're fifth-generation
Harvard." I stripped off my jeans and sweatshirt and
grabbed the black dress I planned to wear, picking Moonpie fur off the hem as I struggled to pull the dress over my
head. Immersed in a thundercloud of velour I could barely
hear Ed's reply.

"But I only got to imagine these kind of family dynamics. Think what I'm learning."

It was lucky for him that I had forgotten to untie the
belt. By the time I found it, and saw daylight again, Ed was
on his way downstairs properly clothed.

I couldn't believe Junie had been foolish enough to think
any of us wanted Ginger present at our family reunion.

Pause.

Okay, I *could* believe it. I'm sure that if and when the
subject comes up Junie will say she can't even imagine her
daughters are hanging onto childhood squabbles. And if
they are, then this visit is exactly what's needed to clear
the air.

Junie never gave enough credence to Sid's problems
with Ginger. To this day I don't think she understands how
badly Sid needed her help and support. But Ginger was far
too clever to misbehave in front of Junie. I'm sure Junie
saw Sid's complaints in the same light I see Teddy's. The
natural whining of a child who doesn't want to share.

Although we had fifteen minutes to go, the doorbell
rang downstairs and I experienced a moment of pure panic.
I had carefully planned this open house, choosing the first
day of the children's holiday break, selecting a time when
people who are still going in to work could stop by on the
way home, debating what to serve and exactly how much
of the congregation to invite. In the end I had decided in
favor of extending the invitation to everyone, assuming
that people will move in and out over the two-hour span of

the party. It's nearly Christmas, after all, and surely there are trees to decorate, presents to wrap, and carols to sing elsewhere.

Now I almost felt nostalgic for that chalk outline that had kept people away for so long. The house looked wonderful; the food was remarkable. My girls understood that this was an important event and we needed their full cooperation.

But I could almost feel the house trembling under the weight of suppressed emotions. I just hoped it didn't explode until the last parishioners were on their way home.

✦ ✦ ✦

As it turns out, I'd been given a short respite before guests arrived. Bix Minard had been at our door. I found him in our kitchen, pawing through the refrigerator to see if anything remotely appealing had appeared.

It's a measure of how much Sid values Bix that despite Ginger's arrival, she could still smile brightly at this new man in her life, a smile that didn't even dent his ennui.

I was sure Bix was starving. This morning our golden-haired guest had refused Vel's freshly roasted Columbian coffee—he prefers Costa Rican—my vegetarian sausage—Bix does not eat "fake" meat—and Ed's scrambled eggs. Our eggs, it seems, are not from genuine free-range hens. How he knows this without examining their teensy little chicken pedometers is the mystery of the day.

"Nothing much has changed in there," I told him. "But the table is overflowing. As soon as the party starts you can eat to your heart's content."

He glanced at me with all the warmth of Frosty the Snowman. And now that I think about it, our boy Bix actually looks a bit like Frosty. Bix doesn't have a carrot nose, but his does protrude noticeably. He may have been hot stuff on the lacrosse field at Princeton, but since his glory days, Bix has developed a Frosty-like paunch. Even his gray v-neck sweater, layered over a striped T-shirt and a crisply ironed dress shirt, can't hide the bulge. Then there's that *GQ* habit of carelessly flinging a long, dark scarf over his sports coats or jean jackets.

"I'll wait." Bix closed the door with unnecessary force. I wondered if his patrician stomach growled in Latin, or maybe Shakespearean English. It was another mystery unsolved. At that precise second Ginger walked into the room. Most likely the growling was from Sid's throat.

"I've never seen a prettier spread," Ginger said. "Agate, you have a knack for starting with modest ingredients and making something wonderful."

Ginger had been an annoyance in my childhood, not a thorn digging deeper and deeper into my flesh. I didn't go for her throat. "Think of it as the loaves and the fishes," I said.

She frowned, or close enough to make her point. "I didn't see any fish. There is a lot of bread, though. Cheap and filling. Always a good choice on a budget."

"Yes, and if I pick up enough cans on the street this year, maybe next Christmas we can afford butter to go with it."

"You were always so funny." She didn't crack a smile.

Ginger turned to Sid. "And what a fabulous fruitcake. I have another recipe you might like to try. Of course the ingredients aren't as easy to find, but I always say it's worth a trip to a gourmet market for the best."

She held out her hand to Bix before Sid could choke out a reply. "I'm Ginger Grable. Sid and I were raised together."

I watched Bix visibly transform from a sulking, slouching pain in the neck. By the time he had finished, he was passably debonair.

"Sid's never mentioned you." Bix held her hand just a little too long.

"I guess screaming in my sleep doesn't count." Sid took Bix's arm. "Bix, come help me tack up the mistletoe. I forgot to do it earlier."

I watched my sister drag Bix into the living room, then I

turned to Ginger. This was my house after all, and we might never be alone again.

"I'm all for you being here if you've come to make amends, Ginger. Or even if you're just here to make Junie happy. That's good enough for me. But make no mistake about it. I'm expecting you to act like the successful, happily married adult you are. Agreed?"

She looked puzzled. "We've all grown up, haven't we? Even Sid?"

The doorbell rang again, and this time I knew the party had begun. Funny how happy I was going to be to see our friends from the church. Twelve sopranos squabbling, eleven board members bleating, ten ladies lecturing. It didn't matter, bring them on. At that moment, I'd never loved my church family more.

3

Shared history is wonderful. My sisters will never forget that the scar on my left forearm comes from a bicycle accident in Topeka. Of course they will also remember that the bicycle wasn't mine, and I spent the next two summers frying funnel cakes so I could pay Junie for replacing it.

Vel and Sid know why I check the inside of my shoes before stepping into them—scorpions—and why I despise cauliflower. Here's a hint. One year during a brief stop in Santa Barbara, Vel and I decided cutting and packing cauliflower would be an easy way to earn spending money.

New friends are wonderful, too. They only know what you've told them, or they've managed to ferret out behind your back. Lucy Jacobs is my new best friend, and frankly, funnel cakes, scorpions, and cauliflower pale in significance to what we've shared. Lucy is even nosier than I am, and without her help, that chalk outline would be a ghost haunting us still.

These days Luce and I have formed a partnership, renovating houses to sell. Our first project, a Colonial across

Church Street from the parsonage, sold just days after we cleared out the junk, scrubbed and sealed the floors, installed a new sump pump in the basement and solid surface countertops in the kitchen. We immediately sank our profit into a turn of the century Victorian on Bunting Street that had been sitting empty for more than a year.

Lucy is a realtor, with the breed's eye for sales potential. I grew up with a mother who could make a home out of the rattiest digs with little more than elbow grease and imagination. Together Lucy and I took one look at the Victorian, which is zoned for both residential and commercial, and guessed that after expenses, we could at least double what we'd made the first time.

Lucy is good for lots of other things, too. Now, as I thanked people for coming to our party and accepted compliments on the food and decorations, I headed straight for her. Lucy was in a little alcove at the end of our bookshelves, chatting with one of the younger members of our Women's Society.

Even in a crowd Lucy is hard to miss. She has red curls she can't tame and the dream body of every Generation X woman. Yvonne McAllister is a friend and supporter. She's also a chain-smoker, and I could tell by the way her eyes kept flicking to the front door that she was ready for another hit. She excused herself the moment I arrived and headed outside.

"Nicotine fix," I told Lucy.

"She was leaping from foot to foot. How do you think things are going?"

I glanced around. People were talking. People were eating. No one had killed anyone yet, but that's why I needed Lucy's help.

"Ginger keeps eyeing Sid's boyfriend." The moment Lucy arrived I had explained my family dynamics. She, like Ed, was fascinated.

"I've been eyeing him, too. He's a loser. Can't you tell?"

"You know better than that. We don't get to decide."

"What do you want me to do?"

Actually, I was most worried about Junie. My mother has a heart big enough to include everyone in the world, no questions asked. She really believes inviting Ginger to our reunion is a gift to all of us.

I was not optimistic we were going to make it through the afternoon without a scene of some sort. I knew Lucy would have no luck keeping Ginger from ogling Bix, but she might have some keeping my mother out of the fray.

"Can you keep Junie occupied? And if it looks like trouble's brewing, can you keep her out of it?"

Lucy grabbed one of her long snaking curls and held it out. "I come from a family of redheads. Look at this. And we never have scenes like this."

"I'm delighted to share."

"What is it about Christmas that does this?"

"You can't blame it on Mary and Joseph. Sid and Ginger would act this way if it was National Kite Flying Day. Can you help me here?"

She must have heard my frustration. Lucy tsk-tsked a time or two, then waltzed off to find Junie. And how hard could that be? Junie's caftan lit up even the darkest corner.

I wasn't sure where to go next, but Sid found me before I could decide.

"Don't start," I said, holding up my hands. "I told Ginger to act like a grown-up. It's up to you now. Can't you just ignore her?"

Normally Sid looks like a twenty-first-century Botticelli angel, but now she looked more like something from Dante's fifth circle of Hell. *"The souls of those that anger overcame."*

"If I ignore her, she'll just keep escalating!" Sid said. "Don't you get it? She thrives on hurting me. She's some kind of emotional vampire."

This was true, of course, which was the reason I really

couldn't jump all over poor Sid. But it was also true that
the only way Sid could stop the cycle was to find a way to
move beyond Ginger's abuse. I didn't know how to help
her there.

I did my best. "Just keep your head down, and maybe
she'll go find another neck to sink her fangs in."

"At least *I* know *why* she's here. Didn't you wonder?"

The question had crossed my mind. I was hoping she
had come out of genuine affection for Junie, but I wasn't
counting on it.

"I'll tell you why," Sid said before I could answer. "Junie won a big award at the international quilt show in
Houston last month. Did you know?"

Quilts are Junie's most recent artistic endeavor. She's
been quilting for a while now, and I don't think she plans to
move on anytime soon. She seems to have found her
medium.

"I didn't know," I said. "Junie never thinks to brag about
herself."

"Well, she just told me her quilt won a prize, then some
corporation bought it to hang in their offices. She came
away with a lot of money!"

I saw where Sid was heading. "So you think Ginger
found out about this somehow? How? I don't see her sub-
scribing to *Sew and Know*."

"I imagine Junie stopped in Indianapolis to persuade
her to come here, the subject came up, and wham, Ginger
was suddenly interested in our reunion."

I wondered if even Ginger was that devious. How much
money were we talking about here? Enough to make the
drive to Emerald Springs in the winter? Enough to face old
enemies who know her for the woman she is?

"I hate to throw myself in the middle of a family feud," I
said, "but I would very much appreciate it if you and Ginger
wouldn't catfight about Junie's money until say, dinner-
time? If we could just get through the open house? Please?"

Contrition defused Sid's anger just a crumb. She sighed. "I know."

"Take Bix somewhere. Go for a ride. Feed him grilled cheese at Lana's Lunch. Tell him the cows are fed on pesticide-free clover and gently herded by Costa Rican milkmaids. You have my heartfelt assurances deserting the party will be okay."

"I'll see if I can pry him from Ginger's side."

I couldn't help myself. "You know you can do better, don't you?"

She whirled, her eyes narrowed. "You never like the men I bring home!"

I couldn't refute it. Ed and I have been married longer than all of Junie's marriages put together. So far neither Sid nor Vel have caught on to choosing men for whom marriage is an acceptable goal. But clearly they come by their confusion honestly.

I touched her arm. "Let me arrange a marriage. It's the best way. You and Vel can sing 'Matchmaker, Matchmaker.' It'll bring you closer."

She couldn't stay mad at me—she had Ginger for that. "You are certifiable, Aggie."

I watched her wend her way toward Bix-the-prick before I wound mine to the front door to greet more of our guests.

I was gratified by the turnout. If people worried they were taking their life in their hands walking into the parsonage, they didn't show it. Bells jingled on corsages; battery-powered Christmas tree ties and Rudolph socks provided spontaneous, festive carols. My arms were filled with gifts of homemade cookies and bottles of wine that had not arrived via the discount bin at Krogers. Six members of the choir were singing "Angels We Have Heard on High" in the hallway where Teddy, in a blinking Santa hat, was stationed to usher people inside.

For a moment all seemed right with the world.

Then the door opened and Fern and Samuel Booth pushed their way past my darling Teddy, followed by their hapless son and daughter-in-law and worst of all, baby Shirley.

Every minister has his or her detractors. Dealing with them is one of those subjects seminaries don't teach. Sometimes the detractors are powerful, and sometimes they're clueless. Often they have unresolved issues with authority figures, usually parents. Sometimes I think they just make trouble for the fun of it. Sometimes, sadly, they are right.

In the fall the Booths took over as Ed's greatest detractors when a woman who tried valiantly to fire my husband disappeared forever from the Emerald Springs scene. She'd had her own reasons, which hadn't had anything to do with Ed, but that little fact seems to have bypassed the Booths. They are watching, waiting, and hoping for Ed to slip up. I know the signs.

Potbellied Samuel Booth is more or less a cipher. Fern is the voice of authority in the family. She's a square-faced woman with a Dutch-boy bob and eyebrows that form a solid, unforgiving line.

Howard Booth, their son, must be an adopted child, because he's a foot taller than either of his parents and has a face that was clearly pleasing enough to attract Mabyn, his wife.

Mabyn is what's known as a catch. She's petite, with shiny chocolate-colored hair, flawelss pale skin, and outstanding fashion sense. Today she was wearing a black dress topped with a delicately beaded gold sweater that had just a hint of shimmer. I would love to go shopping with Mabyn.

Actually I'd settle for just having enough money to go shopping with Mabyn.

Then there's little Shirley. Maybe Howard Booth isn't adopted after all, because at eighteen months Shirley is already the spitting image of Fern. I really love children. If

Ed didn't expect to see me sitting in a pew, I'd cuddle babies on Sunday mornings. Or I would if Shirley Booth weren't among them. Unfortunately little Shirley resembles her grandma in every possible way.

Right now Shirley was dressed in green organdy with a red velvet bow clipped to a black topknot. She was squealing furiously. Had she been my daughter I'd have eased her out of the stiff, itchy dress in a heartbeat, but she wasn't mine. And Mabyn looked as if she wished Shirley wasn't hers, either.

"Welcome," I said pleasantly. "I'm so glad you could come."

Of course Fern did the talking. "Yes, well, considering everything that's gone on here, it's nice to see the parsonage in happier times."

"Yes, isn't it?" I smiled. I had the feeling I'd have to slap my cheek three or four times to melt back to a normal expression.

But Fern was ignoring me. She had turned her churlishness on her daughter-in-law. "Mabyn, can't you stop that child from fussing?"

Mabyn looked suitably cowed. I felt a spark of camaraderie. "We've got all kinds of goodies in the other room," I told Mabyn. "I know there'll be something Shirley will like. Why don't I clear a path for you?"

"I think we know where the dining room is," Fern said. "You're not the first family to live in *our* parsonage."

Since this was "our" parsonage, I wanted to ask why Fern didn't help me scrub and wax the antique linoleum floor in the kitchen. I'd been promised a new one, but it had yet to materialize. Meantime I threw biweekly paste wax parties, but nobody came.

I stepped back, smile still firmly in place, and resisted the urge to remove the flailing Shirley from her mother's arms and tuck her into Teddy's bed for a nap.

The stream of partygoers slowed to a dribble, and the

carolers moved off toward the punch bowl, now brimming with Vel's spectacular nonalcoholic eggnog. Arteries might clot today, but no eggnog imbibers would stumble out my door.

I went into the living room and found poor Cliff looking lost beside our Christmas tree. I hadn't seen him with Ginger at any point during the party. When not pursuing Bix, Ginger was busy introducing herself to every male in attendance as my "special little sister," and no matter how old the men, they were clearly appreciative of her efforts. Although I hadn't yet had a chance to talk to him, Cliff didn't look like a man who would be comfortable introducing himself to anyone.

I whisked into the dining room and stole two cups of eggnog, then made it back out again before Fern could corner me for a lengthy critique of everything from my salted nuts to Sid's taffeta bows.

"Here," I told Cliff when I found him again. "You look like you need it."

"I'm afraid I don't drink."

I smiled. This was a plus considering the fate of Ginger's mother. "You're safe with that."

He looked pleased, more because I was talking to him than because the eggnog was alcohol free. I felt a stab of warmth for the guy. Cliff was not the man I expected Ginger to choose as a husband. He seemed too nice and, well, too ordinary. I was curious—so what's new?

"Tell me about you." I raised my crystal cup to tap his. "How did you and Ginger meet?"

"At a party." His first sip of eggnog left a streak over his top lip. "I couldn't believe she noticed me."

Me neither, although, of course, I didn't say so. "And you've been married . . . ?"

"More than a year."

"Well, congratulations." I wanted to welcome him to the family, but I couldn't force out the words.

"That a real antique, isn't it?" Cliff gestured to Ed's train set that circled our lovely blue spruce.

"It was Ed's father's. It doesn't work, but we put it up every year."

"I can get it working." He smiled. Cliff has even, white teeth, and for a moment I saw maybe a hint of what had attracted Ginger. "I know a lot about electronics," he said.

We gazed down at the set together. I don't know anything about trains, but Ed's told the girls about this one so many times I have the spiel memorized. It's a Lionel O-gauge passenger train, with a steam locomotive that once tooted merrily, two passenger cars, and an observation car. The cars are bright red and the engine is a rusty sort of green. Sometime in Ed's youth, the train stopped moving and tooting. I had a nasty suspicion my mother-in-law had helped it along.

"Ed would love to be able to run it again," I said. "His dad died when he was little."

"If you let me know when he's not going to be around, I'll see what I can do. It would be a nice surprise on Christmas Day, wouldn't it?"

"He'll be gone all day tomorrow."

"Then I'll stop by."

I was touched. Cliff really *was* a nice guy.

When I left him he was kneeling beside the tree looking closely at the train set. I'd hardly seen my husband, who was busy making sure everyone was happy, but now I found him chatting with a man who looked vaguely familiar. I joined them, and when it was clear I needed one, Ed performed an introduction.

"Aggie, you remember Peter Schaefer? He's the pain relief specialist who was so much help when Marjorie Witkins was dying."

I did remember. Mrs. Witkins, a longtime member of the church, had succumbed to a particularly virulent cancer last month, and Dr. Schaefer had been called in to help

her internist find the right combination of drugs to ease her
suffering. Ed had worked with both doctors and the family,
to be certain everything was done. With Dr. Schaefer's
help Mrs. Witkins had died more humanely than she might
have. I had met him briefly at her funeral.

"I appreciate the invitation," the doctor said. "Not everyone in Emerald Springs is so happy to entertain me."

Peter Schaefer was a distinguished-looking man in his
midforties. Black haired, tanned, and lean, he did not look
like anyone's version of a social pariah. I wasn't sure what
to say, but Ed clarified. "Peter's having a few problems
with public sentiment in Emerald Springs."

"Fears of drug abuse," Peter said. "Ours is a society that
believes suffering's good for the soul."

I do read the newspaper, and I know all about the hospice
movement, so I was surprised at his words. "I thought these
days doctors give cancer patients all the drugs they need."

"That's more or less true. But nonmalignant pain is a
different story. You'd be shocked at the degree people suffer from other conditions, and the little that's done to help
them."

"Peter's made a real difference for some members of
our congregation." Ed didn't volunteer for whom and I
didn't ask.

"I suspect there are other members of your church
who'd like to ride me out of town on a rail," Peter said.

This was clearly the prelude to a conversation on medical ethics. I told the doctor I was glad he had come and excused myself.

Vel was readying more food in the kitchen, so I followed her from counter to counter, apologizing for sticking
her with what should have been my job.

"Don't worry, I love doing this," she assured me. "The
food's a big hit." She paused and met my eyes. "But Sid's
fruitcake?"

I waited.

"Junie scarfed up Ginger's beef satays, but she claims she's developed an allergy to almonds. She didn't touch the fruitcake."

Sounds like small stuff, I know. But it was another slap in the face to our little sister, who had worked so hard.

I thought of Ginger and her interest in Bix. "Since Ginger's cooking is such a hit, why don't we tell her we need help whipping up something exotic and chain her to the stove."

"That's the funny thing. She doesn't seem to know her way around a kitchen. She was in here warming the beef when I was finishing up the eggnog, and I asked her to hand me the egg separator. She couldn't find it, and it was right in front of her. Then I asked her to grind some nutmeg, and she didn't have a clue how to do it."

I'll confess I'd never seen a nutmeg grinder before Vel arrived with hers. It has this tiny little prong that holds the nutmeg, and tiny little teeth at the bottom. I thought it was some exotic torture device until Vel explained. But *I* didn't go to culinary school.

"I don't care if she stands here and burns chocolate," I said. "At least she'll be out of commission."

"Good luck."

Before I could find Ginger or even join Lucy and my mother, who were laughing together in the family room, Fern and Samuel tackled me. The crowd around the dining room table had thinned a little, and I'd forgotten to don my invisibility cloak. Both the Booths had filled their plates, so I guess the food, at least, was above reproach. They were staring through the open doorway at Ed and Peter Schaefer.

"Your husband is talking to that doctor," Fern said.

Since clearly this was true, I had no idea how to respond. I waited.

"I can't believe he was invited," Samuel said. "Surely someone else brought him along?"

"Dr. Schaefer's been a real help to Ed."

I saw their eyebrows shoot up, and hastened to explain since, of course, they would think the worst. "By helping our *members* who need a pain specialist."

Fern lowered her voice. "The man is a drug pusher. Everyone knows it. Now that he's moved in, our little town's just a way station for addicts. I have a granddaughter! I will not allow this man to poison Emerald Springs and hook my little Shirley."

I tried and failed to picture baby Shirley, Big Bird, and the Teletubbies strung out on the corner of Church and Cardinal Streets.

I struggled to take her seriously. "He's our guest. I'm afraid that's the only thing I know today."

First that bookstore, then that incident in the park, and now this!

Okay, in Fern's defense, she didn't say this out loud. But I swear, I could hear her thoughts. So yes, I had been temporarily employed at a bookstore with a few questionable books. And yes, too recently I had played hide-and-go-seek with a murderer. But I was reformed. I was trying to live an exemplary life.

"We are watching Dr. Peter Schaefer." Fern gestured frantically to a woman who looked only vaguely familiar. Others were glancing our way, and I tried to smile my reassurance.

The woman stomped over. Hers was one of those faces I remembered but couldn't put a name to. She was probably a member, but one who only came for special events and holidays. Christmas is a magnet for even the most liberal churches.

"You know Ida Bere?" Fern asked.

This sounded like a test, so I didn't answer directly. "Welcome to our open house, Ida."

"Mrs. Wilcox doesn't know the story behind Dr. Schaefer," Fern told Ida, who was an athletic-looking woman

close to Fern's age. Ida had muscular arms and a square
jaw that could probably grind up nuts and bolts.

Ida wasted no time. "He is polluting Emerald Springs.
He feeds on our young!"

I pictured the urbane Dr. Schaefer in a Godzilla cos-
tume. "You sound very concerned."

"He writes prescriptions for hundreds of pills, then he
writes more. Where do you think those drugs go? Why do
you think he does it? You don't think he's really trying to
help people, do you?"

"Isn't pain relief a valid medical specialty? Alleviating
suffering sounds like a good thing to me."

Ida leaned closer. "He prescribes drugs to addicts. And
if his patients aren't addicts when they arrive in his office,
they are by the time they leave. I'm organizing a coalition
to stop him. I hope we'll have your support."

I held up my hands. "It sounds like a complicated issue.
But you're obviously worried. I hope you'll make an appointment to talk to Ed. He's keeping office hours right up
until Christmas Eve."

"I don't know why you invited that man," Ida said. "I
don't know what he's doing here."

"Enjoying himself, I guess. Which reminds me." I was
desperate to change the subject, and I knew how to do it,
although it pained me enormously. "Fern, every year we
ask the youngest child at our holiday party to put the angel
on the top of our tree. And I'm sure Shirley is the youngest
this afternoon. Do you think she'd like that?"

Fern was too smart not to know what I was doing. But
she was also a proud grandma. I watched her struggle and
felt more kindly toward her. Say what you will, but Fern
does love her granddaughter.

"I'll go find her," Fern said.

I was relieved to see Ida falling into step behind her.
Gratefully I made my party rounds.

By now the house was packed, and there was activity everywhere. Deena and friends from her religious education class were tying garlands of tinsel in their hair. A young couple Ed had married in November were smooching under the mistletoe Sid and Bix had tacked between the kitchen and dining room. From the living room sofa I heard a debate about the annual Christmas Eve Nativity, which this year was in the parking lot of the largest Catholic church in town. Several Women's Society members, bless them, were quietly clearing away plates and cups. I didn't see Lucy, but Junie was showing off her caftan to an admiring group of needlecrafters who work all year making saleable items for the Christmas bazaar.

The choir had taken a brief break, but I knew when Shirley put the angel on the tree they'd be thrilled to do another impromptu carol. As I went to corral a soprano, I heard music from the hallway. But it wasn't any carol I knew.

"Delta Xi, means to me, loyalty, truth, and honor. I pledge with my heart, to make a new start, with the brothers of Delta Xi."

I stopped at the door into the hallway to see the most unlikely trio, Bix, Cliff, and Peter Schaefer, heads together, right arms hooked, singing happily.

I'd vetted the eggnog, but I guess I should have warned Cliff about the mulled wine.

They finished, and I applauded, along with a couple of other people who, like me, were delighted the song had ended.

"Fraternity brothers," Cliff said sheepishly. "They noticed my ring."

He held up his hand and I saw a gold ring with a crest and Delta Xi in raised Greek letters. I thought it was great Cliff had new friends. I thought it was even greater Cliff hadn't taken a swing at Bix, who was unfortunately not eating grilled cheese at Lana's Lunch with my sister.

Peter had his hat and coat in hand, and before he left I wished him a happy holiday. I just hoped that he hadn't felt the waves of acrimony lapping in his direction. At least he'd found brotherhood as he was leaving.

I dug up a soprano, and managed to catch my husband and ask him to retrieve the angel from the coat closet. I rounded up all children in attendance, and finally, to get everyone's attention, I rang the silver bell Sid had hung from evergreen swags draped over the bannister.

When it was almost quiet I told everyone about our angel tradition. People were tolerant of the sentiment. After all, it was Christmas time.

Mabyn and Howard came around the corner with Shirley in her father's arms, but Shirley didn't look any happier than she had when she arrived. Ed joined us and presented her with the angel. Shirley reached for her mother, but Mabyn stepped out of sight, as if she knew that Shirley would try to cling to her if she stayed nearby. Howard lifted his daughter high and told her to put the angel in place. Ed stood by to help.

The house actually had grown silent, except for the choir members who had chosen to perform "The Little Drummer Boy." Their off-key "rum pum pum pums" were like a drumroll, building up the tension.

Shirley's a smart little girl, and when she realized every eye was riveted on her, she stopped fussing. This was a child who knew she was meant to play a starring role in life's little play, and I bet she thought the rest of us had finally realized it, too. She lifted the angel with a dramatic flourish. Her dad held her away from him, then higher to reach the top. Ed stood by to guide her to the branch and help slip the angel in place. When it was secure, everybody applauded loudly.

I guess it was the applause that did it. Shirley gave a loud screech and a lurch, and startled, her father lost his balance and stumbled backwards. Shirley made a grab for the closest branch and grabbed a string of the old bubble lights instead. She yanked; the lights flickered wildly, then shot sparks into the room.

Somebody screamed, everybody leaped backwards, and to top things off the unmistakable sound of splintering glass rang from the direction of the dining room.

I was the first one to get there, or almost. Mabyn had ducked into the hallway so not to distract Shirley, and she reached the dining room before me. But I still got there in time to find Ginger sprawled on the table, swimming in eggnog. Sid was standing over her, and she wasn't attempting rescue.

Worst of all, much much worse, the Women's Society sacred punch bowl was now only jagged chunks of crystal on the dining room floor.

4

I had an entire night to think things over, and the next morning, over a breakfast of whole wheat pancakes and real maple syrup, I was nothing short of chipper.

"Well, I'd say overall, things went well. Almost nobody saw Sid slam Ginger into the eggnog. Only one gift caught fire when the lights short-circuited, and that was Nan's toothpick holder. Plus people cleared out of here so fast that there are more leftovers than I'd expected. Nobody will have to make lunch for the rest of the reunion."

Sid's head was in her hands. Between moans she'd drained two cups of coffee and was well into her third. Clearly I was not the only one who'd experienced a sleepless night.

Vel was at the stove making more pancakes on the off chance my girls felt safe enough to come downstairs at some point. Ed was already next door choosing between "Joy to the World" and "Oh Come All Ye Faithful" for the Christmas Eve processional. Bix was wherever Bix disappears to. My theory? Old Bix likes to pretend we are really an offshoot of the Kennedy or Bush clans. He needs a lot of distance for this.

"Aggie, I said I was sorry yesterday. About a thousand times." Sid lifted her head to peek at me, then stared down at the table again. "Damn that mistletoe, anyway. Whose idea was that?"

How often in my life does somebody else cook breakfast? I took another pancake. "Your idea. You said every Christmas party needs mistletoe, then you took Bix off on a mistletoe hunt."

"Oh, shut up."

"Maybe you shouldn't have put it up, knowing Ginger was going to be there—"

Sid lifted her head and glared at me. "It's not Bix's fault. I walked in, and she was kissing *him*. Right there between the kitchen and the dining room. It wasn't a mistletoe kiss!"

I don't need a definition that measures proximity, pressure, and length. I know the mistletoe score. I can imagine what Sid saw.

She struggled with the rest of it. "And then when Bix lit out of here, she turned to me and she said . . . she said . . ."

I knew what Ginger had said. I'd heard it from Sid yesterday. It had been more of a chant than an explanation. *"First I got your mommy, then I got your boyfriend . . ."*

"So what do we do now," I said, cutting off one more recitation of Ginger's taunt. "Junie's no dope. Maybe she likes to look the other way, but yesterday was a 360-degree view of the problems with you and Ginger. Maybe she doesn't know exactly how Ginger ended up nearly drowning in eggnog . . ."

All morning I had tried not to picture that scene, but now my own words brought it back. Ginger, awash in nog, skidding on the floor as she pushed away from the table. At least two partygoers were cut by glass trying to help, but luckily not badly. The only good thing was that Ginger didn't tattle on my little sister. She escaped outside, maybe to think over her story. When she returned, Ginger simply claimed she'd tripped, and no one contradicted her.

Personally, I think she just didn't want people to know Sid got the best of her in a fight.

"I could talk to Junie," Sid said. "I could try to explain."

There was a long silence. We adore our mother. We also know her faults. Junie hears only what she wants to. She would listen, then she would probably rhapsodize about karma, about the Golden Rule, about all the wonderful things Ginger brings to our lives. It was quite possible that after two paragraphs of this, Sid might baptize Junie in eggnog, too.

Maybe my party and my reputation were on the line, but Vel has strong opinions about the way people should conduct themselves. And Sid, no matter what the provocation, had failed us all. When she finally answered, Vel's voice was molten steel.

"I'll tell you what you can do. You can sit quietly at dinner tonight and behave yourself."

"Oh, lower your voice," Sid said. "My head is about to come off my shoulders."

"Well, if that would keep you quiet, I'd be in favor," Vel said.

I'm used to this. Vel lectures, I find something to laugh about, Sid reacts. Junie's girls, all grown up.

Welcome to my world.

"Vel has a point," I told Sid. "The only way Christmas won't be spoiled is if I invite Ginger and Cliff to dinner tonight and you're at least icily polite to them. You've dunked Ginger good. Let that be enough retribution, okay? Suck it up and be a grown-up."

Sid narrowed her eyes at me. Generally I try not to side with either sister, all too aware of the dynamics of triangulation-family therapy speak for two against one. But the only way we were going to salvage the holiday for

Junie was to pretend that the eggnog episode was an accident, and that Sid and Ginger did not, in fact, despise each other still.

"And what about Bix?" Sid demanded.

Vel and I were silent again. Sometimes silence is the best weapon. Ask any woman with sisters.

"Ginger was kissing *him*; *he* wasn't kissing Ginger," Sid said.

Silence stretched and stretched and stretched. . . .

"You just don't see the things in Bix that I do," Sid said at last.

Vel's voice was a bit gentler. "If he's the man you say he is, dinner won't be a problem."

Sid rested her head in her hands once more. "It'll still be a problem for Junie. I tell you, Ginger's here to get her money."

Vel applied logic. "I don't know exactly how much Junie got for her quilt, but I really doubt it was enough to lure Ginger to Emerald Springs. Ginger's a success in her own right, and last night Junie said something about Cliff being an inventor with a pocketful of important patents. What does Ginger need Junie's money for?"

"Then why is she here?"

Since wanting to renew a relationship with old pals was clearly not Ginger's reason, we fell silent again. I'd asked myself the same question all night long, and no answer had occurred to me.

Junie saved us from a round of pointless guessing. She appeared in the kitchen doorway wearing a vintage pink dressing gown, trimmed at the edges in dyed ostrich plumes. It was worthy of the Smithsonian.

"I had the most wonderful dream." She smiled brightly. "Just so very, very wonderful. Is there coffee, precious?"

"Precious" is a little Junie joke. Junie polished rocks and made jewelry for many of the years she traveled the craft fair circuit, roughly—as one might guess—from the time I was born until little Obsidian came into the world. Unfortunately Vel was born and named first, when velvet paintings of Elvis and fierce Siberian tigers were a sure route to crafting success.

Technically agate and obsidian are *semi*precious stones, but Junie has never been tempted by accuracy.

I got to my feet. "I made enough coffee to fuel a truck stop. And Vel made great pancakes."

"I need sustenance!" Junie plopped down on the closest chair and poured herself a glass of orange juice. "Sid, precious, hand me a plate."

Sid managed to lift her head from her hands and give a sickly smile. She handed Junie a plate from the stack near her elbow, and a napkin wrapped neatly around the morning's choice of cutlery. That, of course, was Vel's work.

"So, my dream," Junie said. "Here it is. I was in a kitchen, one of those sterile, white kitchens. You know, the kind nobody really cooks in. But it was open to the sky, and now that I think about it, the whole kitchen was floating on clouds."

I tried not to look at Sid. I poured coffee into the largest mug in my cabinet and topped it with whipping cream before I put it in front of our mother. "How many pancakes would you like?"

"Four to start. So there I was in this celestial kitchen. And guess who else was there?"

Vel caught my eye. I could swear she was signaling me to peel open the remaining napkins and get the knives out of Sid's reach. We both knew what was coming.

"Ginger!" Junie said, before anyone else could.

Sid moaned and put her head back in her hands.

"Agate precious, give your sister something for that headache."

Nothing manufactured would make a dent in Sid's headache, but I searched for and found a bottle of something generic with a childproof cap that requires a hacksaw and jackhammer. I handed the bottle to Vel, who glared at me. I shrugged. She began to struggle.

"I suppose I shouldn't drag this out, but it's just too good." Junie was beaming. She took her first bite of pancake and rolled her eyes in pleasure. "So there was Ginger, and she had a huge chef's knife, you know, the kind they always show on infomercials?"

"This is beginning to frighten me," I said. "Better make it fast."

"Well, this is just the best, best part." Junie chewed, swallowed, then beamed some more. "Ginger was chopping beef, like that fabulous beef she served yesterday."

Sid took the bottle from Vel, who had managed to wrench off the cap. "Who brings beef to a vegetarian household?"

"I'm sure Ginger doesn't know Aggie and Ed are vegetarians," Junie chided gently.

As a matter of fact, Ginger's Kobe beef had looked mighty good to this vegetarian. But now was not the time to say so.

"So there she was, chopping away," Junie said. "Chopping, chopping, chopping . . ."

The gleam in Sid's eyes was more frightening than the thought of Ginger with the knife. "And then?" I prompted.

"The knife slipped," Junie said triumphantly.

Sid's eyelids snapped shut. I could tell by her smile exactly what she was imagining.

"So far, this isn't all that nice a dream," I pointed out.

"Because I haven't told you the best part! The knife slipped, and it turned into a dove and flew away. A white dove! Now do you see?"

I didn't. Call me clueless.

The silence was thick enough to pour on the pancakes. No one seemed to get it. Junie looked from face to face, and hers clouded with disappointment. "I thought for sure you'd understand. It's prophetic. Ginger's culinary career has turned her into a peaceful, loving woman with endless spiritual potential! My dreams are never wrong."

Actually, Junie's dreams are never *right*. But after years of pointing this out to her, my sisters and I have given up. Junie believes she has great prophetic powers. When the evidence goes against her, she's willing to say her interpretations aren't perfect, but that's as close to reality as she gets.

"While you were at it, did you have any dreams about how long Ed will keep this church?" I was afraid the answer might depend on how many people had seen the fight, and how many people *they* told. Right now I was pretty sure Mabyn Booth had witnessed the demise of the punch bowl, and if she told Fern what Sid had done, my family's reputation would be blackened beyond recognition.

Junie understood. "I am so sorry about that lovely punch bowl, but last night, I thought of just the man to replace it for you, a dealer in fine glassware. He's at the Jacksonville Art and Antique Show every single year. We always spend the best time together. I'll give him a call myself."

I pictured returning all my Christmas gifts for the necessary cash. I hoped they were expensive gifts.

"He owes me a favor," Junie said, lifting one eyebrow provocatively. "A big favor. It won't cost you a thing."

This was territory I did not want to explore. I could tell from my sisters' faces that they felt the same way. "That's, uh, so generous of you," I said.

"Well, it's my responsibility. I was the one who asked Ginger to come here. I just had no idea she was so clumsy."

Unfortunately Sid had been in the process of swallowing tablets. Now she choked at Junie's words, and Vel whacked her between the shoulder blades.

With unnecessary force, I thought. But I could relate.

+ + +

The house Lucy and I are renovating on Bunting Street was built in 1897, at a time when detail and craftsmanship weren't add-ons but expectations. In my year in Emerald Springs I had probably driven by the house a dozen times, but I had never noticed it until Lucy made me.

The sand-colored house sits behind a hedge of sickly, gnarled viburnums that are as tall as the first floor. Beyond the hedge is a fussy little yard with nondescript evergreen shrubs pruned within an inch of their lives, and a standard-issue sidewalk lined with statues of gnomes, fairies, toad-stools, and gargoyles. Built in an era of larger families, the house is surprisingly small, just 2,500 square feet counting an ample attic. But it's a proud house and seems larger. The moment I got past the shrubs, I saw the potential.

A porch graces the west side of the front while a bay window graces the east. There are two stories, and along the way someone had the sense to open the tiny rooms downstairs and combine them into larger spaces. The tin roof is unusual around here, and the gingerbread was care-fully restored or replaced in the last decade. The house is a style known as Stick Victorian, with wonderfully detailed roof trusses, cornices, and brackets.

Unfortunately the last owner settled into the house in the forties and continued to live there until her death last year. Along the way she collected every relic of the Victo-rian era she could afford on a fixed income. Lucy had warned me, but I had an instant attack of claustrophobia the first time I walked through. The woman wasn't a hoarder. There were no empty cans or cardboard boxes, only enough doilies to smother an army. And on those doilies? Knickknacks, paddy whacks, give the dog a sim-pler home. The Bunting house was a museum of tacky Vic-toriana. Lace, ruffles, angels, dried flowers, mass-produced porcelain tea sets adorned with violets and shrub roses, potpourri. I could go on.

Two weeks ago, after countless hours sifting through

the flotsam and jetsam to be sure nothing of value was hidden away, we had a garage sale. A furniture dealer bought the furniture we didn't want to keep, and everything that didn't sell either went to the dump or a local charity. Everything except the garden ornaments. The house next door—an aluminum-sided Colonial—is still occupied by a friend of our former owner, and I promised her the garden ornaments as mementoes.

I kept a few things to sell with the house: the nicest of the tea sets, a collection of porcelain spaniels, a leather-bound copy of *Alice's Adventures in Wonderland*. We kept just enough furniture to make the rooms look lived in and made enough money on everything else to help with our renovations.

The key that unlocks the front door is an antique, solid brass with a barrel stem and ornate head. Lucy wanted to replace it, but I think whoever buys this house might treasure a nod to the past. Our Victorian is in a transitional area of Emerald Springs. It's zoned for commercial use, but in addition to the woman next door, there are other people living on the street. Luckily no developer bought this one as a teardown, so Lucy and I can fix it up, perhaps as a gift shop, perhaps a tearoom, with a cute little apartment upstairs for the shop owner. There's something about the old wreck that calls out for one more chance. We aim to please.

I used the key and the front door with its oval, etched glass pane swung open with a creak. The creak I can fix easily, the blackened varnish on the old wood will take warmer weather and a lot of stripping. The outside is not our priority just now. We hope to redo the inside just enough to expose the potential, then put it back on the market. If it doesn't sell right away, we'll wait until spring and tackle the exterior before we try again. Although I like the idea of a finished product, selling and moving on is our new livelihood.

"Up here," Lucy called from the second floor, when the door banged shut. "Bring the mop and bucket."

I set down the grocery bag of cleaning supplies I'd brought with me and grabbed the mop and bucket at the bottom of the stairs. I found Lucy in the smallest bedroom—and the one with the ghastliest wallpaper. Let's just say the wallpaper in the house fits the overwrought decor. I'm not even sure how to describe the pattern. The background is dirty gray, covered with large pink and red daisies poised at angles with Japanese screens and other geometric shapes in bronze. The effect makes me dizzy, particularly since some of it is hanging in curls where seams have come unglued or torn. It seems more psychedelic than Victorian, and even the most devoted enthusiast of the period would remove it.

Lucy had begun the task using a clothes steamer, a mixture of fabric softener and water, and a tool that scores each section once it's soaked through. She was standing on a stepladder working near the ceiling.

"You're just in time," she said. "You can start scraping. I started in the corner and it ought to be wet enough."

"What got into you?" Lucy and I took one look at this place right at the beginning and knew we had to hire help. This renovation is too big a job, and our time too limited to do it alone. We've been searching for the right handy person, but not successfully.

"I had a couple of free hours between appointments. I'm going to keep work clothes in the closet so I can dart in and out. You should, too."

Sadly most of what I wear can be called work clothes. There's rarely a reason to change.

I rolled up the sleeves of my black turtleneck and reached for the Sheetrock blade. "I only have a little time. I have to meet Teddy's teacher before she heads home. This could have waited until after the holidays."

"I figured you had a lot to scrape off."

She wasn't talking wallpaper. "Like sisters?"

"You're going to give me the scoop. The whole scoop, right?"

"I already told you about Ginger and Sid."

"Not everything, I bet."

I tried to remember what I had told her. "Well, I told you how Ginger came and went, how she always managed to make Sid look like the villain, how she stole her boyfriend. We called him the Prom King."

"Uh huh. But, you know, those don't seem like good enough reasons to shove Ginger into the eggnog."

I stopped scraping. "What makes you think Sid did?"

"Oh puh-leeze! Of course she did. You as much as warned me it was going to happen."

I relaxed a little. "Just keep that to yourself, okay? I don't want the world to know."

"Well, good luck with *that*. So, come on . . ."

I sized her up. Lucy was wearing farmer overalls and looked darned cute in them. She had a bandanna over her wacky red curls and a skinny corkscrew of wallpaper nestling beside one ear.

"Who put you through college?" I asked.

She looked down. "My parents. They started saving the moment I was born."

"My dad helped with whatever he could." My dad lives in an Indiana survivalist compound. Life there is not what anyone would call expensive, although new body armor sets him back every time they improve that technology.

"I figured your dad for somebody who doesn't believe in education. At least not the kind they teach at universities," Lucy said.

"He has a master's degree in Asian Studies."

"Which he puts to good use planting corn and shooting intruders?"

"He's really a very peaceful person."

"Just cautious."

"Ummm . . ." Ray Sloan was not the topic of this conversation. "Junie helped with whatever expenses she could afford, too. Between them, with loans, scholarships, grants, I got myself through school."

"And your point is?"

"Well, Sid's father couldn't help much. He's, well, let's just say that Patrick Kane was busy with the IRA at the time."

"You mean IRS."

"No, IRA."

Lucy clicked her tongue. "Aggie, is just *knowing* you enough to get me a file at the FBI?"

"You might want to shield your face when we're in crowds together."

She looked as if she might consider that. "So what happened to make Sid hate Ginger?"

I noted the volume of the question; she was getting cranky. "Sid's dad wasn't much help with her college plans, and Junie?" I shrugged. "Junie got a small inheritance that year, which would have helped Sid a lot. Instead she used it to get Ginger into the Culinary Institute of America."

Lucy was silent. I went back to scraping. "It was the final slap in the face for Sid," I said. "She thinks Junie chose Ginger over her."

"So what did Sid do?"

"She settled on a state university instead of a private one, scraped up loans, worked part-time, put herself through in five years instead of four. Junie helped when she could, but by then the inheritance was gone and Ginger had quit school."

"Eggnog was too good for Ginger."

"Pretty much."

We worked in silence for a time. The wallpaper was coming off without a lot of effort on my part. And it was curiously satisfying.

"Did this destroy Sid's relationship with your mom?" Lucy asked at last.

It was time to go. I set down the scraper and wiped my hands on a rag. "It's a silent hurt. Once Junie decides something, there's no point in trying to talk her out of it. Sid set out to show Junie she didn't need help. And she's made a success of her life, but nothing like Ginger has. I'm sure that rankles."

Lucy climbed down and walked me to the bedroom door. "I'll stop by on Christmas Day. I bought Hanukkah presents for the girls."

"Stay for dinner. See the fireworks if Ginger and Cliff are still around."

"And speaking of fireworks?" Lucy reached up and flicked the light switch, which was older than I am. Nothing happened for a few seconds, then the light blinked and finally went off. "I had the inspector look at these. The wiring is sound enough, but we need new switches. And a couple of new plugs in the bathrooms."

I should have been able to put in switches myself. Junie might look like a fluff ball, but no daughter left her home without basic wiring and plumbing skills. I was going to replace the innards of all the toilets right after Christmas, a job I could easily manage. But I have this problem with technology, and it extends to simple wiring, as well. In a nutshell, everything I touch goes berserk. Last week our phone service was disconnected when I tried to use the call-waiting feature. The phone company swears this isn't possible, but we went for three days without service before it mysteriously turned itself back on.

We'd have to find someone else to do the switches.

Lucy went to clean up so she could show a townhouse later in the afternoon. I let myself out and decided to make the ten-minute walk to Teddy's school. Emerald Springs experienced its first big snowfall last week. Our landscape is white, but the snow is dry and powdery and our sidewalks are clean. Later in the winter walking won't be as easy. I wanted to take full advantage.

Okay, the truth. I wanted to delay the return to my house after I met Miss Hollins. Walking back and forth to my minivan would buy me an extra ten minutes. It would also give me time to gird my loins for dinner with the whole glorious tribe. Vel was cooking. I hoped Ginger was bringing her own poison taster and his name wasn't Cliff.

Emerald Springs may be provincial, but it's really a pretty little town. Old hardwoods and evergreens tower over picturesque houses. Yards are large enough for children to have swing sets and puppies. Streets are quiet.

Right now the streets of this part of town caroled Christmas. Wreaths adorned front doors, and reindeer skeletons pranced in yards, waiting to light up the night after sundown. A wilting blow-up Santa had his arm around an equally flaccid Grinch, and a corner house had a Technicolor nativity scene with a giant plastic Frosty in an attitude of prayer—a sight I doubt the Holy Land ever witnessed. In the middle of the third block, children were pulling each other on sleds, although the snow was only a few inches deep.

Teddy's school, Grant Elementary, is a two-story, red brick rectangle, built in the early fifties. It's a baby boomer school, and the hallway closest to the office displays endless photos of classrooms filled with little girls in crinolines and little boys with Howdy Doody plaid shirts and slicked back hair. There have been extensive updates, of course, but the building retains the feel of another age, when computers were comic book fantasies and the media center consisted of one rattling movie projector.

Teddy's classroom is on the first floor looking over a playground that nowadays houses state-of-the-art climbing equipment. I'd enjoyed my first look at the room during the annual fall orientation for parents. Miss Hollins was young and enthusiastic, a bit huffy when questions were asked but otherwise pleasant enough. I think she's so new at this that she's not ready for anything that sounds like criticism.

She's feeling her way. In a few more years her confidence will soar, and she will smile indulgently at our fruitless attempts to control our children's education.

She was waiting for me when I arrived, her head bent over papers. Jennifer Hollins looks a lot like her first graders. She wears her brown hair loose to her shoulders, with jumpers and soft flowered dresses that remind me of pinafores. Her glasses are round, very Harry Potter, and her skin is warmly freckled.

Her expression, however, is prim and all business. At least with parents. She donned it the moment she looked up to find me there.

Miss Hollins got to her feet and waited for me to approach the desk. She smiled, but I could tell her heart wasn't in it.

"I'm sure you're really busy," I said. "I bet you're looking forward to the holiday."

She relaxed a centimeter. "How are you, Mrs. Wilcox?"

I am Aggie *Sloan*-Wilcox, but I know when to make a point of that. Definitely not now. "Harassed. The holidays can really do that to you, can't they?"

She smiled again, thinly at best. There was no point in softening her up. She knew I'd come to take issue with something. I cut to the chase.

"Teddy refuses to write a story about angels. She's decided that angels don't exist, and she refuses to be part of any conspiracy. I wondered if—"

Miss Hollins blinked. "This is one of those Civil Liberties problems, isn't it?"

I blinked. "I'm sorry?"

"You're complaining because I asked the children to write on a religious topic."

"Well, actually, no, I—"

"Because I researched this very carefully." Now her eyes were sparkling with anger. "I am not unaware of the need for diversity at this time of year. There are angels in almost every religion. The Buddhists have their *devas*. These are very close to angels, if I may say so, and *devas* show up in Hinduism, too. And Muslims believe that angels are emissaries from Mohammed. The earth-centered religions believe in spirits—"

I held up my hand to stop her. "*Teddy* doesn't believe. History of world religions isn't going to do it for her."

"So what would you like me to do about *that*?" She folded her arms.

I'd had enough uppity women in my life lately. I came out fighting. "Even if every religion in the entire universe believes in angels, you have to face the possibility that not every child in this school is religious."

"Like Teddy?"

I counted to nine; ten took too long. "My husband is a minister."

Her eyes widened. She really hadn't known, I guess.

"Teddy is a child who questions things." I remembered to breathe. "It can be a problem, I know, but we encourage her to think things through."

"Well, maybe you shouldn't."

Okay, now I was *ticked*. I made it to eight and spaced my words carefully. "Right now Teddy only wants to believe in the things she sees." I didn't share my daughter's disenchantment with Santa Claus. I wasn't sure this young woman could see the connection. "This may change and it may not, but for now, she doesn't want to write about angels. Is . . . there . . . something . . . else . . . she can write about instead?"

She screwed up her freckled face. No one has ever looked disdainfully at me through Harry Potter glasses. It was something I never hope to see again. "Yes, certainly. She can write about something she *sees*, Mrs. Wilcox. But if I were you, I would question giving in to her on this."

I questioned it for, oh, one and a half seconds. "She'll have a story written. And you won't take off points because she couldn't bring herself to write about angels right now? We have an understanding?"

She gave the briefest of nods.

Mine was even briefer. I turned and headed for the door. Halfway there I saw a stack of Christmas gifts the children had left for Miss Hollins. Teddy's decorated tree and star cookies were wrapped in silver paper at the very top.

I am a virtuous woman. Well, maybe not so much, but my husband *is* a minister. I did not snatch back the cookies.

5

When I got home Vel was alone in the kitchen, preparing pasta for dinner. Pasta is the logical standby when meat eaters cook for vegetarians. Of course Vel's sauce, made with grilled eggplant and a plethora of vegetables and spices, was complicated and smelled luscious.

I'd half expected to find her rolling out sheets of dough and cutting angel hair pasta with an Exacto knife, but she wasn't that stressed. Vel's meals get more intricate as her anxiety increases. As girls, on the nights it was Vel's turn to cook, Sid and I were not above pretending that report cards had arrived or her best friend was moving. We had some fabulous meals until she caught on.

"I've poached pears to go with this," she told me. "And I thought the girls would like farfalle pasta with the sauce because it looks like butterflies. Your little Italian grocery has a good quality import."

The pancakes had finally worn off. I sneaked a leftover piece of carrot that hadn't made it into the sauce. "We have a little Italian grocery? Here in Emerald Springs?"

"I can't believe you don't know. It's a charming little store. Signore DiBenedetto handpicked pears for me. Everything he has is top quality."

I vaguely remembered what store she was talking about. From the outside, it's tiny and dark and looks like a dump. Which says everything about judging a book by its—well, you know.

When Vel didn't slap my hand I took another piece of carrot. "How did you find it?"

She looked up. "Well . . ."

I was suddenly *really* interested in the answer. "Well . . . ?"

"I was heading for Krogers, and I spotted Ginger."

"Doing what?"

"Standing on a sidewalk just down from the store, looking around like she thought somebody might be following her."

"So you did? Follow her, I mean?"

"Well, just a little ways. And I wasn't very good at it, because I lost her. That's when I found the grocery."

"Maybe she thinks Sid hired a hit man."

"Sid did pretty well without one yesterday."

I took the last piece of carrot and got the sponge to clean off the counter. "You were pretty hard on Sid at breakfast."

"No more than she deserved."

"I think she feels bad enough."

"She's all grown-up now. Why can't she just let this stuff roll off her back?"

"For the same reason I expect you to return the yellow mohair sweater you borrowed your senior year of high school."

"Give me a break."

I laughed and hugged her hard, releasing her quickly, since Vel's not a touchy-feely kind of gal. "What can I do?"

For the next half hour I took instructions. For dessert we were going to serve a platter of leftover goodies from the open house, but Vel had bought Italian dessert wine and a very ripe Gorgonzola to serve immediately after the meal, the way Signore DiBenedetto had suggested. If Vel was following the old guy's advice, I had to meet him and discover his secret.

The parsonage dining room is the least-used room in the house. Invariably we eat in our too large kitchen at a farmhouse-style table that divides the room. Tonight called for more formal surroundings, and Vel and I set the dining room table, despite it being more or less a crime scene. The room is long and narrow and the old walnut-veneer table has been here through several generations of ministers. We just managed to squeeze ten chairs around it, including an office chair from Ed's study. Unfortunately dinner was going to be cozy.

"Place cards?" I suggested, calculating the best way to keep Sid and Ginger at opposite ends. "Teddy would be happy to make them." I went up to cajole her and also tell her about my meeting with Miss Hollins.

Teddy and Deena were both in Teddy's bedroom when I arrived. My daughters looked suspiciously angelic, the way children often do when Christmas is right around the corner. We don't do the naughty or nice thing in this house, but even children without the threat of coal in their stockings know that behaving well during Christmas week is in their best interest.

Teddy's room is simple, almost somber. To brighten Teddy's choices Junie made a wonderful country church quilt for her bed, and I noted that Teddy had carefully folded it back so that neither she nor Deena were sitting right on it. Had I checked the ID bracelet on this baby before I brought her home from the hospital?

The girls were playing a board game Teddy had received last Christmas and never, to my knowledge, opened until now. I suspected that this, too, was an example of what lovely and *grateful* daughters they were.

"Having fun?" I went to the bed to peer over Deena's shoulder. "She's beating you, isn't she?"

"I'm letting her."

"You are not!" Teddy jumped her little plastic thinga-majig six spaces.

"Junie's taking a nap in my room," Deena said.

I know it's unusual, but my sisters and I have never called Junie anything but Junie. To this day I'm not sure how this happened. But faced with *Grandma* or *Granny* or *Nanna*, my sisters and I decided that *Junie* would work for the girls, as well. In my family the word means love, which is what all grandchildren need.

"I need a favor." I explained about the place cards. "Can one or both of you make them?"

"You don't want Aunt Sid and Ginger to sit near each other, do you?" Deena asked.

I shook my head. So much for family secrets.

"I think I even like *Teddy* more than Aunt Sid likes Gin-ger, and that's saying a lot."

"Way more," I agreed.

"Will there be another fight?"

I guess if my daughter figured out the eggnog baptism wasn't an accident, the jig is up at church. "Not if I can help it," I said with a certain amount of force.

"I asked Bix to help me find Moonpie after lunch," Teddy said. "He was lost again."

Moonpie hides from Teddy, but we don't point this out, since she'll have plenty of other reasons to need therapy by the time she grows up. "And did Bix help?" I asked.

"He told me to go away."

I wondered where Bix was hiding right now, and what I could do to him before dinner.

"I don't like children," she said, in Bix's whiny voice.

Teddy is a mimic, an eerily good mimic. "Did he really say that?" I asked.

She looked up at me, as if to question my intelligence.

I changed the subject and told her what Miss Hollins had agreed to.

"Good grief, Teddy," Deena said. "Who cares if you believe in angels or not? Just make it up. You can write about stuff you don't believe in."

"I can't." Teddy jumped six more spaces, and Deena rolled her eyes.

Ginger and Cliff hadn't arrived by the time everyone else came downstairs for dinner. I suspected Ginger planned to make an entrance, and I was right. The Grables were ten minutes late, and Ginger was dressed to the hilt. Most of the time I shop in Emerald Springs, and if I'm not at a discount store I'm at "Here We Go Again," the consignment store that benefits our local hospital. Ginger clearly shops where Mabyn Booth does, in some exotic location with taxis and skyscrapers. The coat was butter-soft, caramel-colored leather, belted with a notched collar. Under it she wore a violet cashmere sweater, suede boots that exactly matched it, and winter-white wool pants. Her amethyst jewelry was exquisite, set in delicate burnished gold.

I was wearing a faded denim skirt and the same turtleneck I'd worn to scrape wallpaper.

Ginger immediately handed me a wicker basket wrapped in red cellophane. "Something just a little extra special," she said. "Luxuries you would never buy for yourself."

I heard the subtext. Luxuries we could not *afford* to buy. I peeked through the cellophane and indeed, did not recognize a thing.

"Flame raisins on the vine," Ginger said. "Italian chestnut honey. And just the most incredible Calabrian fig puree. I'm sure you'll enjoy the new tastes."

Since I was determined to show Sid how this was done, I smiled my thanks. "We'll put them out with dessert. That way we can all enjoy them."

"I certainly hope some of that wonderful fruitcake is left," Ginger said. "Sid, it wasn't ruined by the eggnog, was it?"

Ed caught my eye. I thought he looked particularly handsome tonight in a sweater Junie knit for him several years ago. I thought he also looked particularly alert, as if he was ready to fling himself between Ginger and Sid.

"It survived just fine," Sid said pleasantly.

"Well, I'm just glad my Kobe beef was eaten so quickly," Ginger said. "Your guests just couldn't seem to get enough, Aggie. But I apologize. I really didn't know your family was vegetarian."

"We don't expect other people to live the way we do," Ed said.

"How unusual. For religious people, I mean."

Ed caught my eye again. I thought maybe he was beginning to understand.

"Drinks this way." Vel pointed toward the living room. "We have some wonderful wine Junie bought today. Girls, I made a special punch for you."

We moved into the living room, and the preliminaries went well, which in this case meant no one threw anything at anyone else. Vel had made a lovely vegetarian antipasto platter, and to her credit she politely asked Ginger to serve plates for everyone.

"No pepperoncini for me," Junie told her. "All those things I used to love." She shook her head.

Cliff had hardly said a word, but I joined him at the Christmas tree. "I popped in this afternoon," he whispered. "To see what I could do about, you know."

"Any luck?"

"Success."

No one had told me, and I was thrilled. "He'll be so happy. You're a genius."

He smiled at me. "She doesn't realize, you know."

I knew we were talking about Ginger now. "Realize what?"

"How she comes across sometimes. She only acts this way when she's insecure."

I wondered if Cliff was as bad at reading everyone as he was at reading Ginger. "Junie loves her like a real daughter. That ought to count for something."

"Maybe things were harder for Ginger when she was with her real mother than you realize."

"I realize a lot, but I'll give her credit for choosing a good man," I said.

He looked pathetically grateful.

I cleaned up plates and glasses as they were emptied, and eventually we moved into the dining room. The girls had outdone themselves on the place cards: Teddy's artwork and Deena's fanciest script. Best of all they had put Ginger and Cliff at one end of the table, and Sid and Bix at the other, with the rest of us as buffer.

Vel brought in the pasta, topped with feta cheese. The poached pears were nestled on fresh greens and smelled of thyme and lemon. A basket of hot rolls appeared, and we all snuggled together in our chairs.

"Fusilli pasta," Ginger cooed. "How clever of you, Vel."

Vel glanced at me, as if to say, *I told you she doesn't know about food*. The table was silent as everyone dished up. Bix disdained the pasta but took five pears, which meant no one else would have seconds.

Ginger took small portions of everything, but when everyone else began to eat, she stopped with her fork halfway to her mouth. More than once I had noticed her staring into space in the living room. At the time I'd assumed she was searching for the perfect way to ruin somebody's evening. But now I noted that she seemed far away. I wondered how many glasses of Junie's vintage cabernet she had imbibed as she'd dished up artichoke hearts and provolone.

"How did my favorite people spend their days today?" Junie was clearly in her element, wreathed in smiles. In her mind, this was the reunion she'd dreamed of.

In random order the others recounted their days, although Bix just shrugged. When it was Ginger's time she looked more than pleased to tell us. "Oh, I was at the spa all day getting wrapped and massaged and pampered. For such an ordinary little town, the spa and hotel are almost up to my standards."

I filled my mouth with pasta so I couldn't respond. It was my turn next, but as a safety measure, I chewed slowly.

"Aggie, tell Cliff and Ginger about the house you're renovating," Junie prompted. "I'll bet you were there for part of the day."

I was surprised, since Junie hadn't seen the Victorian yet. Then I remembered that Lucy had been her guard dog during the open house. I swallowed. "Lucy must have told you all about it."

"My talented daughter." Junie's proud smile turned her plump cheeks into shiny red apples. The apples went perfectly with her red velour sweatsuit and the blinking Santa hat she'd borrowed from Teddy.

"We'll see how talented once it's finished," I said modestly. "It's a lot of work, and we haven't found anyone who can help us yet."

"It's a great old house," Sid said. I had taken Vel and Sid to see it when they first arrived. Bix had come, too, but he had waited on the porch when I mentioned there might be mice.

"What needs to be done?" Cliff asked.

This was a safe topic, so I expounded. "The big things? Wallpaper removed and walls painted. Old linoleum and carpet hauled away. Possibly new floors downstairs. We'll see when everything comes up. Woodwork refinished in a couple of rooms. One of the bathrooms has to be gutted and completely redone—we'll bring in the pros to do that. The kitchen needs new appliances and the backsplash needs to be regrouted." I thought about my session that afternoon. "Some simple rewiring. New light switches to start."

"I might be able to help there," Cliff said.

"Oh, I couldn't ask you to do that."

"No, really. I'd enjoy it. We're leaving for Michigan Christmas morning to visit my grandmother, but I have all day tomorrow."

I started to repeat my last sentence, then I realized there was a note of desperation in Cliff's voice. He sounded like a man who needed something to do. And who could blame him?

"Well, that would be great." I smiled down the table at him. "Help is always appreciated."

"I've got just the thing for you. My newest invention. It combines several different technologies, but best of all it can be programmed as a motion detector and turn itself on and off when someone walks in or out of a room."

I'd been thinking simple switches. The kind that go on and off when they're flicked. I could just imagine what would happen if I tried to program Cliff's, or even use them.

"That's so kind of you, but Emerald Springs isn't the same as real estate in a bigger city. This house won't sell for that much," I said. "I just can't let you waste such a wonderful invention on—"

"Oh, let him." Ginger sounded more petulant than usual. "He wants to show off. He thinks he's going down in history with Einstein—"

"You mean Edison," said Sid, always helpful.

"I'd like to do it for you," Cliff said. "My treat."

And what could I say to that? It's hard to explain that I'm technology-challenged, without opening myself to offers of advice and tutoring, neither of which makes the slightest difference. And how many of these switches could he install in a day, anyway? Lucy can turn *those* lights on and off for me.

"Well, great," I said, trying to sound enthusiastic.

"I'm glad *that's* settled," Ginger said. "Cliff is so boring when he starts talking about his inventions."

"I'd love to hear more about them," Sid said, leaning forward as if she was enthralled. "Every single detail."

"No, let Ginger tell you about her new cookbook," Cliff said.

I figured Cliff knew that Ginger would continue the insults if he tried to talk about himself. Some relationships mystify me.

Vel leaped in before Sid could add another word. "Yes, tell us about your career, Ginger."

"You're sure?" Ginger purred. "Well, it's been just such a surprise to me. But I guess I had the right combination of brains, looks, and talent to make a success."

I kicked Sid under the table, because without looking, I knew she needed it.

Ginger put down her fork. "I was discovered while I was still in school. A Cincinnati television station was looking for somebody pretty and bright to demonstrate recipes on their local news show. Somebody told me and I went to audition. They thought I'd be perfect. Of course I worked hard, and before long they gave me a holiday special, and after that was a huge success, they gave me more. Then I was offered a weekly show all my own on our PBS affiliate. It was picked up by several stations across the country and would have made me a star, only . . ."

She shrugged sadly. "I was in a car accident. I injured my back."

I remembered several years ago Junie had mentioned the accident to me in a phone call. I had even sent Ginger a get well card.

Sid perked up. "That *must* have been hard for you, Ginger, considering how much time you spent on it—"

I cut her off quickly. "I hope you had a good doctor. I know back pain can be awful."

"It never really goes away. I've just learned to suffer in silence."

I stared daggers at Sid, who had opened her mouth again. She clamped it shut.

Ginger continued her sad saga. "The show was cancelled, of course, since I couldn't do any new episodes for months and months. And standing for any length of time was just excruciating, so I couldn't get a restaurant job."

"There's a happy ending coming." Cliff smiled fondly at his wife.

Ginger didn't spare him a glance. "I realized that what I really wanted to do was set down some of my wonderful recipes for other people to enjoy. You know, a gift to all those people who'd loved my shows. So I started work on a cookbook. I called it *Splurge: Decadent Dining for Gutsy Gourmets*. It hit at just the right moment. Of course I'd planned it that way. But everyone was so tired of eating nothing but lettuce and carrots and brown rice. It was a naughty cookbook for naughty people. The talk shows loved me."

I was so glad I had never turned on my television to find Ginger rhapsodizing about her own talents. This was bad enough.

"Tell them about the *new* cookbook," Junie said.

"Well, if you promise not to tell anyone else." Ginger lowered her voice. "I'm calling it *Binge: Fattening Foods for the Delinquent Dieter*. Don't you love it?"

No one spoke. Appealing to gourmets yearning for the richer food they loved was one thing. But what woman would be caught with a book called *Binge* on her bookshelf? Even if she locked herself in the bathroom twice a day to scarf down a gallon of rocky road ice cream, she wasn't going to advertise.

Ed finally rescued us. "It's certainly a unique approach. Do you have a publication date?"

"Some time next year. We need to get all the promotion in place. There's talk of another television show, maybe the Food Network." She looked at Sid. "But enough about me.

I'm sure the rest of you have made *huge* successes of your lives."

"Girls," I said quickly, "you've been so quiet."

"You told us to be quiet." Teddy frowned. "You said that—"

"Well, it's your turn now." My smile was as bright as a Christmas star. "I was thinking our guests don't know about the big Christmas Eve pageant on the Oval." I looked away from my daughter to include everyone. "That's what we call the park across from the church. This quite a deal here. It's been a tradition for twenty years. Deena will tell you all about it."

"I will?" Deena looked disappointed. I wondered if she'd been hoping there would be another dustup at the table.

"You will." I aimed the smile at her.

Deena shook her head, as if to point out what she was forced to put up with. Luckily it's Christmas, and there's enough little girl inside her to hope for the best.

"Every year one of the churches near the Oval puts up a nativity scene. You know, the kind with real animals? Sheep and donkeys. People play shepherds and Wise Men and Mary and Joseph."

"Nobody plays Jesus." Teddy gnawed her lip and looked straight at her father. "Was Jesus real?"

"No question about it," Ed said.

"Was he born in a manger?"

"Teddy, let Deena finish," I said, before Ed started a lengthy overview of the scholarly debate about Jesus's birth. Teddy will tackle these questions in seminary in oh, twenty years or so. Why spoil the fun?

"So, as I was saying"—Deena narrowed her eyes at her sister—"It's a tradition. And each church gets to do something special, as part of it. The stable's behind the Catholic church this year. And the Baptists get to choose Mary and Joseph. I think the Methodists get to choose the shepherds. Somebody else gets the Wise Men, and last year one person got to lead a camel there on Christmas Eve, but nobody got to ride it. That's pretty lame. I offered to ride a horse, but they said there weren't any horses at the manger. Like they'd know for sure."

"What does your church get to do?" Junie asked. "Costumes? Lights? Music?"

"Nothing fun." Deena looked at her father.

"All the churches meet on the Oval as the sun goes down," Ed said. "Together, we process to the nativity and sing carols. The Lutherans lead the songs this year. Afterwards we all leave and go to our separate services. And while we're inside our churches, somebody puts the baby in the manger. It's just a doll, of course, but this year I choose the person who gets to do it."

Junie wiped her eyes. Junie gets weepy whenever something touches her. "Why, that's so beautiful. What a lovely, lovely thing. Who did you choose?"

"It's always a secret," Ed said. "A person who might need spiritual recharging. Supposedly nobody is left outside to see."

Teddy finished. "And then we come out with lighted candles, only the little kids have to use electric ones which isn't fair, and we march back to see the baby in the manger."

"We sing 'Silent Night,' then everybody goes home," I finished. This particular nativity pageant may be a wee bit corny, but I'm already outrageously fond of it.

"Choosing somebody to put the baby in the manger is a lot better than having to clean up sheep poop every day," Deena said.

I squelched her with a look, but Junie laughed. "From what I hear somebody in this family wants her own little animal to clean up after."

"Me!" Teddy said. "I want guinea pigs for Christmas, two of them. So they can have babies."

"No guinea pigs." I was sorry I hadn't gotten to Junie first. "We have a cat. A cat who hunts."

"But that's the only thing I want for Christmas."

"I don't want animals," Deena said. "I want tickets to the Botoxins concert in Columbus on New Year's Day. But apparently that's not going to happen, either."

"Aggie, I can't believe you aren't giving the girls what they really want for Christmas," Ginger said. "Now, if they'd asked for a Porsche, I could understand." She giggled.

Ed and I locked eyes for a moment. Mine said: *"Your turn, buster."*

Ed's tone was pleasant and measured. Just. "Deena's too young to fend for herself at a rock concert. And none of her friends will be going."

"Because Mom got together with their mothers and made sure of it!"

She got me there. Deena is one of a group of girls who call themselves the Green Meanies. Emerald green, of course. I did organize an informal gathering of Meanie moms that meets when necessary so our daughters won't play us off against each other. It's slightly better than nothing.

"Everybody agreed you're too young," I said, although strictly that wasn't true. Before she would go along with the rest of us, Crystal O'Grady, mother of Carlene, had to be bribed with the name of the woman who had painted tiny holly sprigs on Grace Forester's nails.

"I remember what it's like not to get what I wanted on holidays," Ginger said. "But I'm sure you two know best. I'm sure you got the girls something nice."

"New socks and a half-price pizza coupon," I said. "We're always more than generous."

"I'm sure it will be a very nice Christmas," Junie said.

✦ ✦ ✦

Later that night Vel sat at the kitchen table with another glass of Junie's cabernet while Sid and I cleaned up. Ed gets a break from kitchen duty at Christmas time, and the girls had gone upstairs, most likely to discuss what a terrible mother and father they have. Junie had gone off with Cliff and Ginger to do a tour of the Emerald Springs Christmas lights before the Grables returned to their hotel. Bix had taken off after his five-pear dinner. Sid hadn't told us why, but if possible, she was in a worse mood than she'd been during dinner.

"If you can just step back and watch things unfold, it's a marvel how quickly and easily Ginger can sabotage a gathering," Vel said. "Really, she has a natural talent."

"I hardly remember her mother, do you?"

"Probably a little better than you do. Fig was even prettier then Ginger, if possible. And manipulative? She could twist Junie into a pretzel."

"Junie's not usually much of a pushover. I bet she was so worried about Ginger, she just let Fig have her way. She thought she had to protect Ginger at all costs."

Sid banged two pans together in the sink. "Why didn't somebody just report that woman to Children's Services and have Ginger settled permanently in a good home? Anybody's home but ours!"

"Well, because Fig moved from town to town like we did, and those things take time. Or at least that's my guess." Vel got up and peeked out the window at what sounded like footsteps. "I thought that might be Junie. But it looks like Bix is back."

"Aggie, can you finish here?" Sid's voice sounded like it was being forced through a strainer. She was gone before I could answer.

"Did you watch Bix help Ginger on with her coat?" Vel asked softly.

Somehow I had missed that.

"He smoothed her hair over the collar, lock by lock."

"Lord."

"Prayer may not be a bad idea."

We listened. There were definitely loud voices coming from the front of the house.

"So," I said. "Let's crank up our volume, so we don't have to hear this."

"Well, did you catch the farfalle, fusilli, gaffe tonight? I told you, Ginger doesn't know a colander from a sieve."

"Maybe it was just a mistake."

"Okay, here's another one. Remember when Junie told Ginger not to give her any pepperoncinis? Ginger gave her three, but she *didn't* give her any of the portabello slices I marinated. I think she mixed them up."

Since the noise out front was growing louder, I spoke louder, too. "Maybe it's some kind of learning disability."

"Or maybe she just didn't pay a lot of attention in cooking school."

"Then how did she have her own show? How did she write a cookbook? The book is real. I've seen it. Maybe she's just not paying attention. Maybe she's got other things on her mind, like wrecking our family life."

"I can tell you she used a packaged sauce on the beef at the open house."

"That's not a sin, Vel. Even for a pro. It was a good sauce."

"How would you know? You're a vegetarian. You didn't eat any of it."

I was caught. "Okay, I'm not such a purist that I didn't dip a little bread in it."

Vel's dimples are deeper than mine.

The moment was destroyed by Sid slamming into the kitchen. "I'm going to become a nun." She sat down at the table, then she stood up, then she sat down again. Finally, she put her head in her hands.

"You're not Catholic," Vel said.

"I could be!"

Vel and I looked at each other. Vel shrugged. We waited.

Sid straightened at last. "He's leaving for Sag Harbor and taking the rental car. I told him I'm tired of watching him drool over Ginger."

"Any chance he could take her along?" Vel asked.

Sometimes the dumbest thing turns out to be the right thing to say. I thought Sid was going to strangle Vel. Instead, she started to laugh.

We were all holding each other and laughing hysterically when Junie walked in.

"My three precious princesses," she said. "What would I do without you?"

6

I woke up early, but not as early as Ed, who was already at the church rearranging the poinsettias or slipping candles into little paper holders for the service tonight. Of course that's an exaggeration. He doesn't really do these things himself. He goes to numerous committee meetings where the jobs are patiently discussed and assigned. Then he checks to be certain the jobs are done. Done well. Done on time. Done without resentment. I understood perfectly why he was gone before I'd even had coffee.

Nobody needed me this morning. I knew the girls planned to do some last-minute Christmas shopping with their grandmother today, and that Vel and Sid would probably sleep late. Ginger and Cliff wouldn't come until after the evening service, when we have a simple meal and everyone opens one small gift. This takes the edge off the anticipation so the girls get a little sleep.

This would be our last glimpse of Ginger, since she and Cliff were leaving tomorrow morning for Michigan. I was counting down the minutes. I'd assigned Vel to buy Ginger a gift until she insisted she was going to buy her a basic cookbook. Now she was buying for Cliff, and I had to pick up something for Ginger on the way home.

I was so thrilled to have a job to go to. I got up and threw on jeans, T-shirt, a red flannel shirt, and my work boots. The flannel shirt and work boots are an affectation, but I feel like such a pro when I wear them. For Christmas I'm hoping for a tool belt.

I was out the door in fifteen minutes, and in five more, I pulled up to the Victorian. The sky was the dull gray of pewter, and the clouds hid all but the faintest trace of sun. I'd caught a weather forecast on the car radio, and there was a chance of snow tonight. We might have some flakes by the time the service began, but the majority of it would probably fall later in the evening when everyone was safe and snug at home. Christmas Eve is one of the few days every year when this forecast is greeted with enthusiasm. Mostly due to Bing Crosby.

Inside I turned up the thermostat and took measurements in the kitchen where a new counter would go in. Then I went back up to the bedroom where Lucy and I had scraped wallpaper yesterday. Last night Cliff had said he'd come by about nine thirty. By the time I heard a knock on the door I'd stripped off the flannel shirt and a few good patches of wallpaper. Cliff was standing on the porch with a bag of cinnamon rolls from the hotel restaurant.

"Well, will you look at this. I knew there was a good reason not to bother making breakfast." I took the bag while he removed his coat. He was wearing a kale green shirt that made his complexion look sallow and unhealthy. The pocket sported three ballpoints and what looked like a protractor. The jeans were stiff and new and an inch too short.

"It's a great old house," he said. "And I like Emerald Springs. I always wanted to live in a small town."

"Can't inventors live wherever they want?"

"I worked for a corporation in Indianapolis. When I left and went out on my own, moving away seemed like more trouble than it was worth."

"And Ginger likes it?"

"She'd be happier in a bigger city, but I need a lot of space for my workshop. She needs a big enough kitchen so she can concentrate on perfecting her recipes. That kind of real estate would be hard to afford in a city like New York or Chicago."

I suspect that even in Indianapolis, real estate is pricey. These two must be doing very well indeed.

I walked him through the house, and Cliff flicked switches and asked questions. He was sorry he didn't have more time in town since he saw potential for a switch in every room. He apologized that he had business calls scheduled for the afternoon. I was glad he only had a few hours to help.

He left for his car to get what he needed. We'd decided to put the first switch in the bedroom where I was working. I was scraping again when he joined me upstairs.

"How many inventions do you have to your credit?" I asked. "I can't even imagine the process."

"Some that never went anywhere. Three that matter, including this one."

"Are they all home improvement gadgets?"

"The switches can be used anywhere a more complicated security system isn't needed. So small businesses will benefit. My last invention was a different kind of valve to use on hot water heaters. It saves energy. It's made a mark in the industry."

"Sounds important."

"Small ideas, big results. Kind of my motto."

"It's a good one."

"Good, but not very showy. I'm not a showy guy, I guess. I'm still surprised somebody like me ended up with somebody like Ginger."

When some people say this kind of thing, they're looking for compliments. But I could tell that Cliff was truly amazed Ginger had settled on him. Frankly, it was a mystery to me, as well, but not for the reasons he thought. In my opinion Cliff was far too nice to catch her eye.

But maybe Cliff had been right last night. Maybe being with us brought out the worst in her and there was more to Ginger than I'd seen.

"Well, I think she's lucky," I said. "You seem like natural husband material."

I caught his grin, and I was glad I'd stroked his ego a little more.

The grin died quickly. "I guess I am. I was married before."

There is no good response to this. I used the standard. "Oh."

"She died. I thought I'd never find anyone else I could love half as much, then Ginger came along."

"I'm sorry, Cliff. That must have been hard."

"Tell me more about your family."

I did, and pretty soon we were laughing at stories about my daughters. Along the way Cliff confessed a desire to have children of his own. I thought the odds weren't promising. Ginger was not mother material.

He disappeared into the kitchen for a while, then came back to poke his head in the bedroom. "Nothing left to do now without turning off your power," Cliff said. "Can you see well enough without the lights?"

I was ready for a break anyway and told him so.

I was halfway down the stairs when Ed walked in the door.

"Hey, I know you," I said. "Aren't you the guy who moved to Emerald Springs for a quieter, easier life? The guy who thought he'd have all kinds of time to work on a book?"

"I'm between meetings. Want to take a walk?"

Me? Alone with my husband? It was too good to pass up. I told Cliff, who was absorbed in decoding our circuit breakers. He nodded on principle, but I doubt he heard a word.

I got my coat and linked my arm in Ed's. With his blue watch cap pulled low over his ears and straggly beard he looked like a longshoreman. It was an interesting fantasy.

"Let's get coffee," he said.

A new place had just opened half a block from the Oval, and I'd been wanting to give it a try. We started in that direction. Give Me a Break is the Emerald Springs answer to Starbucks, lots of different blends of coffee, a skimpy display of baked goods, the eternally hopeful tip jar. I can tell they're working on ambience but haven't quite figured it out yet. The white walls and chrome chairs make the big room feel cold and empty, even though about half the tables were taken.

We found one in the corner, and Ed treated me to the coffee of the day, Jamaican Blue Mountain. I thought of Bix.

"You're smiling," Ed said, handing me coffee made just the way I like it.

"I wonder if this is where Bix hid out every day while he was here? I'm glad he's not around to growl at our children anymore."

"Another defeat for Sid."

"She's got to grow up and stop keeping score."

We clinked coffee cups. Carefully. The coffee smelled too good to spill even a drop.

"So meetings went okay?" I asked.

His lips twisted into half a smile. "I had one I hadn't counted on. Ida Bere tackled me today. It seems I'm contributing to a surge in the drug culture of Emerald Springs."

"By inviting Dr. Schaefer to our open house?"

"Exactly."

"What gives with that?" I settled back and sipped and did not ask if she'd mentioned the punch bowl.

"I told her Peter's interested in joining the church. He's been to our newcomer's meetings. I explained that it made sense to invite him."

I hadn't known Peter Schaefer might want to join our congregation. "Ida strikes me as somebody who needs a cause to make her feel alive."

"Maybe, but some of her concerns could be legitimate."

"So what are you going to do?"

"I don't stand at the door and bar entrance. Peter's as welcome as anyone else. But I do have a few feelers out, just to see if there's anything to what she says. Ida swears he's giving out ridiculously large prescriptions for oxycodone, which patients are selling on the street. She called it hillbilly heroine."

"Cute. And not a mountain in sight."

"Most of what she told me sounds like rumor, but I'm checking it out." He sat back in his chair. "It's nice of you to let Cliff work on the house. You didn't want to, did you?"

I smiled seductively. I had this little fantasy running through my head. Ed, the longshoreman, me the poor little stowaway on a Chinese freighter. Clearly we'd had company for too long.

"What's he doing for you?" Ed asked.

I came back to earth in wintry Emerald Springs with my relatives strewn through every room. I told him Cliff's plan. "The switches do everything except vacuum the floors, and if I mentioned that, he'd probably find a way. He swears they're simple to use, and no one looking at them will know there's anything special about them. Something about microscopic computer chips in the housing . . ."

"I'm sorry." Ed understood.

"I limited him to two rooms. I'm hopeful."

He glanced at his watch. "The ministers are meeting in a little while. One quick troubleshooter before the pageant tonight. I've got to get going."

"First tell me who you've chosen."

"Chosen?" He pretended not to understand.

"Yes, to put the baby in the manger. Ida Bere maybe?"

"I don't think the baby would make a dent in Ida's crusade. She'd probably drop it on its head in the manger and go find somebody else to complain to. No, I chose somebody who might really benefit from a little faith and hope."

"And that person is?"

He gave me that smile I can never resist. "It's a secret."

"From me?"

"Most especially from you. I don't want the world to know."

"Oh, low blow!"

He leaned across the table and kissed me. Give Me a Break wasn't the cargo hold of an Asian freighter, but it didn't really matter.

Ed left for his meeting, and I went back to the house to check in with Cliff and lock up. It was time to shop a little and go home. Cliff was just cleaning up when I walked in.

"You're done?" I was amazed.

"I told you it's a very simple process. Unfortunately I only brought the prototype with me. I'm going to install the rest of them in my grandmother's house in Michigan, and she only needs the motion detector feature. I don't want her crossing rooms to turn on lights in the dark. Anyway, I've programmed yours the same way, to go on when somebody walks in the room and off when they leave. If we were doing more switches I'd hook them into a simple alarm—"

"Not necessary," I said quickly.

"Anyway, these are the simplest version. But this is all I had with me."

I was more grateful than he could imagine. And my enthusiasm bubbled over. "Well, thanks," I said. "You've saved me so much work, Cliff. And thanks again for fixing Ed's train set."

I guess I laid it on too thick, because his face lit up.

"After you left I realized that I'll have some time late this afternoon and evening. I have more switches than I need for my grandmother, I could put in more."

"Oh, no, you don't want to—"

"It's no trouble. They went in without a hitch. I'll put in a couple more before we meet back at your house for dinner. I'll start as soon as my phone calls are finished."

I was caught. "Oh. Great." He stood there waiting, and I realized he needed a key. I fished an extra out of my pocket. I'd lucked out and discovered a hardware store that could make copies of our unique original.

We parted outside. He seemed happy. I was resigned. Halfway to my van I realized I'd left my flannel shirt upstairs with the measurements in the pocket. I went back inside and up the stairs. Sure enough, the moment I walked into the room the lights came on. Considering my usual luck, I was surprised and encouraged. I grabbed the shirt and left, but the lights stayed on. I waited a moment in the hall, hoping this was just due to some kind of delay, but nothing happened. Resigned, I went inside and taking the old fashioned approach flipped the switch. The lights went off.

I scooted out the door, but before both feet were over the threshhold, the lights came on again.

We played this game for awhile, the lights and I. The lights won. When I left the Victorian, they were still burning brightly through the upstairs window.

✦ ✦ ✦

Unless I wanted to drive to one of the strip malls on the outskirts of town, my shopping choices were limited. I needed more wrapping paper, which I could probably find at one of the local pharmacies. I needed a gift for Ginger, which was easier than it sounds since nothing I bought, ranging from a full-length chinchilla coat to a Chia pet, would please her anyway. I decided the pharmacy would suffice for that purchase, as well.

The closest one to the Victorian was a chain store, with nine long aisles of cosmetics, school supplies, and groceries and two short aisles devoted to pharmaceuticals. The staff gives out maps at the door on the long shot a customer might need antacids or antihistamines.

The crowd was thick, but I squeezed my way in and dove for one of the last rolls of Christmas paper, a dull silver sprinkled with demented-looking Santas. I held it against me, arms wrapped tightly around it, in case the desperate-looking mother with two toddlers in a shopping cart made a grab for it. She grabbed the last roll instead, a bright purple foil with yellow and orange candy canes and glared at me.

Next I was faced with finding something for Ginger. After squeezing my way through the aisles I was trying to decide between a Christmas CD of the Vienna Boys Choir—the nice choice—or a DVD of *Psycho*—the naughty choice—when somebody cleared her throat behind me.

I turned to see Mabyn Booth with Shirley riding on her hip.

"Well . . ." I said. "Umm . . . Merry Christmas." I was going to brazen this one out—I just wasn't sure how. I knew I would not mention the punch bowl.

"You waited until the last minute, too, didn't you?"

"There's always something I need on Christmas Eve. What are you here for?"

"Shirley's had a little cold. I'm picking up a prescription." She smiled. "Plus tape, three more Christmas cards, ribbon, a small present for the little girl down the street because Shirley pulled her hair yesterday, and hard liquor. Oh, if they really had it, to help me get through Fern's holiday dinner tonight."

Shirley started to fuss, and Mabyn shushed her. Shirley fell silent.

Since I'd never seen Shirley take direction, I was impressed. "I'm buying a last-minute gift."

"Someone you're ambivalent about?" Mabyn nodded to the copy of *Psycho* in my hand.

I popped it back on the shelf, then I laughed because clearly, I'd been caught. "Ginger."

"Oh, of course. If you're deciding between that and the CD, I'd go with the movie."

I had to probe. "You probably have some idea why I'm having a small lapse in Christmas spirit."

"I had a bird's-eye view of the entire incident in your dining room. To my mind your sister—what's her name?"

"Sid."

"Sid struck a blow for scorned women everywhere."

I went limp. "I think you were the only one who saw it."

"And you're wondering if I've told everyone my version, aren't you?"

"Crossed my mind."

"Not to worry. I have a few relatives I've wanted to shove a time or two myself. If Fern tells me how to raise my daughter one more time, I'm going punch bowl shopping myself."

Shirley fussed again and Mabyn switched her to the other hip, rummaged in her purse for a small stuffed toy, and handed it to her. Shirley quieted immediately.

Gratitude loosened my tongue. "This isn't any of my business, but Shirley seems to do fine when you're alone with her."

Mabyn brightened. "You think?"

"I'm really impressed. When she's at church or whenever Fern's around—" I stopped myself. This was not an appropriate conversation.

"No, now you have to go on, Aggie."

"Well . . . Shirley's probably a little confused about who's in charge. And kids love to pit grown-ups against each other. They figure it out quickly, or at least mine did."

"I know you're right, but I'm terrified of Fern. Howard is, too. We should never have left Cincinnati. Fern's criticism is like sandpaper wearing us down. I used to be in public relations and advertising. I ate bullies for breakfast. But Fern?"

"She really loves Shirley." I paused, considering my next words. "That can work to your advantage."

"How?"

"Well, tugs-of-war aren't good for children." I really didn't want to put ideas in her head or say more, but I hoped she understood what I hadn't said.

"So if Fern realizes the conflict is hurting Shirley, she might stop?"

"With a little nudge." I held up my hands, the wrapping paper still firmly clamped under my arm, just in case. "But you have to find your own way on this."

"You haven't said anything I didn't know already." She smiled. "But it does help that you think I'm doing okay with my daughter."

"Better than okay. Don't let anybody shake your confidence. You have a lot of years ahead as her mom."

"I'll think about this."

"Thanks for keeping my secret."

"And thanks for the advice."

I wanted to tell Mabyn this wasn't really advice, that I was just making an observation or two, and that most of all, I was not telling her to declare out-and-out war on her in-laws—who give generously to the church and are always looking for an excuse to clear out the parsonage.

But Mabyn and Shirley were swept away in the sea of last-minute Christmas shoppers, and I was left with my jealously guarded wrapping paper and my own family problems. While I stood there shaking my head at my own interference, somebody who probably had more problems than I do bought the last copy of *Psycho*. This had to be a sign. Silently I asked for forgiveness and took the Vienna Choir Boys home for Ginger.

7

Our girls have never known a Christmas Eve without a candlelight service, so as darkness approached they got ready without prompting. Junie was excited about the pageant, even though she has temporarily settled on interplanetary colonization as an answer to life's biggest questions. Junie's personal theology is like a river that rushes downstream, gathering and encompassing everything in its path. Sometimes the waters move too swiftly.

Vel and Sid had volunteered to come to the service, too. Sid may have spent last night punching her pillow, but now she looked as if she was determined to get over Bix Minard. At least she doesn't have to ask herself what *she* did wrong. She was that far ahead in the recovery game.

Vel finally dragged herself away from the stove. For our dinner Junie had made honey wheat bread and vegetable soup that would simmer in the slow cooker until we returned from church. Ginger and Cliff weren't coming to the service, but they would meet us at 7:00 for one final family love feast.

There are disadvantages to living where we do. The church is beside and behind the parsonage, with only a narrow alley and postage stamp parking lot to separate us. This means that everyone who needs a key or wants to discuss whether to use organic or chemical fertilizer on the church lawn finds their way to our door. On the other hand, Ed can be at work in a minute, and if I need him, I don't have to wait.

Tonight I was delighted to live so close, both to the church and the Oval. We were able to leave at the last minute, filing quietly out the door and walking to the park in silence. Teddy slipped her hand in mine, and even Deena stayed close to me. The Oval is roughly a tree-studded acre of grass with a bandstand in the middle. The bandstand is embellished with gingerbread trim that tonight sported beribboned pine swags and twinkling white lights woven through the lattice work.

Browning Kefauver, the town's unfortunate choice for mayor, sat in one of the six chairs that had been set up in the bandstand for the gathering, along with some of the town's most prominent ministers. Brownie is a nondescript little man with protruding ears, no backbone, and few principles. I know things about Brownie that would curl the straightest hair. Let's just say letting Brownie preside over a nativity pageant is like letting the CEO of Exxon preside over a Greenpeace rally.

Maybe it's that pesky church and state split, or maybe just that Brownie does know how to quit while he's ahead, but once the festivities began, he was only a figurehead. The ministers took over the event. There were to be no prayers or readings here, but someone has judged that singing carols is legal as long as a few secular songs are sung as well. I can imagine the session that led to making specific choices. Yes to "Good King Wenceslas," because it's a history lesson about helping the poor. Yes to Longfellow's "I Heard the Bells" because it's a nondenominational story of hope vs. despair. Still, count me among those who are pleased and relieved we're trying to respect all the citizens and religions of Emerald Springs.

The Lutheran choir was in front of the bandstand, all thirty of them in white robes with red stoles over heavy winter gear. Men and women with red and green armbands walked through the crowd distributing lyrics to almost a dozen carols. A quintet of shivering high school students began to play. Their counterparts would be waiting at the nativity.

I scanned the crowd for Ed, but he wasn't sitting in the bandstand. I thought he was probably gathering our church members, and after two verses of "Here We Come a-Wassailing" I spotted him. We wound our way to the east and found about forty Tri-C members huddled around my husband. Unfortunately, Fern and Samuel Booth were among them, along with Howard. Mabyn and Shirley were noticeably absent.

I shepherded my family to the other side, hoping to avoid the Booths, but Fern spotted me and came right over.

"A-Wassailing" ended and there was a brief pause as the orchestra shifted their music. Silently I egged them on, hoping to avoid a conversation.

The strains of "Let There Be Peace on Earth" began, and even though no one appreciates the finer qualities of my voice, I joined in with enthusiasm.

Fern cared not one whit. "I see you have your entire family with you."

I smiled at her and didn't quit singing.

"You'll notice *I* don't," Fern said. "I understand you and Mabyn had a little talk today."

I glanced at Howard, who looked only a bit chagrined.

I stopped singing where everybody else took a breath. "I always enjoy a chat with Mabyn."

"Mabyn refused to bring Shirley tonight. The child is at home with her mother on Christmas Eve. They won't even be at our holiday dinner after the service."

I looked sympathetic. "I'm sure you'll miss them, but of

course you wouldn't want Shirley out in this weather or up late when she's got a cold. You're lucky to have a daughter-in-law with such good sense about children."

"I don't know what you said to Mabyn, but I hope you're not interfering, Mrs. Wilcox."

I paused, but not long enough. "Well, no, honestly, if I was going to interfere, I'd just tell you right to your face how important it is to step back a little and give your children some room to do their job. Because that's going to be best for Shirley, and I know how much you love her. Grandmothers have such a special place in families." I nodded to Junie in her fake zebra skin coat, her arms around both my daughters.

"And *your* mother never tells you what to do?"

"My mother makes me feel like everything I do is right, even when she has suggestions."

"I suppose that explains a lot about your family."

I put my hand on her arm and squeezed gently. "Thank you. It really does."

She was clearly furious. She turned with military precision and marched back to her husband and son. I tried to figure out how I was going to explain the shortfall in next year's church budget to my husband. Goodbye to my new kitchen floor.

Three carols later I was more or less back in the spirit of things. Our little group had arms around each other's waists, swaying back and forth as we sang. Night was like a curtain swiftly drawn. One moment the Oval was suffused in winter's gray light, the next only the street lamps provided a glow.

The orchestra switched to background music, and people began to line up informally to march to the nativity. No camel arrived to lead us this year, since the cost of camel rental had been so astronomical that last year's pageant committee had been forced to sponsor bake sales all the way into July to pay for it.

Now on cue, three young people in ornate, kingly robes, followed by "servants" bearing gifts, came out from behind the Baptist church and processed majestically to the head of the line. I was delighted to see that one of the kings was actually a queen, a teenager who babysits for us occasionally, with her long blonde hair pinned and hidden under a gold crown.

Brownie, whose signature bow tie was visible under his wool coat, joined the ministers who formed a phalanx behind the kings, followed by the robed Lutheran choir. Then, as the orchestra played, we headed for the Catholic church.

Five of the major Emerald Springs churches are directly on the Oval. Six more are set just a block back. I guess in the earliest days, churchgoing was a major form of recreation here and splitting into factions must have been, as well. For such a small town there are a number of choices. We have several Catholic churches, but St. Benedict's is the only one on the Oval.

The procession took a few minutes. The nativity had been set up in the parking lot behind the church because the front is narrow and taken up by marble steps and a portico. We wound our way to the back along the driveway. I hadn't viewed the scene, which had been set up here for the past week, but someone at the open house had reported it was particularly impressive.

Impressive was the right word. The stable took up a good tenth of the lot. The doorways leading into the stalls were cleverly arched, and the crenelated detail above them suggested Holy Land architecture. Hay bales and animals peeked from doorways and windows, and a donkey stood with his head over a stall door. The actual manger scene was in front of the facade, however. The manger itself looked like the real thing. I guessed that some Emerald Springs farm was temporarily missing a feed trough. Small leafless trees with burlap-wrapped root-balls outlined the scene, and more bales of hay completed the ambience.

Through the years the costumes have been perfected. To cover their heads the shepherds wore the traditional keffiyeh of various homespun prints, held in place with a rope circlet. Their robes were simple, of roughly woven cotton tied with more rope. They leaned on staffs with the traditional crook at the top.

The wise folk and their servants had come to rest at one side where a sheep and a goat were tethered. The animals seemed to be old pros, or else they were so interested in the feed scattered at their feet that the horde of two-footed beasts that had descended on the scene didn't impress them. They stood quietly, as did the animals tethered inside.

Maybe it was the presence of angels that had calmed them all. There were half a dozen in white robes, with impressive feathery-looking wings and gold circlets bobbing over their heads. One adorable little angel looked to be a kindergartener. I wondered if she and Teddy had discussed theology.

Mary and Joseph were high school students, serene under the traditional costumes and focused on the empty manger. They didn't look up when a brass sextet began the strains of "It Came upon a Midnight Clear." The animals, too, were resigned to the noise. The pageant was going off without a hitch.

Just about the time my gloved fingers were starting to freeze and people were stamping their feet to stay warm, the choir launched into "Oh Little Town of Bethlehem." I knew this was the signal to leave for our own service and my watch confirmed it. Ed caught my eye and nodded. He took off before the last verse was sung so that he could be at our church to greet the congregation when they arrived.

Since everyone was cold, the manger scene was quickly abandoned. Up the driveway and back to the Oval, people streamed in all directions, some sneaking home, having completed their Christmas Eve ritual, some to services at the nearby churches. We walked toward ours, but near the door Sid drew me to one side.

"Save me a seat, will you? I've got to make a quick trip to the parish house."

I noted other people making trips that way. The restrooms were up on the second floor and there would be a line. "If the service starts, the ushers will ask you to wait in the narthex until there's a break. It might be quicker to run home."

"I'll be okay. I'll catch most of it."

I waved her off and let my daughters pull me inside with Vel and Junie following behind.

Our church is nearly as old as the town of Emerald Springs. Old churches of every denomination have a special feel, as if generations of prayers and hymns still echo silently. I think of the people who have come to this sanctuary at times of sorrow and joy, as a step toward moving on to a new phase of their lives. I feel honored to be in their company.

Tonight the old windows were lit with candles in brass candlesticks. A Christmas tree adorned with colored bulbs and ornaments handmade by church children sat in the side of the room away from the pulpit. Esther, our organist, was playing a prelude of French carols, and our choir was assembling in the back for the processional.

I hadn't realized until that moment how little Christmas spirit I'd absorbed this year. I was grateful to be here, sitting quietly, with nothing to do except celebrate.

The processional began. We stood and Ed walked in at the head, wearing a black robe and a bright Christmas stole. I lost myself in the music and the flickering light of candles.

The service had almost ended before I realized that Sid had never rejoined us. As we lit our own candles and stood to walk out to the Oval with members of the other churches, I looked around the sanctuary but didn't spot her.

"Have you seen Sid?" I whispered to Vel. "She was supposed to meet us here."

She shook her head and shrugged. The lights were so low I knew if Sid was sitting in the back of the church, I might not see her anyway. The pews in the back emptied first, and we waited our turn. Deena complained when wax dripped over her finger, but she didn't blow out her candle. I gave her a tissue to pad the hole in the paper candle holder, and Teddy looked on, jealous that she was stuck with an electric candle this year.

When it was our turn to file out, I realized that it had begun to snow. The sky sparkled with it, silvery flakes that were only just beginning to stick. We walked across the street where all the trees were now ablaze with tiny white lights. Deena's candle flame wavered then died, followed closely by mine. I promised her we would relight them when we reached the manger scene. For the first time Teddy was glad to have batteries fueling hers.

We crossed the Oval on the way toward St. Benedict's, when I realized the crowd had stopped. Although there are always police cars blocking the road that circles the Oval so people can cross to the various churches without incident, now at least two police cars were blocking the driveway that led to the St. Benedict parking lot. The twinkling of Christmas lights on the Oval had been eclipsed by rotating red lights on their roofs.

I put my arm out to hold Deena back and held tightly to Teddy's hand. "There's a problem," I said.

Junie and Vel stopped on either side of us. "What do you think this is about?" Vel asked.

"Maybe somebody had a"—Junie's gaze flicked to Teddy then to mine—"an incident." She splayed her hand over her chest.

I'd thought the same thing. But these were police cars, not the Emerald Springs rescue squad. And if the squad was back there stabilizing a patient or worse, would the police block the exit? I tried to remember if there was another way out of the lot and realized there was a two-lane drive that separated the St. Benedict Primary School from the rectory. It ended at Cardinal Street.

"That's probably it," I said.

"What's *it*?" Deena demanded.

"Somebody probably got sick, and they had to call an ambulance."

"Does that mean we won't get to see the baby in the manger this year?"

This was little-girl-Deena talking. Apparently she's already adopted this ritual as one of her own.

"It might," I said. "Why don't you stay here with Aunt Vel and Junie and I'll see what's up. If it's going to be awhile, we might not want to wait."

When Deena opened her mouth to protest, Vel rested her hand on her shoulder to keep her in place.

I wound my way through the murmuring crowd, looking for Ed or someone who might know what was up. I spotted a couple of church members, but they didn't know any more than I did. Closer to the police cars I saw that one of the policemen was stringing crime scene tape across the driveway behind their cars. My throat went dry. This was no heart attack.

Ed found me before I found him.

"Aggie."

I turned, and he put his arms around me. That simple gesture said it all. In a matter of moments the situation had gone from an unknown delay to one that was going to be personal. I knew this from the look in his eyes and the warmth of his embrace. For a moment I wished this would all go away, that I was back in the church listening to Ed read the story of the birth of Jesus.

Finally I looked up at him. "Sid?" I whispered.

He shook his head and frowned. "Sid's not with you?"

I felt such relief I could hardly push out the next words. "No. Ed, who?"

"I'm afraid it's Ginger. Father Carnahan slipped out at the end of their Mass to turn on the lights in the stable. He found her body in front of the manger."

8

Together Vel and I sat at the kitchen table and killed what was left of a bottle of wine, but maybe, under the circumstances, that wasn't the best way to think of it. Alcohol is not a helpful response to shock and grief, but for now it was all we had. Junie was upstairs trying to cope with the facts as we knew them, and my daughters, having been given an abbreviated, sanitized version, had gone to sleep with more to worry them than what would appear under the Christmas tree in the morning. Ed hadn't even been home yet. He had left from the Oval to find and comfort Cliff. And Sid?

We had no idea.

"No more," I said, when Vel offered to pour what was left of another bottle in my glass. "It's just giving me a headache."

"I doubt that's the wine." Vel didn't pour more for herself either.

"Where could she be?"

Vel isn't one for false comfort. She shrugged, but not in

an offhanded way. The shrug said everything. I'm afraid. I'm confused. I wish I had stayed in Manhattan and gotten my holiday jollies at Rockefeller Center and Radio City.

Once the girls were in bed and pre-merlot, I had bundled up and used my van to search the local streets for my sister, widening my grid until I was forced to admit I'd gone farther than Sid would have on foot. Snow dusted the road when I left, but by the time I'd turned and driven the same route one more time for good measure, the roads were solid white. They were also quiet, and for the most part, empty. Sid was nowhere to be seen.

"The husband is always the first suspect," I said.

"We don't even know Ginger was murdered."

"Come on, Vel. What are the chances she was so awed by the manger scene that she died on the spot?"

Vel massaged her temples. "Jumping to conclusions isn't helpful."

"But coming up with a hypothesis might be."

"So if it was murder, you think it was Cliff?"

"I didn't say that. I just said he'll be the first suspect. And if he was working on putting new switches in the Victorian, he was only seven or eight blocks from the manger scene."

"From everything I saw he was nuts about her."

"And from everything I saw, she treated him badly."

"Okay, so he finally figures out Ginger doesn't love him, kills her, and puts her at the nativity scene, making it easy for someone to find her?"

"Or as some odd sort of plea for forgiveness."

"Who else?"

Cliff had been easy. This was harder. I said what hadn't been said yet.

"Sid."

"Sid despised Ginger, but not enough to kill her."

I was surprised Vel hadn't started with the usual: *My little sister would never commit murder.*

"Obviously, I don't think so either," I said, "but others might see this differently. Sid shoved her into a punch bowl, oh, let's see, day before yesterday?"

"Let's be completely accurate, please, in case we're questioned. Sid shoved Ginger, and Ginger tripped and *fell* into the punch bowl."

"The fine points aren't going to impress the police."

"So what, Sid left the church to find Ginger and murder her? Then she planned to slip back inside for the final chorus of 'Bring the Torch, Jeanette, Isabella,' but got busy elsewhere? Doing what? Packing Santa's sleigh?"

I knew Vel was upset. I ignored the sarcasm. "The point remains that she wasn't with us at the time Ginger was murdered. I hope she was with somebody else who can vouch for her, but she doesn't know anybody else."

"So who else might have done this?"

"A stranger. A burglary gone wrong. Maybe Ginger was on her way over to the church for our service and got waylaid."

"We can probably assume that's not true. She didn't seem like a churchgoer to me."

"Okay. Maybe she was downtown finishing her shopping and was cutting across the Oval on the way to her car and—"

"You told me yourself on Christmas Eve everything closes at five except the drugstore."

"Darn it, Vel, maybe she had to get a prescription filled. Maybe she was getting a sore throat. Maybe she needed bubble bath."

"Okay, maybe a stranger killed her. Who else?"

I'd run out of options. Who did Ginger know in Emerald Springs other than us? And the only "us" who wasn't accounted for was Sid.

"She was at the open house," Vel said. "Did she hit it off with anybody? Somebody she might have been with this evening?"

"Apparently she hit it off with Bix. But by now he's back in the Hamptons drinking hot buttered rum with Steven Spielberg and Jerry Seinfeld."

"Anybody else?"

"She talked to every male at the party. They were hanging all over her, young and old."

"Maybe she struck up a friendship, or worse. We have no idea what she did during the hours she wasn't here."

"She said she spent all day yesterday at the spa."

"Yes, but it wasn't true." Vel sat up a little straighter. "Remember? I saw her on a sidewalk near the Italian grocery."

We couldn't go any further with that because we heard the door open and close, and before either of us had moved, in walked Sid. Her arms were clasped around her chest, as if she was trying to protect what little heat she was generating. From the bright red of her cheeks and nose, I was sure that was exactly what she was trying to do.

Her eyes were red, too, and not from the weather.

Vel jumped to her feet first. "We've been worried sick."

"I-I-need something hot to-to drink."

"I'll make a pot of coffee." I sprang up, but Vel was already at the refrigerator, reaching for freshly ground beans.

"Sit, Aggie. Sid, you do the same."

Instead I headed for the living room to get a pile of Junie's hand-crocheted afghans. When I returned Sid had managed to slip out of her snow-dampened coat and I tucked them around her. Vel had already soaked a dishtowel in warm water, and Sid held it to her face.

It was too soon to ask. I knew this. But still I asked anyway. "Where have you been?"

Sid shook her head. "Can't . . . t-talk."

Vel grimaced but went back to the coffeemaker, which was dribbling hot coffee into the glass decanter. She got a mug and poured a large dollop of milk in it and set it in the microwave. By the time it had heated there was enough coffee to make café au lait.

"Here." She thrust the cup at our sister, who put the towel on the table and took the cup gratefully. Sid sipped slowly, as if her lips and tongue were half frozen and she was afraid she might burn them.

I got down on my knees and pulled off Sid's boots. They were more of a fashion statement than real winter protection—after all, she lives in Georgia. Once they were off I was able to cover her feet with an extra afghan.

"Better?"

She nodded and sipped some more.

She finished the coffee and closed her eyes. The kitchen was silent until she opened them again.

"I know . . . about Ginger."

I took my chair and Vel took hers.

"I'm . . . so sorry!"

My heart nearly froze in my chest. I could tell from the look on Vel's pale face that hers was chilled as well.

"I can't believe . . ." Sid shook her head. "How could something like this happen? Who would *do* something like this?"

My gaze had been locked with Vel's. Now with relief we turned to stare at Sid. "Where were you?" I said. "And why did you leave the church and not come back? Don't tell me you're too cold to talk. We're too worried to wait!"

Sid thrust out the cup. "More coffee?"

Vel snatched it out of her hand and poured a full cup, hot and black, and thrust it back at her.

Sid cupped her hands around it and held the steaming coffee under her chin. "Ed picked *me* to put the baby in the manger."

"What?" This was not what I'd expected to hear.

"I know. I know." Sid's eyes filled with tears. "I was really surprised. Just like you are. But he said my anger at

Ginger was controlling my life. He said this was the right time for me to come to terms with it, to forgive and move on. He said . . . he said that until I did, I would never be happy with myself or with anybody else."

This sounded like something Ed would say. I was surprised and warmed by his concern for my sister. Also not at all pleased about his ability to keep his thoughts secret from me. "And that's why you left and said you'd be back? You weren't going to the bathroom?"

"I-I really thought it over. For most of the day. I wasn't sure I should be the one, but in the end, I saw he was right. Ginger wasn't the only person who was at fault. I was just as much to blame. So Ed left me the key to his office. When the parish house cleared out, I went in and got the baby. I just stayed there for a while." She gave a quick sob. "It-it was so peaceful, and when I held the doll I just started to think about how important it is to let our best emotions rule us, how important hope and faith and love are in the world."

I got her a napkin, and she took it gratefully, wiping her nose and eyes. "I knew it was just a doll. But that didn't matter. And I knew I'd probably be furious with Ginger again someday, but that didn't matter, either. I-I felt like maybe I could forgive and move on, that I could, you know, break the hold this has on us."

I nodded. "What happened then, Sid?"

"I went outside. Ed told me to cut through the Baptist's parking lot if I didn't want anyone to see me. So that's what I did. I went into the nativity the back way. I thought somebody would probably be there, like somebody taking care of the animals, but there wasn't anybody at all."

That surprised me, too, but the animals were docile. And tethered.

"So nobody saw you there?" Vel said.

"Nobody. Unless someone was watching from a window or something. I put the baby in the manger." She sighed and sipped her coffee. "I felt so peaceful. Like I was giving up a lot more than a doll. I said a little prayer, then I decided I needed to be alone. The snow was so beautiful and the town was so quiet. I wanted . . . I wanted to hold on to what I was feeling. I wanted to figure out my life. So I decided to walk. I planned to come back when the services let out. I wanted to be at St. Benedict's when people went back and found the baby in the manger. So I walked through neighborhoods. I could see Christmas trees in houses, and Christmas lights were lit. I was so happy. Then I started back to the Oval, but I guess I'd walked farther than I thought, because it took awhile. And when I got there, I heard people talking about a woman who'd been found . . ."

She didn't say any more.

Vel leaned forward and took the cup out of Sid's trembling hands. "How did you figure out it was Ginger?"

"Some guy saw the body, a young guy. He was pretty shook up. He was describing her to his friend. He said he'd never seen her in town. He said she must have been pretty . . . before. Brown leather coat, long red hair. Purple boots." She shuddered. "I knew. The boots were too unusual."

"Why didn't you just come home?"

Sid looked up. "Aggie, I know how this looks. I know what the police are going to think. We'd been seen fighting. I was alone at the manger scene right before . . . before. I realized I needed to retrace my steps, figure out exactly where I'd been and try to calculate exactly when. In case somebody had seen me walking by. But I was so upset, after I went a block, I couldn't find my way. I couldn't remember if I'd turned here or there or anything, and the snow was falling harder." Her voice caught. "And then I was just scared."

Vel chafed Sid's hands in hers.

"Ed knows I was the one who put the baby in the

manger," Sid said. "The baby must have been there when Ginger . . . when Ginger . . ."

Vel nodded. "Okay. But that just means you were there first."

"Come on! I was there. I've had a running feud with Ginger most of my life. I just broke up with my boyfriend because he was flirting with Ginger!"

Put that way . . .

I sat silently, the weight of the evidence against Sid sealing my lips.

"We don't even know for sure this was murder," I said at last. "And if it was, maybe the police already know who did it. Don't borrow trouble, Obstinate-Sidian." Times like these call out for childhood nicknames.

"I was going to get Ginger to one side tonight and tell her I wanted to start over, that maybe we'd never be friends but there was no reason to be enemies. That I was sorry for every time I'd ever hurt her."

"Really?"

Sid looked up. "Well, I was going to *try*. I could have managed some of it. And meant it."

We didn't have time to make plans on how to approach whatever came next. The front door opened again and we heard heavy footsteps. In a moment Ed and Detective Kirkor Roussos walked into the kitchen.

Detective Roussos is one of the most attractive men I've ever known, in a brooding Greek fisherman sort of way. He's somewhere in his early forties, intelligent, and distinctly reticent. Roussos and I are, well, I don't know what we are. Not colleagues, although I did manage to help him close a case. Not friends, since our only connection is murder. Not adversaries, since even though we didn't agree on how involved I should be in solving two recent Emerald Springs homicides, we did agree that solving them was an excellent idea.

Although I'm a happily married woman, I'm aware that

if I weren't, I'd be looking for more than murder to connect me to Kirk Roussos.

"How's Cliff?" I asked, rising to greet them.

Ed stripped off his coat and gloves. "About like you'd expect. He had just finished up at the house, and he was washing up to come over here."

"Where is he now?"

"He's back at the hotel. He doesn't want to see anybody. Detective Roussos has already questioned him."

I waited, but nothing was forthcoming about that.

I nodded at Roussos, who nodded back. He was wearing his detective mask. If he had any feelings about being back in our kitchen, they weren't in evidence.

"This is my older sister Vel Forrester," I told him. Vel rose and shook his hand.

"This is my younger sister Sid Kane," I said.

Sid didn't get to her feet, but she held out her hand.

"Detective Roussos would like to talk to you," Ed said. "Individually. He wants to find out everything he can about Ginger. He'll need to talk to Junie, too."

"Can't this wait? It's been an awful night."

"I'm sorry, but it can't," Roussos said. "Would you like to go first, Mrs. Wilcox?"

I looked at my sisters. Sid gave a slight nod. I looked at Ed and mouthed "Jack." Then I turned to Roussos. "Okay. Where shall we talk? The living room? Remember where it is?"

"I'll get Junie," Vel said. "It might take her a few minutes to pull herself together."

While Ed stayed in the kitchen with Sid, I led Roussos to the other room. I perched on the edge of the couch and he took a chair. He looked uncomfortable, and the parsonage furniture really isn't that bad. I suspected he was sorry to be here under these circumstances.

I pondered the point of questioning my sisters and me separately, but the reason seemed obvious. Roussos really didn't care what Vel and I might say in each other's presence since we're clearly not suspects, but he did want to get Sid off by herself. Doing it this way, like some sort of package deal, he called less attention to that fact and stood to make her more comfortable.

Only nothing was going to make Sid comfortable. I hoped Ed was already on the telephone to Jack McAllister. Jack is a new associate in the best law firm in Emerald Springs. His real interest is criminal law, which is why he agreed to come back to the town of his birth and work for the firm. He grew up in the church, and his mother, Yvonne, has been a friend and a supporter. If nothing else, having Jack here when Roussos questions Sid will provide some protection.

Jack is also something of a hunk, and for some time I've wished I could introduce him to Sid. Although not like this.

"You've known the victim how long?" Roussos asked.

I concentrated on saying nothing that would incriminate my sister. "Since she was a little girl. I'm sure Ed told you that Ginger lived with us on and off when we were growing up. Her mother had an alcohol problem, and my mother tried to shield Ginger from the worst of it."

He nodded. "Before this visit, when was the last time you saw her?"

"Years ago."

"And why was that?"

"Because Ginger had a lot of problems."

The questions went on that way for awhile. He asked, I gave the briefest answer I could. I didn't want anything I said to come back and haunt Sid.

His eyes never left my face. The experience was disconcerting. The last time we'd spent any real time together, he'd been armed and trying to save my life. It's hard to work up animosity toward a man who is responsible for the air in your lungs.

"Okay," he said at last. "We're almost done. Just tell me where you were tonight."

I did. Succinctly.

"And who was with you?"

I named everyone in the family, including Sid. "Ginger and Cliff were going to meet us here after the service. For dinner and a gift exchange."

"And everyone you named, they were with you the entire evening?"

"No. Sid left before the service at our church began."

"Did she tell you where she was going?"

"She indicated she was going to the parish house next door to the church. I thought she was going to use the restroom."

"Did she come back?"

"You know she didn't. Ed gave her the job of putting the baby in the manger."

"When did you see her again?"

"When she came back here."

"And when was that?"

"Maybe half an hour ago. I didn't look at a clock."

"Anything else?"

"Just that you're wasting time. You should be out looking for whoever did this."

I thought something like sympathy shone from his eyes, but it was gone before I could be sure. He just nodded and stood.

I stood, too. "Can you tell me how she died?"

He considered. I knew he didn't want to share details, but this would be public soon enough. "It's looks like either she was hit with something, or she fell and struck her head. Hard."

I nodded, trying not to picture this. "I'll send Vel in."

"I think I'll need to talk to Miss Kane next."

The doorbell rang, and I went to answer it. Jack was

shivering on our porch in ratty jeans and a down ski jacket. Not the usual young attorney gear, but it would certainly do. I hauled him inside. "He's about to interview my sister. I'm so glad Ed called you."

"He called from the hotel while the detective was talking to the victim's husband. I was at a party out in the country. And the roads are slick. I couldn't drive any faster."

I should have known Ed would call Jack without my prompting. "They're in the kitchen."

Jack followed me in, just in time to find Sid getting to her feet. Jack strode over to her like an older, more experienced man in a suit and held out his hand. "Sid, I'm Jack McAllister. Ed and Aggie asked me to sit in on your interview with Detective Roussos."

"Jack's a lawyer," I said.

"Why do you need a lawyer?" Roussos asked her.

"Why do you need to ask?" Jack asked Roussos.

Roussos shrugged. "This way?" He started toward the living room.

We could hear them talking, but not what was said. Ed put his arms around me and pulled me close. He smelled like snow and fresh air and peppermint. I saw candy canes in his suit pocket. Some child had probably given them to him at the service.

"How's Junie taking this?"

"You know Junie. She'll get through it, and she'll make sure we never know how badly it hurts her. She won't want us to worry."

"How about the girls?"

"I don't want them to remember Christmas as a scary time. I told them as little as I could. They were sad something happened to Ginger, but they don't—didn't know her well. We can probably salvage a lot of tomorrow for them if we work hard. I'm sure this whole situation seems more puzzling than anything."

"It puzzles me, too. Did you have a chance to talk to Sid?"

In a low voice I told him what Sid had said about the evening. "What about Cliff?" I asked.

"You mean how he's doing? Or did he kill her?"

"Both."

"He's broken up. Considering what we saw of their relationship, it's hard to fathom, but Cliff believes his marriage to Ginger was rock solid."

"I don't think reading people or feelings is his strong suit. He's one of those guys who lives in his head."

"As for his alibi?"

"Ed, did you hear his conversation with Roussos?"

"When I went over to the Victorian to find him, the old woman who lives next door was sitting in the kitchen with him. Seems she was curious about what anyone was doing there tonight. She saw him go in before dark, then she saw the lights going on and off. Since it was Christmas Eve it seemed odd to her that anyone might be working, so she finally came over to check. They were chatting like old friends."

"He could have slipped out at some point."

"According to her, the light show never stopped. I'm sure Roussos will do some more checking though."

"He suspects Sid, doesn't he?"

"It's possible when he talked to Cliff, Cliff mentioned that Ginger and Sid didn't get along."

I heard noise on the stairs. In a moment Vel and Junie arrived in the kitchen. Junie was wearing an old flannel robe of Ed's and she looked as if she had aged a decade. I went over to her and put my arms around her. She rested her head on my shoulder a moment, but only a moment. Then she straightened.

"I'm going to make cocoa," she said. "And everybody's going to drink it."

We did, too, as Roussos finished with Sid and Jack, then

did cursory interviews with Vel and my mother. We sat at the kitchen table and finished mugs of cocoa topped with marshmallows, just the way we had as children when something was wrong in our lives.

As I finished the last of mine, I remembered a night when I was thirteen and Ginger was seven. I'd heard her murmuring and tossing from side to side in her sleep, and I had gone in her room to wake her. She was upset and confused about where she was, and she began to cry. Ginger rarely cried real tears, so I suppose that the tears, as much as anything, were memorable.

I remembered that I had taken her downstairs and made cocoa. And as she drank it, she sat close to me, as if the unexpected warmth and comfort were new and worthy of further exploration.

Then when we finished, I tucked her back into bed, and while I sat beside her, she went to sleep.

Now upstairs in my bedroom, cuddled close to my husband, I finally cried, too.

Sleep well, Ginger. And may you find peace at last.

9

I awoke the next morning to the smell of sausage. Okay, it was soy-based sausage, but in the months we've been vegetarians, I've made some headway forgetting how the real stuff tastes. I've gone maybe 1 percent of the distance. That's a breakthrough.

This morning the sausage smelled delicious. Since Ed wasn't beside me I suspected he was downstairs cooking, and there would be omelets to go with it, maybe even waffles. Opening presents makes everyone hungry, and Ed always makes sure we're well fed. I swung my feet over the side of the bed in anticipation.

Then I remembered the events of last night.

I stayed there, considering how to make Christmas a good one for my daughters. As if on cue Teddy pushed the door all the way open and came through with Moonpie clutched in her arms. Moonpie, being the gentleman he is, was bearing up under the strain. The moment she put him on our bed, he would disappear for the day.

As expected he launched himself off and under our bed

when Teddy set him down, but she didn't seem to notice. She wriggled up beside me.

"Did Ginger really die?"

"I'm afraid so."

"Why?"

"We don't know, honey. But people are trying to find out. In the meantime there's nothing we can do but remember she was our friend."

Teddy considered this. "I don't think she was really our friend. People always seemed mad at her."

"Do you think so?"

"She said things that sounded nice, but they weren't." She paused. "Aggie, you're just so funny," she mimicked Ginger's voice.

Out of the mouth of babes. I hugged her. "Your grandmother cared about her very much."

"Junie likes everybody. Last night she said Ginger is an angel now. How does Junie know what Ginger is?"

"She's making her best guess."

"I don't believe in angels."

"I think Junie really means that Ginger is with God."

"I don't believe in God, either."

Again I was reminded how much had disappeared with Old Saint Nick.

I tried to point out the differences. "That's something you'll have to decide for yourself, too, but just so you know, a lot of people *do* believe in God, even if they don't believe in Santa Claus. We get to pick and choose."

Teddy was frowning at me. I felt I had to say more. "It's not all-or-nothing."

She continued to frown.

"You don't have to decide before breakfast," I said.

She nodded thoughtfully. "I guess we can have Christmas anyway, can't we?"

"I know a little girl who has presents under the tree." I

slid off the bed and lifted her down. "Let's go tickle Deena awake."

"She's helping Daddy cook."

I suspected Ed was providing Deena with the fatherly version of the same talk. Two parents, two children. For once I was glad we didn't have more.

Since eating a relaxed meal before gifts isn't possible, Ed put the waffles and sausage in the oven to stay warm, and as soon as everyone else joined us, we took juice, coffee, and cranberry bread into the living room. I insist on order of sorts. This means we finished in twenty minutes instead of ten. Ed had thoughtfully rewrapped my mother-in-law's Christmas toothpick holder after the bubble lights set the package on fire. Toothpick holders were only popular for a limited time at the turn of the twentieth century, when picking teeth in public was acceptable. So the collection that Nan has amassed for me would have looked right at home in the Victorian—before the garage sale. This newest addition was made of fragile opalescent glass. It will look stunning on top of my cabinets.

Everyone tried hard. Junie had made both girls "quillows," quilts that tuck into an attached pillow to take to sleepovers or to cuddle up inside on a cold evening. Teddy's was made from pastel cat fabric and Deena's fabric was covered with brightly colored flip-flops. Junie had pieced complicated stars in matching colors to top them off. I suspected they would be the hit at any slumber party.

I got my coveted tool belt, an encyclopedia of home repair, a fancy color wheel from Junie for picking out wall colors, and a lacy white blouse to help me remember I am not Al on *Home Improvement* reruns. Ed got a new wool overcoat and a simple MP3 player, which I promised I wouldn't touch. The girls got clothes and games, and for Deena, an MP3 player to match her dad's. Vel and Sid gave Teddy a sled.

Junie and my sisters got lots of presents, too. As we had every Christmas since childhood, we addressed our gifts to each other in the code we'd invented to keep Junie at bay. Teddy found this interesting. Deena found it lame and made sure we knew. We cooed over and discussed every gift. I felt sorry for Ed, who was forced to listen to all the female chatter, but when I turned the switch on his train set and for the first time in decades it chugged and tooted around the track, he was delighted to forgive us.

At least the mood was light enough to pass for a real Christmas morning. Although I knew my mother and sisters had Ginger's death at the forefront of their thoughts, they made sure our girls did not.

We were in the middle of breakfast when I saw the girls whispering to each other. "Christmas secrets?" I asked and hoped the topic didn't have anything to do with Ginger.

"Teddy was asking if I thought the guinea pigs might come later."

I frowned. "We're done with presents, Teddy."

She seemed okay with that, as if she thought it hadn't hurt to ask. But Deena looked less pleased. "I bet my friends got tickets to the Botoxins concert."

"I bet they didn't."

She really does have a spectacular pout. It's a little too Angelina Jolie to make me comfortable, but she timed it exactly right. Had it continued one instant longer, I would have taken her aside to discuss the importance of gratitude. But under the eleven-year-old facade, Deena really is fairly solid, so she stopped pouting and moved on to a second helping of waffles. After breakfast she asked Sid for help with her MP3 player, and the two of them went up to her room to download Deena's favorite CDs. Botoxins, most likely.

Ed and Teddy bundled up to try her new sled on the closest public hill, although it was iffy whether we'd had enough snow. Vel went upstairs to pour over the Italian cookbook I'd given her, and Junie and I stacked the dishwasher.

"How are you doing?" I asked when we were alone in the kitchen.

"It's hard."

I put my arm over her shoulders. "You did your very best to help Ginger turn her life around. You know that, don't you?"

It was a measure of how sad Junie felt that she didn't try to comfort me. "Every time we started to get Ginger on her feet, Fig came back, claimed she'd straightened out her life, and carted Ginger off again."

"You did a whole lot more for her than anybody else ever did. Short of kidnapping her, there wasn't anything else you could have done."

"I know how hard it was on you girls, especially your sister."

I knew which sister she meant. And I was surprised to hear her admit this. I pointed to a chair. "Sit. I'll finish the dishes in a minute. Let me make some tea."

Again, the fact that she let me said everything. For our Christmas celebration Junie was wearing overalls of a large floral print, heavy on poinsettias and holly. Under it she wore a gold lame pullover, but even the bright fashion statement couldn't disguise the circles under her eyes and her grayish pallor. For the first time I was face-to-face with the fact that Junie was growing older. My flirtatious butterfly of a mother looked as if she needed a good rest in the cocoon. I wondered how much longer she would keep up the craft fair circuit.

I made the tea strong and added a dollop of real cream. Junie will always be plump, but she's not one to nibble all day. It's just that when she does eat, she sees little point in not enjoying it.

I sat across from her, sipping mine.

"I had hoped . . ." Junie tried to smile. "Well, I had hoped Ginger's problems were behind her."

"It's possible this was just a random act of violence."

"That seems unlikely."

I wasn't sure how much she understood about last night. She'd been trying so hard just to cope with Ginger's death. "Junie, Sid doesn't have an alibi, and I think the police know about her feud with Ginger."

"I wanted the girls to get along. I did what I could to make it happen. But Ginger was too needy. She knew Sid was the greatest rival for my attention. And she needed so *much* attention. Your sister was caught in the middle."

"Ginger took up a lot of time. And space." I hesitated. "And money."

Junie looked up. "Don't you understand why I paid for culinary school for Ginger?"

"Not really."

"I thought it was her last chance to make something of her life, that it would give her a goal, a career, some real self-esteem." A tear trickled down her cheek.

"I guess I knew that. It's just that—" I realized this wasn't the right moment to sound critical, but Junie sighed.

"That I didn't help Sid, as well? Agate, precious, despite her rivalry with Ginger or maybe because of it, your sister was the little princess in our family. We waited on her, petted her, listened sympathetically to every little complaint she had, and we let her slide by. When it came time for her to go to college, she wanted that handed to her, as well. She'd never really had to work for anything the way you and Vel had. We'd spoiled her. Maybe we were making up to her for Ginger being such a thorn in her side. I don't know. But when she got her high school diploma, I realized it was time to reverse that trend or Sid would expect other people to take care of her for the rest of her life."

Junie never fails to surprise me. But this was more on the order of a revelation from on high.

"You need to tell Sid," I said after a long silence.

"Your sister would never kill anyone."

I knew this. Sid was the sister who had inspired Deena

to confront a parishioner in our last church because she wore a fur coat to services. Sid gives money to any organization that works to stop violence. She once inserted her slender body between two men arguing on a street corner because she was afraid fists were about to fly. Sid shoved Ginger at the open house, yes, but that had been completely out of character. Murder was out of her universe.

"This could get nasty, Junie."

Junie wiped away another tear. "No, this will be resolved the way it should be. I'm sure nobody will think your sister's a murderer. I had a dream last night. I saw Sid happily married. She had three children, and she named the oldest girl Ginger."

I'm afraid that the new Nostradamus is not alive, female, and temporarily residing in Emerald Springs, Ohio.

+ + +

In the early afternoon Roussos dropped by with more questions for Sid. I guess the good guys don't take a break on holidays. I wondered where Roussos usually spent them, and if he had family in the vicinity.

Jack doesn't live far away, and he walked over to sit in on the interview. Afterwards Sid told us it was clear Roussos knew she had shoved Ginger at the open house. Maybe Mabyn had been confronted and forced to tell the truth. I thought this didn't bode well for my sister.

I *knew* it didn't bode well when, once Junie was out of the room, Sid pulled me to one side to say that Roussos had asked her not to leave town. Neither Sid nor Jack thought she should force the issue.

Lucy came by with gifts for the girls, but she didn't stay long. She told me we would talk later, and I knew she'd hold me to it.

Late in the afternoon Ed came into the kitchen where I was pretending to help Vel make Christmas dinner and asked if I wanted to visit Cliff with him.

"You go," Vel said. "I can finish without you."

I nodded, but without enthusiasm. "This isn't going down as one of our best Christmases, is it?"

"Not likely." Ed kissed my forehead and pulled me close for just a moment. "Shall we invite him to dinner?"

I looked to the cook for answer. "You can try," Vel said, "but I doubt he'll say yes."

I went upstairs to tell the girls where we'd be and comb my hair. Once Ed and I were in the car heading toward the Emerald Springs Hotel, he told me that Cliff wanted to talk about Ginger's funeral.

"You can't mean he's going to bury her here?"

"That's what he said on the telephone."

"But why? That doesn't make sense. She never lived here. I mean, it's the scene of the crime. You think he'd want to bury her as far away as possible."

"Cliff said that at least *here*, someone will come to her funeral."

I didn't know what to say to that. According to Ginger she had a legion of fans if not friends. She'd had her own television show. She was the author of a successful cookbook and at work on the next one. Since their marriage she had lived with Cliff in Indianapolis. Surely she had met people along the way.

"The only people he could think of who might want to attend were *his* family, a grandmother and great-aunt whose health won't permit a winter trip," Ed said. "It's a sad statement about Ginger's life."

I couldn't have agreed more. It was also strong evidence that the people Ginger *had* known hadn't liked her. Exactly how many people had she alienated and how badly? Had any of them disliked her enough to kill her?

Was Roussos going to look into this? Or was he going to settle on my sister as villain?

The Emerald Springs Hotel and Spa wants to be a premiere resort, with its own heliport to accommodate jet-setters, and famous chefs vying to direct its kitchen. That's what it wants to be. In reality it's a sprawling brick building with two hundred or so rooms and suites, a funky old spa with museum-worthy fixtures, and a restaurant that treats vegetarians like recalcitrant children. I learned that last fact on my wedding anniversary.

The hotel, built just after World War I, sits on the site of the first Emerald Springs Hotel, which was built before the Civil War. Until the old frame building went up in flames, the original hotel was a popular destination for Ohioans eager to "take" the waters. The mineral springs that flow underground are said to have healing properties, not a one of which has ever been proved. The mouth of the springs "springs forth" in a nearby public park where swimming and wading are allowed in the summer. I can truthfully say that last summer the water did nothing for my ingrown toenail. Call it evidence.

In the summer the lobby smells faintly of mildew, and when the wind blows, the walls creak. Now, in winter, the lobby smelled of wood smoke and fresh evergreens. Small tables were occupied by guests playing cards or chatting over drinks. I liked the ambience, as if we had jumped back a century to a simpler time. I was ready for a simpler time.

Ed asked a clerk at the reception desk to announce our arrival to Cliff. Then we took the elevator to the fourth floor, which is as high as it goes. The hallway carpet was gray, patterned with pink and lavender roses. Below the chair rail the walls were painted the same green as the carpet's foliage and above it a paler green. Watercolor landscapes were spaced at intervals.

Cliff's room sat at the end of the hall. Ed knocked, and we waited.

Cliff let us in with a sad little smile. "Thank you for coming."

Trying to figure out what to say in these situations is so

hard. It never gets easier, and being married to a minister doesn't help. I don't think it gets easier for Ed, either.

"I'm so sorry," I said, touching Cliff's arm. "I can't even imagine how you feel."

"It just seems impossible."

"It does," Ed agreed.

The room was actually a suite with a kitchenette to the right, and a sitting room straight ahead with a bedroom off it. Cliff led us to wingback chairs in the sitting room in front of a fireplace with gas logs that looked as much like real ones as Mickey looks like a mouse. He must have ordered a pot of coffee when Ed told him we were coming. Coffee was the strongest fragrance in the room, but I could still detect a note of Ginger's spicy perfume. I pictured Cliff trying to pack up Ginger's belongings, and I knew what I could do to help.

"One of the last things Ginger did was buy gifts for your girls," Cliff said. "If you would take them back with you?"

I nodded, trying not to think about what Ginger had selected. "We'd like you to come home with us and have dinner."

"No. I'm really not . . . up to that."

"Cliff, would it help if I packed Ginger's things while you and Ed talk? It might be easier for you to let me do it."

His eyes filled, and he nodded. "The blue suitcase was hers."

I imagined Cliff hauling the suitcase home and being forced to unpack it. "Are you . . . I mean is there anything she had with her that you want to keep? Because I could pack those things separately for you to take back, and just take care of the rest of it here."

Again, he seemed grateful. "When my first wife died I had to dispose of her things." He shook his head. "I don't want anything. Ginger had some jewelry with her, I think. I'd like you to have whatever you want."

That was a wrinkle I hadn't thought of. "Oh no, that seems like a lot—"

"Please. Just take it all."

I nodded. If Cliff was planning a real funeral, the funeral director would expect us to provide a dress. If nothing hanging in the closet was appropriate, at least I'd know her size. This was something I could do for Cliff, as well.

I left Ed to discuss arrangements and went into the bedroom, closing the door behind me. Ginger's perfume was stronger here, and her belongings were strewn all over. This was going to be harder than I thought. Ginger still seemed alive in this room, and I could almost hear her ask why I was going through her things.

I found the suitcase lying open on a stand, but she had unpacked completely, and it was empty. I opened drawers and began to fold and place items inside. Lacy lingerie, sweaters I hadn't seen her wear, silk pajamas. I finished the drawers, leaving the row of drawers filled with Cliff's things untouched. Her jewelry was rolled in a satin case on top of the dresser. I was surprised how much she had brought with her and wondered if Junie might want it. I was sure my sisters wouldn't.

I cleaned out the closet and found a rust-colored wool dress with a matching paisley shawl that would be appropriate for her burial. I packed it on top, then I tackled the bathroom, assembling and packing everything that was clearly hers in a carry-on bag that had been next to the suitcase.

Fifteen minutes later I was finished. The only trace of Ginger was the perfume lingering in the air.

I joined the men in the sitting room. Ed stood when he saw me. "I can take that." He came over and got the bags. Cliff averted his eyes. Ed wheeled them just outside the door and left it ajar when he came back in to say goodbye.

We stood in the suite's hallway. "Cliff has decided on a simple memorial service. He's already talked to a funeral director. She'll probably be buried at Memorial Gardens. We'll know for sure tomorrow."

I didn't ask Cliff if he was certain this was what he wanted. I was sure Ed had covered that. Cliff was determined to leave Ginger in Emerald Springs with us.

Cliff seemed to cast around for something else to talk about, as if he was afraid he might cry. "I got two more switches in for you, before the police . . ." He shook his head and his eyes grew moist. "And I replaced the one in the room you're working on. It was defective."

I was surprised the switch had been the problem, not me. "Thanks." I touched his arm.

"Oh, I almost forgot. The girls' gifts are in the kitchen."

He took a few steps into the kitchenette and removed something from the counter beside the refrigerator, which had been blocked from view. He came back and handed me an envelope with Deena's name printed on the front in violet ink. Then he left again and returned with a cage. Inside was a guinea pig that was almost the exact red of Ginger's hair.

"Ginger said Teddy really wanted this for Christmas. I hope it's okay?" He held it out to Ed. "There's food and some other stuff to go with it."

I glanced at Ed, who was staring down at the guinea pig. Cliff had been through so much. I didn't know what to say.

"Teddy definitely wanted a guinea pig," Ed said, without looking at me. He took the cage from Cliff. "And we didn't get her one. She'll be thrilled."

Suddenly I knew, without opening the envelope in my hand, what Deena would find inside.

I was sure Cliff believed Ginger had chosen well. He was not the kind of man to pick up on the undercurrents at a dinner table. "You're a very thoughtful man," I said with as much sincerity as I could dredge up.

He returned with a bag filled with all the basics for the guinea pig. "Ginger wanted the girls to have a good Christmas. It meant a lot to her. She said giving them these gifts was like making up for the past."

In the hall Ed and I didn't say a word. Juggling the guinea pig and cage, the food and litter and Ginger's luggage, we made our way to the elevator.

Making up for the past.

Ginger was laughing at us from the grave, and we hadn't even buried her.

10

On the night after Christmas Sid and I hiked a block-by-block grid of Emerald Springs, starting at the Oval. I hoped with Christmas lights still shining, she would recognize at least a portion of the area where she had walked through falling snow on Christmas Eve. She was fairly certain which street she had taken after she placed the baby in the manger, but just two blocks away she thought she might have taken this turn, or maybe that one.

Frankly, I couldn't blame her. Emerald Springs is a lovely little town, but there's a definite trend toward icicle lights hanging from porch eaves and colored spotlights on evergreen plantings. The Frosties, Rudolphs, and Grinches are one big holiday cartoon commercial. Sid thought she recognized a brightly lit Santa, then we saw an identical one three blocks away. And so it went.

In fact, by the time we got home, the map we tried to create was a hopeless tangle of "maybes" and "not so sures." There was little point in giving it to Roussos as a way to check Sid's alibi. Short of knocking on every single door in a twelve-block radius, there was no way to prove my sister hadn't gotten the last laugh in her lifelong war with Ginger.

Meantime Ginger's last laugh at *my* expense was happily inert in the cage Ginger thoughtfully bought to house it. A delighted Teddy named the new guinea pig Cinnamon, Cin for short. As far as I can tell, Cin likes to sit in his cage. Or sit in Teddy's lap. This is his entire repertoire. I'm just grateful that either the stores in Emerald Springs didn't yield two guinea pigs or that Ginger somehow missed that part of Teddy's Christmas wish. Cin posing as a rock is one thing, but Cin humping a girl rock is a sight I hope never to see.

So far Moonpie has not tried to develop a more intimate relationship with Cinnamon, but oddly, he seems to miss Teddy's devoted attention. Maybe a cat can't sulk, but Moonpie's doing an excellent imitation.

As I had suspected when Cliff handed me the envelope, Deena is now the proud owner of three tickets to the Botoxins' concert in Columbus. Rather than humiliate Cliff, Ed and I agreed to let Deena keep them. When concert time comes, one of us will make the grand sacrifice and chaperone. I made myself buy one more ticket.

Of course three tickets mean that Deena has to choose two friends from her vast circle to go with her. All those not chosen won't just be hurt but furious. After all, it was Deena's mother who successfully preached that eleven-year-olds were too young for the concert.

Deena is nobody's fool. She figured this out while her excited squeal was still echoing through the parsonage. Judging from the times since then that I've caught her staring into space, she's struggling over how to resolve it.

Ah, Ginger. Your legacy lives on.

Since Emerald Springs is not a hotbed of violent crime, the autopsy was completed quickly, and Ginger's body was released for burial. The memorial service was planned for the Thursday afternoon after Christmas, and our Women's

Society volunteered to take care of the reception. I was
touched and grateful, and I suspected that the committee's
presence at the service would keep the sanctuary from feeling so empty and sad. Afterwards Ed would do a short
commitment service at the grave side with only Cliff in attendance. Cliff had asked that we respect his desire for a
private good-bye.

On Thursday morning I woke to a silent house. The girls
had spent the night with their friends the Frankel girls. Considering the circumstances of Ginger's death, we had decided not to require their attendance at the memorial service,
and May Frankel had volunteered to take them ice skating
instead. Junie wanted to do the flowers and was probably in
town driving our local florist crazy. Vel, who had extended
her vacation time for Ginger's service, was helping Junie—
or more likely, running interference. Ed was at church working on Ginger's service. That left only Sid and me.

I threw on sweats and went downstairs to see if Sid was
up, but the coffeemaker was off and the only sound was
Moonpie crunching cat food. I figured if Moonpie was hungry, Teddy and Vel, who was staying in Teddy's room, had
been conscientious about closing the bedroom door. Cin
was still with us.

I hadn't had the house to myself in such a long time that
I wasn't quite sure what to do with it. I love my mother and
sisters, but a mother probably coined the phrase "Silence is
golden." For a few minutes I felt rich.

One English muffin and a cup of hot chocolate later, I
knew how I wanted to spend my temporary wealth.

For the most part the Emerald Springs police department is good at what it does. We citizens are safe from
speed demons who enter intersections a second after the
light turns yellow. Our teenagers are routinely treated to
high school assemblies on the dangers of drinking and
driving, and Officer Jim does a puppet show for elementary school students on stranger danger.

But finding a murderer? In a town where homicides are rarer than a sunny day in February, practice never has time to make perfect. I thought that Detective Kirkor Roussos and his cohorts were fair-minded, intelligent, and tenacious. But did they have the training or experience to find Ginger's killer? Or were they going to settle for arresting my sister, who in their opinion had motive and opportunity to commit the crime? For all I knew they suspected Sid of having the means, as well. No new details had emerged on the way Ginger died. But I was afraid that once they had determined Sid could have committed the crime, an arrest was imminent.

My efforts to provide Sid with an alibi hadn't panned out, but I saw no harm in trying to provide another suspect or two for Roussos to investigate. None of us knew much about Ginger's life, just the sanitized and glorified version she'd recounted at dinner the night before she died. I'd seen Cliff once since our visit to the hotel, and I had tried as subtly as possible to get him to tell me more about Ginger, citing my desire to help him notify her friends. But Cliff is still in a fog and seems unable to put thoughts together coherently. So at the moment I had little to go on.

I may live in a town with no escalators, no airport, and no Asian restaurants, but there is absolutely nothing wrong with our telephone service. I could make a few calls before Sid got up or Ed discovered I was meddling again. Call the man old-fashioned, but he would prefer I take up Pilates or hooking rugs. He's not that fond of people shooting at me.

I remembered the name of Ginger's publisher from my short stint at Book Gems in the fall. It was easy enough to get the number in New York, so I made a list of questions. I hoped to track down someone chatty enough to share details that shouldn't be shared. When were they expecting Ginger's next book? Who was working with her on it? What kind of plans did they have for this one? On the list of people who had come in contact with Ginger during the publication process, which ones were most likely to have wanted her dead? In order from one to a hundred.

I dialed before I could talk myself out of it. In a supremely bored voice the receptionist explained that nobody in publishing works between Christmas and New Years and I should call back after the first of the year.

Strike one.

Since I couldn't canvass Ginger's Indianapolis neighbors, I went back in history and decided to discover what I could about her television show on the Cincinnati PBS station. Then if necessary I planned to work my way back to the news station where she'd gotten her first taste of the limelight. From there, the Culinary Institute. Surely someone would remember her.

Publishing might shut down over the holidays, but television doesn't have that luxury. The viewing public expects programming, even if it's reruns. I got the number for the most likely station and told the receptionist who I was. Clearly it was a slow morning because right from the start, he seemed thrilled to commiserate over Ginger's demise.

"Oh yes, I heard about it!" The man sounded youngish, and his voice was breathy and dramatic. I immediately imagined us as lifelong friends, sitting in a tapas bar over sangria and calamari dishing the dirt on everybody we knew. Not in Emerald Springs, though. A tapas bar is another one of those things we don't have.

"Ginger was my foster sister," I said, choosing my words carefully. "You can imagine how we all feel." I wasn't sure he could, but it seemed like the smallest of white lies.

"I came here just as she was leaving. Gawd, she was gorgeous, wasn't she? That hair, that skin."

"She was always beautiful. From the time she was a little girl."

"She photographed like a dream, you know. The camera loved her. It's too bad she—"

He chopped off that last word. Too bad she what? Died? Left the station? Was heartless and manipulative?

I felt my way. "I hadn't seen Ginger for a long time. And there's a gap in her life that I don't know anything about. I'd like to fill it. You say you knew her at least a little? Was she well liked there at the station?"

"Oh, I, well, I . . . Wait, I have another call."

I lost him to Muzak. Great. Clearly my new buddy had gone away to figure out how to answer without compromising every flutter of his integrity. Apparently he'd been at the station long enough to discover the real Ginger. Now he was trying to figure out how to let me down easily and get off the line.

A loud click cut short a particularly heinous instrumental of "Country Roads," and I launched in before he could recount whatever lie he'd concocted.

"Okay, look, I'm going to be honest with you. I *am* Ginger's foster sister, and I *am* trying to fill in the gaps in her life. But mostly because I don't think the police are doing a good enough job of figuring out who killed her. And they suspect somebody I love."

"Oh my gosh." He sounded thrilled. "You mean, you're looking for . . . for . . ."

"A murderer. You bet I am. And I'll find him. Or her. I always do." Okay, always is an exaggeration since I've only gone this route once before. But it sure sounded good.

"Wow! What can I do to help?"

We were going somewhere now. His voice was breathier. I was encouraged.

"Here's the thing," I said, lowering my voice, as if I were recounting a secret. "I know Ginger was hard to get along with. I know she could be difficult. I know she probably made enemies. I need to know who they were."

"Honey, she didn't have one friend here by the time she was fired. She—"

"Fired?"

"What? You didn't know?"

"No. She told us she quit because she was in an accident and couldn't do the show any more."

"Well . . . she was in an accident. That part was true. But it was more of an excuse than a reason for firing her."

I loved the way he had warmed to this. I imagined us sharing a plate of grilled chorizos. "I'm not sure I understand. Can you tell me more?"

"Well, just what I heard through the grapevine. But people here say that she was impossible, just impossible to work with! She didn't come in on time. Half the time she wasn't prepared. She made this demand, that demand. She'd throw a fit if something went wrong, and they'd have to start from the beginning. You know how bad it was? These days the production crew calls a tantrum 'Doing a Ginger.'"

"You're kidding!"

"I kid you not! And that's a no-no. Time is money. The show did okay. I don't think that was an issue. But it just wasn't worth the trouble."

"Was there anybody in particular she didn't get along with?"

He gave a throaty laugh. "Was there anybody she did?"

"Ouch."

"You got it."

I pictured an entire television station filled with people ready to murder Ginger. She had been a genius at alienating people. How very sad.

"So the list of suspects is a mile long," I said.

"You know, the person to ask would be her assistant."

I perked up. "Assistant?"

"Yeah. I think she left sometime after Ginger did. She went to help with Ginger's cookbook, so I never got to know her. But I bet she'd give you an earful."

"She sounds perfect. You have her name?"

"Hmmm . . ." He was silent a moment, and I pictured him going through a directory or a Rolodex. "Nope, don't have it. Like I said, I was coming in when they were going out. I don't remember the name."

"Will somebody else remember?"

"Not anybody who's here right this minute. We've got a skeleton crew on account of the holidays. You could call me this afternoon, though. One guy who might know comes in later. I'll see if I can find out something."

I could tell he liked being involved. I thanked him. "You've been a big help already."

"I'm Randall. Just ask for Rand. I'm the only one."

I thanked him again, hung up, and mentally paid our bill at the bar. The sangria had been heady.

"What are you doing?"

I turned to find Sid in the doorway, one brow lifted in question, her dark hair down and flowing over one shoulder. Sid looks good before her eyes are fully open. It really doesn't seem fair.

"I thought I'd do a little checking on Ginger, that's all," I assured her.

"You ought to stay out of this. I've brought you enough trouble already."

"I'm just asking a few questions. I don't want to disappoint Roussos. He knows I'll be snooping around. He depends on me."

She gave a pale imitation of a smile. "Junie expects me to go to the memorial service. Is that going to complicate your life? Do people in your church know I'm the prime suspect?"

"I don't care what they know. And you should come if that's where you want to be."

She gave a short nod. "I need to say good-bye. But it's so sad, Aggie. I'm not sure Ginger and I ever even said hello."

+ + +

We did say good-bye. All the family except my girls, and dozens of members of our congregation who came to support us. Cliff sat with Junie, and they shed their tears together. My sisters and I sat at the end of the row and listened as Ed read several poignant poems about death, then talked about Ginger's life. Junie had told Ed stories of Ginger's childhood, and now he recounted some of the memories that hadn't involved lashing out at everyone in her path. He talked about her television career and the success of her cookbook, then a little about her marriage to Cliff. Junie had provided a few childhood photos for a table in the front, and Ginger looked luminous and dewy-eyed.

During the final prayer, I opened my eyes before the "amen," looking for a tissue in my purse. As I turned my head I saw a woman, a stranger in a red coat, sliding out of a pew at the back of the church and heading for the door.

The service concluded. Since we were "family" our row was the first to leave the church. We were supposed to stay in the narthex and greet visitors and accept condolences, but once we'd gotten there, I told Sid I'd be back and left by a side door.

At first I thought the woman had vanished. But just as I was about to give up, I saw her crossing the Oval. The coat was a definite. She'd been hidden by the bandstand, but now she was in plain sight. I didn't think twice. I crossed the street and started after her.

She sped up, but so did I. On the other side of the Oval I caught her just as she was unlocking the door of a green Pontiac Grand Prix with a front bumper that looked as if it had tangled with a tree trunk.

"Excuse me."

Startled, she whirled around, her hand to her chest. "Oh, I didn't know anybody was there!"

I examined her a moment. She was somewhere in her forties, hair already mostly gray, eyes a washed-out blue. She looked tired, but I was afraid that was as permanent as the droop of her lips. She looked as if life had taken more than a few swats in her direction, and she no longer bothered to duck.

"I saw you at the service," I said, holding out my hand in a show of friendship. "I'm Aggie Sloan-Wilcox. Ginger lived with our family sometimes while she was growing up."

She shook quickly. "Your husband's the minister." It wasn't a question. She spoke softly, and the accent matched the license plate on her car. Both from Kentucky.

"I'm sorry, but I saw you leave. And I thought . . . well, I wondered if you were an old friend of Ginger's? I wanted to invite you to the reception."

She shook her head. "No, it's a long drive home. I'll be doing too much of it in the dark as it is."

"Do you mind if I ask if you knew Ginger?"

Something crossed her face. If I'd had to guess I would have said it was *Boy, did I ever*.

I could relate.

"I see you did," I said, taking a chance. "And you weren't always glad about it. Don't worry, you're not the only one who felt that way."

She seemed to relax a little. "I'm sorry. She wasn't . . . easy."

"Easy she wasn't."

I knew I wasn't going to get this woman back to the church. But I didn't want her to leave without talking to her. "Look, it's cold out here and you've got a long drive back to Kentucky."

She nodded.

"Let me treat you to a cup of coffee before you go. There's a nice little place just a block away."

"Why?"

The question was blunt but called for. Again, as in my conversation with Rand, I figured the truth was the only way to go. "Because I'm trying to fill in some of the gaps in Ginger's past to figure out who might have killed her."

"It wasn't me."

"Well, that saves us some time." I smiled, and after a moment she smiled a little, too. "It's just a cup of coffee."

She hunched her shoulders in defeat. "Okay."

We didn't say much on the way to Give Me a Break. She did tell me her name was Carol Ann Riley, and she had known Ginger in Cincinnati.

I bought two mocha lattes, and she cupped hers gratefully in her hands, inhaling the entwined scents. We found a corner table.

"That should help you stay awake," I said. "At least the roads are clear."

She nodded and took a sip. "I saw a notice about the service on a trade e-mail loop. I already knew she was dead. I saw that in the newspaper."

"So you came up from Kentucky to pay your respects?"

"No, to make sure it was true." Carol Ann put down her cup and shook her head. "That's not fair. I came because sometimes a funeral's the only way to write the end to a chapter in your life."

"Carol Ann, would you mind telling me how you knew her?"

"I was Ginger's assistant at WKLM. And later I helped her with the cookbook."

The planets were perfectly aligned. That had to be the answer. Only this morning I'd learned of Carol Ann's existence, and now here she was sitting right across from me.

I told her about my conversation with Rand. "I was going to find you and ask you to tell me anything you could. I gather Ginger wasn't very popular at the station?"

"About as popular as a drop in the ratings."

"Assistants work awfully close to their bosses. Seems to me you probably got a good look at all the reasons she wasn't liked."

"Pick an adjective, any adjective, as long as it's negative."

"What did she do to you personally then?"

Carol Ann sipped. I thought she was sorting her thoughts,

or else she was numbering Ginger's offenses in order of importance.

"She used me," Carol Ann said at last. "You can say whatever you like about Ginger, but she wasn't stupid. She could spot weakness at thirty paces, and she had a deadly aim. She figured me out right away. I had every quality she needed in an assistant and no self-esteem. I was eager to hover in her shadow. Here was this bright, pretty woman on her way to the top who needed my skills. And she knew just how to keep me working for her. Large dollops of criticism and crumbs of praise."

I suspected Carol Ann had indulged in a year or two of therapy since leaving her job with Ginger. This knowledge sounded hard won.

"How did she use you?" I asked. "And I'm not surprised, sad to say."

That seemed to give her confidence. "As a cook Ginger was a no-talent hack. There, I've said it and I'm not sorry. She couldn't plan a menu. She was too disorganized to assemble ingredients or tools. And her ideas were terrible."

I thought of the new cookbook title. "So how did she get her own show?"

"She got the show because she looked great on camera. She was flunking out of culinary school and grabbed the job at that first TV station. She was too short to be a fashion model, but she did fine standing in front of the cameras reading somebody else's script and demonstrating basics. Later when she needed more expertise, she hired me. I put the shows together, came up with the concept, and organized everything. I even taught her some of the elementary skills she needed. Of course how much I did was hush-hush. Ginger didn't want anybody to know she wasn't in complete control."

"And that explains why nobody questioned her abilities when she proposed doing a cookbook?"

"Most of the recipes in that cookbook? The entire

concept? Mine! She promised me she was going to share
the royalties and give me proper credit, but of course, I
never saw a dime except the small salary she paid me."

I gave a low whistle. This made Sid's reasons for dislik-
ing Ginger sound anemic. "Is that when you quit? When
the book was finished and you realized she wasn't going to
share the royalties?"

"I started to get the picture earlier than that. So I did some
checking. I looked at the contracts, talked to some people at
her publisher, and finally figured out that I wasn't getting a
thing. Ginger had hidden my contributions on the show, and I
realized she was going to do it again. One afternoon she blew
up at me when we were working on a recipe, and it all just
came flooding in. So I quit. Left her high and dry. She had to
finish the book by herself. And she didn't have the skills."

I tried not to imagine all the people at the church who
were wondering where I had disappeared to. "So she finished without your help."

"Yes, but the work she did was bad. Really terrible. Her
editor found me and begged me to go back and help Ginger
finish the book. She actually had the nerve to appeal to my
loyalty. And the only reason she wanted me was because
she knew the house would have to pay somebody else a lot
more."

"I bet that made you angry."

She smiled without any warmth. "I hear that's what they
did, too. Hired staff to test and fix every single one of the
recipes Ginger submitted on her own. It cost them money
and time. But they had to do it. It was so late in the game
that the book had been advertised and the orders were already in."

I sat back. "I guess they weren't too unhappy though,
were they? I mean the book did well, didn't it?"

Carol Ann took another sip. "Not as well as you seem to
think."

"No?"

"Do you know how many cookbooks are published every year? It was a flash in the pan. If she'd had the savvy to stay on top of things, Ginger could have made something out of it. But she couldn't focus, and the publisher was fed up with her. They probably took every cent they'd had to spend to get the book in shape out of her future earnings. I don't know that for sure, but I do know that the new ideas she gave them didn't go anywhere."

"Are you saying she probably didn't make a lot of money off the book?"

"That's what I'm saying. She was paid all right up front, but knowing Ginger the money was probably gone almost immediately. And I doubt there was much left in royalties. And no prospects of more for a second book."

This was all new information. I swirled what was left of my mocha. "You had lots of reasons to dislike her," I said at last.

"I was sitting in my mother's church in Frankfort on Christmas Eve. Four hundred people saw me. You can check it out." She finished her drink and set the cup on the table.

"Who else then?" I leaned forward and touched her arm. "Carol Ann, it sounds to me like you knew Ginger better than almost anybody else. Was there anybody else she worked with who hated her enough to kill her?"

She rocked the cup back and forth. "She made life miserable for a lot of people. But hate enough to kill?"

I realized I had overstated things. "Then how about this? Whose life did she make the most miserable?"

"Besides me? A long list. But at the top? There was one woman in marketing. She was new at the station. She did this really cute campaign for Ginger's WKLM show, *Spice It with Ginger*. Cute title, huh? My idea. Anyway, when Ginger saw the concept she threw a tantrum. A real full-blown, no-holds-barred tantrum. She hated everything about it. The station owner kind of had a thing for Ginger, and the woman in marketing was on probation since she was new. So he fired her."

My ears perked up. "The station manager had a thing for Ginger?"

"Not that way. He was pushing seventy, and the whole thing was completely professional, not an affair. He just thought Ginger's show was going to be so big it would immediately go into syndication, and he wanted her to be happy. That was one of the first tantrums she threw, before everyone realized tantrums were going to be the norm. By the end, he was as glad to see her go as anybody else."

For a moment I'd been excited about the station manager connection. A jealous, thwarted lover. A Christmas Eve tryst gone bad. At least it would have been something to chase down.

Carol Ann stood, and I stood, too, knowing that I was already so late for the reception, eyebrows would be hanging from hairlines. "Will you give me your phone number, in case I have more questions?"

Carol Ann fished out a business card and handed it to me. "I'm at school during the day. I went back to teaching. Family and consumer science. That's what we call home economics these days. I teach life skills and cooking. Teenagers are a lot kinder than Ginger ever was." She smiled, and this time it reached her eyes. "I'm working on a cookbook for young people striking out on their own."

"Good luck. I mean it."

"You don't have to worry about me. I've got my life in order."

We walked out of the shop and started back toward the Oval. I tried to figure out how to explain my absence to the Women's Society.

"I wonder if Mabyn ever got hers in order," Carol Ann said. "It was such a blow to her to be fired like that."

I had been mentally honing the story of my disappearance. A moment passed before Carol Ann's words sank in. "I'm sorry. What did you say?"

"That poor young woman in marketing. Mabyn somebody or other."

Mabyn is *not* the most common name in a baby names book. I tried to sound nonchalant. "You don't remember her last name, do you?"

"Like I said, she wasn't at the station very long. I only remember the first name because it's unusual."

"It certainly is." And hadn't Mabyn Booth told me that advertising had once been her career? B.S. Before Shirley? Hadn't she also said that she and Howard had moved here from Cincinnati?

I tried to picture the faces in the small crowd at the memorial service. Had Mabyn been among them? I didn't think so.

"Funny thing," Carol Ann said as we were parting company. "For a long time I wished I were Ginger. I thought she had everything. How wrong could I be?"

I had to agree. I was beginning to think that the only thing Ginger had possessed in abundance was bad judgment.

11

The explanation for my absence—that I had left the church to comfort an acquaintance of Ginger's—seemed to satisfy nearly everyone, and after I'd made my apologies, I chatted with the kind souls who had turned out and thanked them for coming. In the kitchen I helped the Women's Society committee wash coffeepots and the trays that had housed bakery sandwiches and cookies. Mabyn hadn't attended the service, nor had any of the Booths, but this seemed for the best. I couldn't very well accuse her of murder just because once upon a time Ginger had been responsible for firing somebody with the same first name. At least, not yet.

I needed more information, and Rand was the man to get it for me. I knew he would be thrilled to learn his first tip had already paid off.

By the time the clean up was finished, I realized my family was gone or going. I caught Vel just as she was walking out the back door.

"Lucy took Junie for a drive," Vel said.

I'd asked Lucy to watch over Junie at the open house, and apparently she was still doing it. I bet she had taken my mother somewhere to get her mind off her troubles. Maybe a stop at the Victorian to see our new project. Or the button museum in an old house in Weezeltown, one of the not so desirable sections of Emerald Springs.

Vel was perfectly dressed for the service wearing her dark suit, an icy pink blouse, attractive but sensible shoes. No Jimmy Choos for Vel. Like the prudent CPA she is, she doesn't want management to think the vast sums they've entrusted to her have plummeted straight to her tootsies.

"Tomorrow I have to get to Cincinnati by three," Vel said. "I couldn't get a flight out of Columbus on such short notice. And Cleveland is booked up, too."

"I'll take you down." I looked around and lowered my voice. "What about Sid?"

"She cancelled her flight. She hasn't rescheduled."

"How will that play at work?" Since the country club had one event after another over the holidays, she'd had to talk fast to get time off. Now with New Year's Eve looming, they must be frantic.

"It's not playing well," Vel confirmed. "And they weren't impressed that she's been asked to stay in town while the cops investigate a murder."

"Poor kid." Sid is so good at what she does, I hoped her boss would remember that and cut her some slack.

"I'm afraid you'll have your hands full for a while. Junie's planning to stay until Sid's cleared. I hear Cliff isn't in any hurry to leave town, not until he knows something about Ginger's murder. And Sid? She's going to be a basket case unless you can keep her busy."

"I would ask her to plan another party, but we're still reeling from the last one."

"You'll need to think of something."

"Maybe she can help me at the Victorian. She can steam wallpaper. Anybody can steam wallpaper."

"I visited Signor DiBenedetto this morning and stocked your cabinets. I'm planning to cook enough this afternoon to help you over the hump."

Translation. There will be enough food in your refrigerator, Aggie, to feed the hungry for the next century. I gave her a spontaneous, acceptably brief hug. "I'll help you."

"Don't. It's my way of coping with . . . everything."

She took off for the parsonage. I went to look for Ed, whose sensitive, carefully edited rendition of Ginger's life had touched my heart. At moments like this I am particularly happy to have chosen a life with this man.

I found him in the parish house foyer, glassy-eyed and mesmerized by his new secretary. Norma Beet was not Ed's first or second choice for this job. Unfortunately Ed's real preferences were incidental. Norma is the daughter of Alfred Beet, an octogenarian in our congregation who consistently refused to let anyone step into his barn of a house to cook and clean. When Norma volunteered to move from South Dakota to take care of him, Alfred relented. Unfortunately Norma also needed a job to make ends meet. She has all the required skills except one. She does not understand the meaning of silence.

"I've told Esther the organ is too loud, but she insists that's the only thing that will keep people from talking during her prelude. I heard two complaints after the service today. I have to bring ear plugs and stuff them in when she starts to play. I won't have any hearing left if I don't."

Ed looked pale. I wondered how long Norma had been talking. Ed is working to dam the torrent, but after a long, emotional service, he runs out of sandbags. Since the woman doesn't have a mean bone in her body, he has to be kind while he's at it. I foresee months of chatter before Norma learns the limits.

"What do you think, Aggie?" Norma turned to me. She's a short woman, round in the middle, graying brown hair blackened to ebony except for an inch at the roots, cat's-eye glasses that sit on a pert little nose. She tends to buy clothing two sizes too small, positive that she'll lose weight. Buttons pop and zippers abandon tracks, but Norma struggles into a size twelve anyway.

She didn't give me a chance to comment. "Esther is a wonderful organist, but I just think the volume is too high." Norma continued the monologue as my gaze flicked to my husband. Ed was draining of color.

"Norma . . ." I waited a second and repeated her name a little louder. "Norma!"

She stopped, looking perplexed.

"I have to talk to Ed, will you excuse us?" I linked my arm through my husband's and steered him into his study. I closed the door the moment we were over the threshold.

"I was paralyzed," he said.

I kissed him. "She's really a very nice woman. Can we buy a set of color-coordinated gags?"

"I've talked to her about listening more and talking less. She says it's a habit. Eventually she'll run out of things to say."

"Nope. She'll just start all over again."

"You disappeared after the service. What happened?"

I told him quickly. "And last but not least, Carol Ann told me Ginger got a woman named Mabyn fired at the station in Cincinnati."

He put his hands on my arms and held me in place. "Aggie, the Booths are off limits."

"No one is off limits."

"Please, find somebody who's not in the congregation to pin this on, okay?" He must have realized what he'd said because he frowned. "What are you doing? You're not supposed to be involved in this investigation."

"Of course I'm involved. My sister's the chief suspect. My foster sister was the victim."

"Good reasons to stay out of it. What is this, some weird kind of family bonding ritual? One sister killed, one sister under suspicion, one sister solving the crime? What's left for poor Vel? Oh, I know, she gets to cater the whole thing!"

I couldn't help myself. I giggled. Call it nerves.

He tightened his grip. "Aggie!" But he didn't look angry enough to worry me.

I disciplined the giggle. "I'm just asking some questions. I'm going to tell Roussos everything I've found out. I'll keep him in the loop, and I won't do anything stupid."

"I've heard that before."

"I don't want Sid going to jail."

Ed dropped his hands to his sides. "You don't have anything there that will interest Roussos."

"Then I'll have to find more." This time I kissed his cheek. "We're going to have a houseful of company until this is settled. And I hear Cliff is staying in town?"

"He says he wants to stay until there's a lead. But I think he's just afraid to go back to a lonely house."

"The hotel isn't cheap. Especially not a suite like he has."

"Apparently money's not much of an issue."

"Carol Ann said Ginger probably didn't make much on the cookbook."

"Then it's Cliff's money."

I told Ed about my conversation with Vel and my plans to drive her to Cincinnati tomorrow to catch a plane home. Then I tiptoed to the door and listened. I didn't hear footsteps. I didn't hear humming, the sound of papers being rattled, the watering of plants, the donning of a coat.

"I think she's gone," I whispered.

"You first," Ed whispered back. "If you're brave enough to find a murderer, you're brave enough to go out there."

I glared at him, then I opened the door. Norma was standing about six feet away, reaching for the ceiling, one arm raised, then another.

I wondered if I could sneak around the exercise session, but it wasn't to be. She turned at the first footfall on the tile floor.

"I didn't even tell you how sorry I am about your foster sister," Norma said. "I can't imagine what that's like. I never had a sister. I had one brother, and he was up to no good my entire childhood. He left home at sixteen and calls now and then but—"

I listened and pictured the *National Geographic* special I'd seen about cobras. First they rise in the air, then they sway and hypnotize their prey. I was slowly being hypnotized. I wondered what Norma would do when I no longer had any will of my own . . .

"Heading out." I shook my head to clear it. "Heading out. I have to go home. It was nice talking to you, Norma."

"Of course I hardly had the opportunity to know Ginger," Norma said, undeterred. "I only saw her that once at your open house. Actually, that's not true. I only saw her outside talking to somebody. Actually it looked more like an argument. Now I wish I'd heard what was being said, but of course I was minding my own business, the way anybody would in that situation. I—"

I'd nearly missed the wheat in the chaff. I moved closer. "You say you saw Ginger arguing with somebody?"

"Well, you know, I got there late. I mean, the party was nearly over on account of this bunion on my big toe and my not finding comfortable shoes. And when I finally got there, things were, well, kind of a mess, you know? What with punch all over the floor and broken glass and—"

"You saw her outside?"

"Oh, yes. She looked so angry. I guess the punch had gotten on that pretty blouse she was wearing and—"

"Where exactly was she?"

"Oh, on the side of your house. The side facing the back of the church. And the other woman—"

"Woman?"

"Yes, she was talking to a woman. Remember how cold it was? Well neither of them had coats on. It's amazing how these young people can tolerate the cold. I mean, I'm from

South Dakota, but you wouldn't catch me outside without a sweater and a coat, hat, and—"

I took her hand and squeezed to quiet her. "Who was the woman, do you know?"

"Well, no, I only caught a glimpse, you see. She had her back to me, and I still don't know everybody, I'm afraid. I just remember because it was odd they were arguing out there in the cold."

"Describe her. And how do you know they were arguing?"

"She was shaking her fist. Ginger, I mean, like she wanted to scare off the other woman, but that one, she was standing her ground. She was young. Let's see. Brown hair, kind of dark and shiny. Lucky hair, the kind that just curves perfectly, if you know what I mean. Not real long or short. And she was wearing a gold sweater. Dull gold, with just a little sparkle to it. And something black under it. But that's all I saw. The sweater was so pretty I wished I had one like it."

I had wished the same thing when I'd seen Mabyn's gold sweater at the open house. Mabyn of the chocolate brown hair and the excellent fashion sense.

"What exactly did you hear them saying?"

Norma looked sad. "Not much, I'm afraid." She leaned closer. "I tried to hear, but they weren't very loud. I only heard Ginger say something about sin in the attic. Or maybe it was Cincinnati. I wasn't sure."

I thanked her and before she could respond, I took off for home. I needed final confirmation that our Mabyn was the same Mabyn Ginger had axed at the television station, but I thought I might be one step closer to solving my foster sister's murder.

+ + +

Cheering up my mother and sisters was out of the question. But providing a little comfort seemed doable. We had gone

through all the party goodies over the holidays, and I suspect Vel was only loading my refrigerator with substantial,
hearty fare. After leaving the church I decided to walk up
to the bakery and see if there was anything interesting left
in the case. Sometimes the owner gives me a bargain at
day's end.

I was so deep in thought that I almost missed Roussos.
This is the great thing about a small town. This is also the
bad thing. You can't walk the streets without running into
somebody you know. In this case, I was glad to see my personal homicide detective on the sidewalk.

"Mrs. Wilcox." He nodded. The smile was tentative, the
greeting formal. Investigating someone's kid sister for murder will do that to a relationship.

"Detective. I was going to look you up." I stopped, forc-
ing him to do the same, but he didn't look pleased.

"Why?"

This was not a man who indulged in small talk. I forced
a smile. "How were your holidays?"

He lifted a brow. As always I was all too aware what an
attractive guy he is. I'm just careful not to let Kirkor Roussos into my fantasies.

"Your holidays?" I repeated.

"I worked."

Unfortunately I knew at what. "As a matter of fact, so
did I. I've found out a few things about Ginger you might
want to know."

He crossed his arms over a black leather jacket that was
just worn enough to be intriguing. I remembered how wonderful it felt from a previous encounter. I want that jacket.

"Why am I not surprised?" he said.

"Don't tell me this isn't any of my business. We know
it is."

"Your business is comforting your family. *My* business
is finding a murderer."

"I can do more than one thing at a time. And who has

more of an investment in the outcome than I do? Besides Sid, of course."

"What have you found out?" He said it with a "so you'll leave me alone" note in his voice.

"Ginger was a big problem to the people she worked with, both at her publisher and earlier at the television station. I talked to her former assistant who didn't have a good thing to say. I can give you her number. She lives in Kentucky, but she claims she has an alibi."

He nodded and didn't look surprised or particularly interested.

"She also told me that Ginger was responsible for getting a young woman fired at the station, and I think that same woman lives here in Emerald Springs. Someone may even have seen her arguing with Ginger during our party."

"She has a name?"

I could just imagine siccing Roussos on the Booth family unnecessarily. Can we picture the Wilcox family packing and moving out of the parsonage and Emerald Springs under cover of darkness?

"She does have a name," I said, "but I want to talk to her first."

"Did somebody give you a badge? Am I missing something here?"

"She's a member of our church."

"I wish you'd leave this alone. You're making me old before my time. I'm not over your last stint as a detective."

"Hey, I was the one in the car trunk."

"Yeah, and you seem to forget it wasn't a trunk full of laughs."

"Just tell me you're looking into Ginger's past and all the numerous people who might have wanted her dead."

"Not a one of whom was known to be in the very place where her body was taken—"

"Taken? She wasn't murdered where she was found?"

Roussos just looked at me. I could tell he wished I had chosen another route to the bakery.

"You think Sid could have carried Ginger to the nativity scene? She works out, but she's not Arnold Schwarzenegger."

He didn't reply.

"We're done here," I said, reading his mind.

"We're done."

"Please check out the TV station and her publisher, okay?"

"We're doing our job. You can count on that." He nodded and left me standing there. By the time I remembered to move, the bakery had closed its doors for the day.

✦ ✦ ✦

Ed was still at the church, doing heaven knows what. I suspected he was working on the order of service for Sunday. Ginger's memorial service had taken a lot of his time.

Junie wasn't home yet. How many old buttons can one woman admire? I was guessing that Lucy had finished off their field trip with a drive into the country. There's a farm store about six miles from our city limits with homemade ice cream that's too good to pass up, even in December.

Sid was on her cell phone with a colleague from the country club trying to finalize plans for their New Year's Eve extravaganza long distance. Vel was simultaneously working on a gourmet version of plain old mac and cheese and a vegetable lasagna. The girls were still with the Frankels but expected home soon. My window of opportunity was brief. I locked myself in our bedroom and dialed WKLM. I was afraid Rand might already have left for the day, but he answered.

"I met her," I said with excitement. "Carol Ann Riley. Ginger's assistant. She came to the funeral."

"Go *on!*"

"I did, and we had a nice little chat. She has an alibi, so no dice there. But she told me about someone else." I recounted the story of Mabyn, then I told him about the fight Norma had witnessed. I knew that the more Rand felt he was in on this, the more help he would be. Me and Rand, old buddies that we are.

"Girlfriend, you are on the road!"

"I know. I know. So here's what else I need to know. Can you find out this Mabyn's last name? Would the records be there somewhere?"

"I don't have to look up records. Our floor manager remembers Ginger like she was still here, and he told me some luscious stuff to pass on. You just sit there and I'll see if he remembers the PR person."

Luscious stuff? I could hardly believe my luck. I sang along with the orchestral version of "Grandma's Featherbed." No question we were into a John Denver retrospective this week.

Rand came back just in time to save me from bungling the words to "Rocky Mountain High."

"He remembers all right," he said triumphantly. "Her name was Mabyn Ross."

I scribbled that down. Now I just had to find out if Mabyn Booth had been a Ross before her marriage. And I was just the gal to do it.

"Okay, you promised luscious stuff!"

"Oh, is it ever." He lowered his voice. "I've got to do this quick. Evening shift takes over in a minute."

"So what did you find out? Tell me quick."

"Well, when Ginger caught on that she was going to lose her job, she started looking around for somebody to support her. But nobody, I mean nobody, thought she'd finally settle for the misfit inventor. He was *so* not her type."

So much to find out, so little time. "What was her type?"

"Oh flashy, darling. And boyfriends with clout, although I hear she wasn't picky about where it came from. The leader of the pack was a guy named Kas, and everybody expected her to—"

I waited, hardly breathing. I heard Rand's voice in the background, like he'd turned his head away from the receiver. "Yeah, all done here and ready for the switcheroo. Just let me finish this call."

He came back on. "Gotta go. Sorry."

Of all the possible threads to pursue, I chose what seemed the most important. "Why'd she choose Cliff, do you know?"

"Some people say he was just ripe for the picking. You know, after losing his first wife that way."

"What way?" I nearly shouted the question, in case the receiver was on its way back to the cradle.

"She committed suicide. Didn't you know? He was the one who found her."

"Rand, there's so much more you want to tell me, right?"

"I'm here tomorrow until six."

I had to let him hang up. I imagined the evening receptionist glaring at him. "Tomorrow, then."

"TTYL, darling." The line went dead.

I scribbled what he'd told me on the back of a Christmas receipt, which is what all good detectives do. Mabyn Ross. Cliff's first wife committed suicide. Somebody named . . . what was it? Something odd. Cass? I held the paper a few inches farther away so I could focus on it. I don't need reading glasses yet, but will soon enough if my arm shrinks.

I couldn't do much about the last item until I talked to Rand tomorrow, but I could do something about Mabyn. I'm the church historian, one of those jobs that's acceptable for the minister's partner to take on since the parishioners I become intimate with are, for the most part, dead or gone. No one can accuse me of playing favorites.

I'm working on a church history, and because I'd rather

work on it here, I keep a lot of the records on the premises. I know that Mabyn and Howard were married in the church by the former minister. Fern had mentioned this several times as in "You would think the church I give so much money to, the church where my only son was married would: 1) ask my opinion on every little matter 2) name the social hall after me 3) fire the minister if he gives a sermon I don't like."

Well, okay, even Fern never says these things. But she has mentioned Howard and Mabyn's marriage. I believe the pews were not polished to her specification, and even though Ed wasn't here at the time, she still holds him accountable.

Since Sid was still on her cell phone downstairs, I went to the guest room and retrieved the list of weddings that had been performed in our sanctuary starting in 1927, when the record first began, to the present. I scanned it quickly and sure enough, two and a half years ago, Howard Booth and Mabyn Ross had tied the knot at Tri-C.

Mabyn Ross. How many Mabyn Rosses could there be in the world? How many hailed from Cincinnati? I had the proof I needed. And now I had one more thing to do tomorrow.

12

The next morning Deena was the second one up. I was the first, starting with a quick trip to the bakery to make up for missing my chance yesterday. The day-old coffee cake is nearly as good as the fresh if it's warmed in the oven. Until Luce and I flip a couple more houses, day-old will do nicely.

I had coffee brewing and orange juice in a pitcher by the time Deena shuffled in. My daughter's not a morning person, but since this might be our only moment alone, I took full advantage. I gave her a hug with one arm and a glass of juice with the other. She poured it down her throat like a desert explorer between water holes. She had pulled her hair into an uncombed ponytail and wore khaki-colored sweats that were two sizes too large. She still looked delightful.

Deena plopped into a chair, and I served her a piece of coffee cake. She nodded and muttered her thanks. I gauged when the sugar would hit and a conversation could begin. I counted to thirteen.

"How did skating go yesterday?"

"Okay."

My calculations had been off. I'd forgotten to factor in preadolescent disgust for adults. I busied myself silently setting out cream, milk, cereal.

Thirty seconds later Deena broadened her reply. "Maddie thinks because we went skating together I'll invite her to the concert."

May Frankel, Maddie and Hillary's mother, had commiserated with me when I told her about Ginger's gifts to the girls. But even though she's a psychologist, she had little advice to offer. I think she's watching to see what we do. If it works, she can include it in her clinical repertoire.

"I assumed Maddie would be one of your choices." I kept my tone casual. For this I deserve a medal.

"Like I know right now. There's so much to think about!"

Whew. All that on a nearly empty stomach. I could only imagine how much Deena was struggling.

The curtain closed on that particular drama when Teddy came in. Unlike Deena, she is fully alert on waking. She carried wide-lined paper with her, and I could see she had filled half of it with her careful printing.

"I'm writing my story about Cinnamon," she said.

A story about angels, with all that vast potential for creativity, had morphed into the tale of an inanimate guinea pig. I could picture the look on Miss Hollins's face.

"There's an idea," I said.

"He's lonely."

I didn't know if this was true, but again, I was glad Ginger had only provided Teddy with one. "So what happens in the story?" I asked Teddy.

"He feels sad."

"That's not a story," Deena said. "Something has to happen in a story."

"He feels sad, then he eats, then he feels sad again."

Deena snorted.

Teddy sensed her sister's disdain. "Then he sleeps!"

I interrupted with a glass of juice and a slice of coffee cake before we heard about the bodily function that so far had gone unmentioned.

"Aunt Vel is leaving this afternoon," I told them. "She thought the three of you might like to go shopping this morning." Knowing Vel my girls would come home with cute tailored suits or chef's aprons.

Both girls perked up, and I knew how I would spend the hour they were away.

I left Vel in charge of my daughters, Sid and Junie planning a walk around the neighborhood and Ed . . . where else? He showered, then took off for his office with his coffee in a go cup to polish up tomorrow's sermon. Frankly I suspect he just wants to get away from the girls' dorm we call a parsonage. Who can blame him?

I considered calling Mabyn to warn her I was on the way, but decided against it. I like the element of surprise. I might find her burying the murder weapon or changing Shirley's diaper. I wasn't sure which would be worse.

The senior Booths live in Emerald Estates, which is adjacent to our one and only country club. Their house is designed to look like a French chateau, with a mansard roof and a marble foyer large enough to host a meeting of the local Democratic party.

I turned the car in the other direction. Wisely Howard and Mabyn settled on the other side of town, in a suburb with smaller homes, fewer pretensions, and a rabbit warren of "Courts," "Trails," and "Places." I found their house after fifteen minutes of asking every passerby the directions to Rosebud Ramble. Turns out the "Ramble" is a cul de sac with only three houses on each side. I suspected an attempt to confuse the senior Booths and foil their visits.

Mabyn and Howard's house is contemporary in style, a one-story cedar with large windows and something of an

Asian feel with its peaked roof and a dry stone stream with a decorative wooden bridge leading to the porch. I parked on the street and admired the effect as I crossed over. Everything was well cared for and of course, in excellent taste.

I knocked, and Mabyn answered quickly.

"Aggie?" She looked surprised but not sorry to see me. "You're a long way from home. Don't tell me you got lost back here."

"No, I came to see you. Do you have a few minutes?"

"You're in luck. Shirley's watching *Sesame Street*."

I remembered those days and the amount I could accomplish while my girls were entranced by Cookie Monster and Oscar the Grouch.

Mabyn opened the door wider to let me in. "I'll make us tea. Sound good?"

I followed her to a kitchen that opened into a small family room where Shirley, dressed in comfortable plaid knit, was watching her show. She didn't look up.

"Shirley looks like she's feeling better," I said.

"She's definitely on the mend."

I'd gotten a nice little tour of the house on the way. The interior decor was minimalist, but there were artful touches, a lacquerware vase of silk cherry blossoms, Japanese scrolls on the wall, a red and black silk kimono hanging over a fireplace in the living room. The effect was soothing, which would surely be a benefit after encounters with Fern.

"Who spent time in Japan?" I asked.

She waved me to a stool at the black granite island. The appliances were stainless steel, but the refrigerator was covered with Shirley's coloring book scribbles. The counters were warmed by ceramic canisters in primary hues.

Mabyn filled an electric kettle. "I was an exchange student, and I lived there for a couple of years after college. I loved every minute of it, but I didn't want to teach English forever."

"You were in public relations, right?"

"More like marketing." She pulled out a canister of jasmine tea and held it out for my approval.

"Wonderful," I said.

I waited until the water had boiled and she'd poured it over the tea leaves before I began. "I came to talk to you about your working life."

"I wondered. You have a reputation as a snoop."

I didn't hear even a hint of malice. We were going to have a grown-up conversation. "Snooping's been pretty well foisted on me."

"I heard that, too. But I'm surprised you figured out my relationship to Ginger so quickly. I've been trying to decide whether I ought to say something, but I wasn't sure there was a point."

"Fast is good. There's not much time before my sister gets pinned for the crime."

"I hate to tell you, but I didn't kill Ginger." She brought the pot and cups to the island and joined me on a stool. "Actually, I don't hate to tell you. I'd be in big trouble if I had."

"And feeling guilty?"

She cocked her head as if considering. "I'm sure I would be. Only I'm not going to pretend I'm devastated by her death. In a way it almost seemed inevitable. It's hard to make that many enemies without repercussions. Of course death is the ultimate repercussion, isn't it?"

"Unfortunately. Shall I ask questions, or do you just want to spill your guts?"

She laughed as if she were perfectly comfortable. "I was employed by WKLM in Cincinnati in their public relations and marketing departments. I'd gone to school there, so it was nice to be back after the years in Japan. I had such plans for that job. And when they gave me Ginger's show to work on, I was ecstatic. I hadn't met her, of course, I'd just seen a sample of her work, but I knew everyone had high hopes for *Spice It with Ginger*. She looked terrific on camera. I think management believed she'd pull in as many male viewers as female."

"And then?"

"Then, I met her. Ginger was marking her territory, so to speak. Now I understand it. She wanted to make sure everybody knew who was boss. Nothing I suggested would have pleased her, because Ginger was determined to use whatever I came up with to show her muscle."

"So you were fired."

"I was so new, I was still on three-months probation. I made the mistake of losing my temper when the station manager came to tell me how badly my campaign had disappointed Ginger. At that point nobody but me had seen Ginger's dark side. I cleaned out my desk, and that was that."

"I'm not so sure."

"What do you mean?" Mabyn poured the tea and handed me mine. The fragrance of jasmine filled the room. I inhaled with pleasure.

"That was some time ago, right? But according to somebody I spoke to, you and Ginger had an argument the day of the open house. *That* wasn't *that*, was it?"

Mabyn sipped, but the tea was too hot and she set it on the island. "I lost my dream job because of Ginger Newton. I ended up with something I liked a lot less, although it paid the bills. For a year I was furious. I knew how unfair it was. That was what bothered me the most, even more than losing the job. The unfairness. When something like that happens, it just fills you up, like a balloon that keeps inflating, no matter how many times you tell yourself to let it float away."

There might be enough outrage here to commit murder. But anger wasn't reflected in Mabyn's voice. I waited. She was staring into space, then she faced me.

"Here's how I coped. I followed Ginger's life, and I

waited for her to screw up and the world to see what kind
of person she really was. I kept track of her. I still had a
couple of friends at the station. They kept me up to date on
what was happening with her show and personal life. Every
time something went wrong, I felt a little better. That's awful, I know, but it was like I needed to see that the universe
had some balance. I wanted to know she was getting a little
of what she dished out."

"Well, in the end, I'm afraid she got more than a little."

"I couldn't believe it when I walked into your house and
saw her there. And you know what? She had *no* idea who I
was. She didn't bat an eyelash. I'd been nothing to her,
just somebody to step on for a boost up. When your sister
nearly drowned her in the punch bowl, I felt like somebody
had finally set me free. Oh, I was over most of it by then,
but there were still the tiniest vestiges lingering. And when
Ginger took off outside afterwards, I followed her. She was
in no mood to listen, of course, but I didn't care. I told her
who I was and what I thought of her, and I told her that she
needed to get help before—"

Mabyn looked up at me. "Before the things she'd done
to other people reaped something worse than a little
eggnog up her nose."

"Ooh . . ." I reached for my tea and immediately changed
tack. "You weren't at the Christmas Eve service."

"No. I was here alone with Shirley, and unfortunately
nobody can vouch for me. Howard came home after the
service and told me about Ginger. Fern is still furious we
missed her big Christmas Eve dinner."

Mabyn held my gaze. "I didn't kill Ginger, Aggie. I
can't tell you how good it felt to confront her. It helped me
stand up to Fern a few days later after talking to you. I will
never be anyone's doormat again. That's my New Year's
resolution, and I mean it."

I believed her. At least most of me did. Was losing a job
years ago reason enough to kill somebody? It hardly seemed

so, not for a stable woman like Mabyn. "I'm going to have to tell Detective Roussos this story."

"I guess I don't blame you."

I finished my tea and stood. *Sesame Street* would be over soon, and I wanted to be well on my way before Shirley was at loose ends.

I thought of one more thing to ask her. "You mentioned that you kept up with Ginger's life after you left the station."

Mabyn rose, too. "It sounds awfully petty. I guess it's a measure of how upset I was. I'm usually not a vindictive person."

"What can you tell me about those years? I don't know much of anything. I've been talking to the new receptionist at WKLM, and he mentioned she was with somebody named Cass, maybe like Mama Cass? But he had to go before he could tell me anything."

Mabyn walked me to the door. "Kas, with a K. Short for Kasimir. Kas Novy. It's a Slavic name, and he's from Eastern Europe somewhere. A real hottie by all standards and something of a local celebrity. And yes, he and Ginger were an item."

"What do you know about him besides his birthplace and ranking on the Celsius scale? Anything interesting?"

"Oh, he's interesting all right. Kas Novy owns Cincinnati's most popular nightclub, a place called Technotes. It's downtown, and it's patterned after some of the famous clubs in New York and L.A., the ones with real attitude. No limbo parties or do-it-yourself martini nights. They pull in the rich and famous, keep it more or less exclusive. They do the velvet rope routine, you know, people on their special list get in without a wait. If you're flashy enough you get right in without being on the list. If you're just plain old, plain old, you might have to wait awhile. Especially on a Friday night."

"There's a market for this in Cincinnati?"

Mabyn stared at me as if my prejudices were showing.

In truth I find Cincinnati with its hills, river, and colorful bridges appealing. Professional sports, a symphony and ballet, major department stores, a rich German heritage that means good wurst and beer always on hand. The list goes on. It's definitely not just a larger Emerald Springs.

"Okay." I held up my hands. "You're right, and I get ten lashes with braided strings of sauerkraut."

Mabyn smiled and I was off the hook. "I heard Kas got funds to open Technotes from some club owners in New York or maybe L.A. Maybe he got advice, too, because he really knew what to do and how to do it. The place has been a success almost from the beginning, although I've heard rumors recently that it's starting to go downhill."

"Oh? Do you know why?"

"Friends say it's seedier, that some people have stopped going because they've seen prostitutes in the vicinity, heard maybe there was some illegal gambling. You know, stuff they don't want to be caught up in if the police show up."

I wasn't sure how any of this related to Ginger, and I steered the conversation back to her. "Do you know how long she and Kas were an item?"

"For all I know right up until the minute she married Cliff Grable. I think Kas either bought her a condo in the city or loaned her the money to buy one. It's supposed to be a real beauty. Practically on the river. The ultimate in luxury."

So Ginger had left a sizzling Slav whose weekends were one big party, and along the way she had abandoned a luxury condo on the Ohio River, as well. All for Cliff Grable, who was as sweet a guy as I'd ever met, but nobody's idea of scintillating.

"You definitely kept up," I told Mabyn at the door.

"It got to be a habit for me and the people keeping track of Ginger. I kept waiting for the other shoe to fall, if you know what I mean? First she's in the accident, then she loses her job at the station, then she publishes a book to no great acclaim."

"Then she's murdered."

"That was more than I wanted, Aggie. Truly. I was finished with Ginger."

I don't know why, but I believed her. I wondered if Roussos would, as well.

✦ ✦ ✦

My daughters came home from their shopping trip with new coats. Vel found a terrific sale and the girls were delighted. Teddy, who has never had one that wasn't Deena's hand-me-down, looked precious in a lavender jacket with white faux fur rimming the hood. Deena's was puffy and reversible, scarlet on one side, silver on the other. Very outdoorsy and perfect for horseback riding or school. I gave Vel a longer hug than she was comfortable with.

I had called Lucy to tell her I wouldn't be at the Victorian today, since I was driving Vel to the airport. She didn't say a word about joining me, but half an hour before Vel was to leave, Luce showed up on my doorstep with a thermos of hot coffee, a bag of chocolate chip cookies left over from an early morning sales meeting, and her lovely cherry red Concorde.

"I just couldn't see you driving all the way to Cincinnati in your minivan."

"Are you giving me the keys, or are you coming?" We were alone in the kitchen while the girls helped Vel finish packing. Junie was upstairs in Teddy's room teaching Sid to knit, something she'd wanted to do for years. Sid was hungry for distraction, and Junie had pounced.

"Just invite me," Lucy said.

"I'd love your company on the return trip. You can keep me awake."

Lucy lowered her voice. "We haven't *talked*."

Of course that's not true. Lucy came on Christmas Day to deliver Hanukkah presents to my daughters and I'd given a brief summary of what had happened the night before.

But I knew exactly what Lucy meant. She thinks we're a team that flips houses on one hand and solves murders on the other. And she was feeling left out.

"I can catch you up on the way back." I added fruit to the cookie stash.

"Now." She made three syllables out of this, which is tough to do but makes a point.

As briefly as I could I told her what I'd learned from Rand and Mabyn. Lucy's green eyes got huge. "I know that club, and I've heard of Kas Novy."

"Have you been there?"

"Yeah. More than once." She looked me up and down. "You can't go like that."

"Hold on. I'm not going. I just mentioned—"

"Of course you're going! What's wrong with you? *We're* going! You want to find out about Technotes, don't you? You want to find out how Ginger was involved. How else are we going to do it?" She glanced at her watch. "How long before Vel has to leave?"

"Fifteen, maybe twenty minutes."

"I'll be back. Go scour your wardrobe and find something clubby." She started toward the door, then she turned. "Do you know what that means?"

"Umm, maybe."

She shook her head, fully aware what a club doofus I am. "I'll bring some stuff. Think young and sexy. Think short and tight."

"It's December. I'm thinking warm and toasty."

"Put comfortable out of your head."

"Bad things happen when I barhop with you."

"Club. It's a *club*."

"I'm just going to call Rand when I get to the city and see what else he can tell me. That's all I'm planning to do."

"Call him? Invite him! He sounds like a party animal." She disappeared. I looked down at my airport clothes. Faded jeans. A navy blue sweater of Ed's over a T-shirt that says

"I Make Matters Worse." Deena gave it to me for Christmas. I hope it's supposed to be funny.

Mabyn had said something about flashy people getting right into Technotes. I figured that in this attire, my hair would turn gray while I waited outside the door. With a sense of foreboding, I went upstairs to see what was cowering in my closet.

13

Rand Garner has spiky bleached blond hair, narrow, rectangular glasses with shiny royal blue frames, about fifty extra pounds on a small-boned body, and a smile that undoubtedly cost his parents thousands in orthodontia. He wore a copper-colored camp shirt with bright renditions of Elvis in his *Viva Las Vegas* period, dark linen pants, and a string tie with a shamrock that blinked on and off when he squeezed the stem. When Rand talks, his eyebrows leap spasmodically. Since he talks a lot, it's like watching two caterpillars dance the tarantella.

"You are *so* not ready," he told me, when I came out of the station greenroom fully attired in the clothes I hoped would vault me over Technotes's velvet ropes. "Lucy!"

Lucy came out in a black velvet camisole with rhinestone straps, a purple lame skirt that barely covered what it needed to, and gray lizard cowboy boots. Her hair was a seething mass of curls that looked like they might reach out and choke an unwilling bystander.

"Back in," she said, hiking her thumb over her shoulder. "Wear my jeans."

I was wearing jeans. My jeans. Jeans that fit me and a long-sleeved white poet's shirt, daringly unbuttoned to hint at my rather substantial cleavage. "I can't get into your jeans and sit, too."

She traded looks with Rand and marched me back in.

I gave up and submitted to torture. Ten minutes later I had poured myself into Lucy's jeans, tied a shocking pink satin halter top in place, dusted my shoulders with sparkly gold powder and donned pointy-toed stiletto heels from the eighties that I'd been too sentimental to throw away. Both Rand and Lucy approved.

Dropping Vel at the airport had gone smoothly, with me promising to keep her in the loop about Sid. Then Lucy and I had whisked through traffic to the station to catch Rand before he left for the day. He had been thrilled about sleuthing at Technotes with us, and we'd agreed to meet back at the station at nine o'clock to change and head over to the club. Lucy and I did some shopping—the lizard boots for her, a really cool set of kitchen sponges for me— then found a quiet little Italian restaurant not too far from the station. We shared a mushroom pizza and caught up on all the house and personal details we hadn't had time for over the holidays.

Rand was waiting by the time we got back, and now we were all ready to go. Oh, somewhere in there I'd made a telephone call to my husband to tell him I would be later than expected—as in it would officially be tomorrow when Lucy and I got back. Rather than go into a lengthy explanation, I told Ed about our plans for shopping and dinner. I'm hoping he thinks the stores in Cincinnati stay open around the clock.

Our plan hadn't left any time to ask Rand what he'd found out about Ginger, and there was no opportunity on the trip to Technotes, either. Rand gave directions without first explaining that he is mildly dyslexic. We saw a lot of Cincinnati before we found the Pendleton area near the Central Business District and at last, our street. We parked Lucy's car in a nearby lot, and she tipped the attendant to keep a close eye on it. Then I limped toward what looked like a warehouse half a block away.

"I'm freezing," I complained.

"You're wearing a coat," Lucy said.

"And practically nothing under it!"

"You've been a wife and mother too long. Free your inner tart."

"If I could get my hands on any kind of tart, I'd eat it. Maybe the calories would keep me warm."

"There'll be no more eating, not in those jeans."

"Ladies, a night of bliss awaits." Rand directed us across the street where a line had formed behind not a red velvet rope but a shocking pink one that matched my halter top.

"Take off your coat," Lucy said. "Aggie, get it off right now. Let the guy at the door see what you're wearing!"

"Are you nuts?"

"Why do you think we're dressed like this? You think he has X-ray vision? Take it off. Show him you match the decor!"

I experienced one of those moments when the world stands still. The kind where everything freezes, but somehow I have plenty of time to think. The kind I tend to have when Lucy Jacobs is at my side. I tried to imagine members of our church walking by and seeing me, half naked, flaunting my best assets wrapped in shocking pink satin just so I could get a jump on the people at the front of the line.

On the other hand, I imagined standing out here for hours, freezing those assets and every other part of my body until blue, not shocking pink, was the color of my night. And after all, I wasn't really here to *party*. I was here to rescue my sister from jumpsuit orange.

I slipped off my coat, and Lucy did the same. Rand had donned a black leather jacket, and he unbelted it and let it hang free so that Elvis bogeyed shamelessly when Rand's extra pounds jiggled against the shirt.

Lucy walked up to the man in charge on the coveted side of the rope. She performed her most seductive smile. "We'd sure love to dance."

The guy, pencil-thin mustache, brown hair slicked straight back from a widow's peak into a tight braid, one diamond stud in an earlobe, gave her the once over. He turned to Rand and took the hem of the camp shirt in his hand. "Nice shirt." He had what sounded like a Russian accent.

"Oh, don't stop now." Rand leaned toward him.

The guy laughed, but he dropped the shirt like it had ignited. He gave me a slow head to toe. I was too cold by then to tell if I'd passed muster, but he jerked his head toward the door. "Have a good evening."

Lucy grabbed each of us by an elbow and hurried us inside. I didn't dare glance at the shivering folks behind the rope. I'm definitely not used to being one of the beautiful people. Lucy paid our cover and told us we could buy her a drink later.

No matter what Lucy calls Technotes, it is, at heart, a bar. There are three bars, as a matter of fact. One on each side of a room the size of our middle school auditorium, sporting thirty-foot ceilings so the clouds of cigarette smoke will have somewhere to go. The other is triangular, and it stands precisely in the center. I looked for chairs, but on this level the only seats were at the bars and every one was at least three rows deep in drinkers. This was a place to mill, drink, and dance, not to get comfortable.

Each of the four walls were a different color. One was metallic gold, one black, the third was my signature shocking pink, and the fourth was a bold lime green. Tonight three men in artist smocks and berets were hard at work on the black one, painting what looked like a psychedelic rendering of a city dump. Huge chandeliers lit the room with ropes of crystal dangling just ten feet from the floor. Areas for dancing were marked with colored lights, like airport runways. Lots of partyers had come in for a landing.

"The minute a mural is finished, they paint over it and start another one," Rand said. Actually Rand had to shout. Shouting was going to be the order of the night because what passed for music was throbbing in the background like King Kong's heartbeat.

"Exactly what are we listening to?" I shouted.

"Techno," Lucy shouted back.

The sound was purely electronic. This was music our computer could write by itself—and might the next time I'm at the keyboard checking e-mail or getting directions. I'm afraid to tell Ed our computer is possessed, since he prides himself on logic.

I waved my hand in front of Lucy's face to get her attention. "Somebody swiped the melody."

"You really need to get out more." Lucy steered me away from the center bar. "For Deena's sake. You won't be able to have a conversation with her in a couple of years. You won't know the language."

"There are a couple of rooms off to the side," Rand said. "Maybe they'll let us in. Let's go."

We were turned away from the first one, which had its own bouncer and guest list. Inside I glimpsed fire engine red walls and a video of Cincinnati's professional baseball team, probably during a winning streak.

The next room was less exclusive, and there were a couple of empty tables. The walls and ceiling looked like a tiger turned inside out, stripes everywhere. This was the Bengal room. No surprise there. Kas Novy might hail from Europe, but he understands that if the state of Ohio had umbilical cords, they would be connected to its home teams.

To mix the metaphor and appeal to the broadest possible audience, each tabletop was a photo of a different man who, judging from the baggy attire, was either a rapper or seriously into Weight Watchers. We took the table closest to the door. The guy staring up at us was doing something with his hands that looked like a bad case of tendinitis in the making. I could sit, but I couldn't bend my legs. I aimed my feet at Lucy, who had gotten me into this predicament. She would have to sit sideways or straddle my stilettos all evening.

A young woman wearing a tiger tail and ears, a sleek black leotard, and gold stockings told us we were welcome, but to stay there we'd have to cough up a hundred dollars for a bottle of champagne, fifty more if we wanted a bottle of hard liquor. She was a perky blonde who could whip her tiger tail from side to side with muscles most of us never think of honing.

After growling for emphasis, she gave us the good news. "It usually costs more. Tonight's a bargain. We won't be nearly as crowded on account of people saving up for New Year's Eve."

Rand grabbed her tail the next time it passed close to him and held it to his cheek. "Oh, I want one of these!"

She ruffled his hair, pried her tail out of his clenched fingers, and went for the champagne.

"This had better bring results!" I hissed the last word. It was quieter in here, but I was in no danger of giving away secrets. We still had to lean into the middle of our table to hear each other.

"Honey, get with the program. This is called fun!" Rand's eyes were glowing with excitement.

"Don't ever marry a minister," Lucy advised him.

I leaned farther forward, and we looked like a Bengals' huddle, minus a few linemen. "Let's talk about why we're here. Before the music gets any louder and Toni the Tigress comes back with our champagne."

Rand's eyebrows leaped. "Oh, the things I found out!"

"You're the man." Lucy winked at him.

"I figured we had questions on two fronts, right? After you dispensed with that assistant thing?" He looked to me for corroboration.

At the station after greeting each other like long-lost friends, I'd given him a brief summary of my talk with Mabyn. So she had been dispensed with, along with Carol Ann, at least temporarily.

"What fronts?" I asked him now.

"Ginger and Kas. And Ginger and Cliff Grable."

"That's it in a nutshell, Sherlock."

"Oh, I am so glad I got it right!"

"You *are* the man." I patted his arm.

"Here's what I know about Ginger and Kas. I wrote it down for you, so I wouldn't forget."

He pulled out a WKLM notepad and flipped to the first page—Rand has yet to master the art of Christmas receipt scribbles. "Ginger and Kas Novy were pretty much inseparable for more than a year. She met him when he came to town to look for a location for a club, and she was with him when he opened this place. They lived together in a penthouse condo looking over the river."

He looked up and grinned. "How am I doing so far?"

"You rock. Go on."

"Then things went sour. I couldn't find out what or why exactly, but it sounds like maybe one of them had a roving eye? I talked to two people heavily into the scene, and neither could tell me for sure. The rumor was vague and I'm just filling in the gaps from my imagination. But Kas moved out, and they weren't seen together after that." He looked up and his eyebrows kept dancing. "Except once."

The tigress came back with our bottle and three glasses. For a hundred dollars you don't get Dom Perignon at Technotes, but it wasn't the worst champagne I've ever had. She popped, poured, and stuck the bottle in a galvanized bucket of ice, asked if we wanted to see the menu and left it for us, just in case.

"Go back to 'once.'" I said. "That last time they were seen together?"

"That's where it gets so good!" Rand lifted his glass in a toast. We clinked.

"Okay," he said after a couple of sips. "That last time they were seen together? In court! She got a restraining order. Seems one afternoon she caught old Kas in the condo tossing her stuff into the hall. *After* she had changed the locks, by the *way*. They had a fight and he slapped her hard enough to leave a handprint. Nobody saw him do it, and Kas came up with an alibi, so they couldn't charge him with assault. But the judge issued the restraining order."

I wondered if Ginger had chosen Cliff because he was such a gentle soul. Had she simply had her fill of glamorous alpha males and settled for somebody she could push around?

"So, that answers that," Lucy said. "If he was trying to get her out of it, Kas must have owned the condo."

I wasn't so sure. "Not necessarily. Maybe he loaned Ginger the money for a down payment, or at least some of it. Maybe that's why he didn't try to go through legal proceedings to evict her, because it was more of an informal arrangement."

"Does a businessman who opens a place like this one make informal arrangements?"

Rand answered. "Maybe he does, if his interest rate is say, over the top?"

"You mean like a loan shark?" Lucy asked.

"Nobody really knows where Kas Novy got the money to open this place. He managed a club in L.A., and he had a lot of connections and probably some investors. But managing clubs doesn't get you what you need to front this kind of an operation."

So Novy might be a legitimate businessman who let love blind him, giving Ginger money for the condo and expecting years of bliss in return. Or maybe he loaned her the

money and called in the loan when they broke up, possibly
at some absurd interest rate. Or possibly the loan was above-
board but he was a man with no patience who didn't want to
wait for the wheels of the legal system to turn. Maybe he'd
just been trying to make a point.

"Whatever it is, it sounds like a motive for murder," I
said. "If he was angry enough to toss her stuff out of the
condo and attack her."

"We only have Ginger's word on that." Lucy topped off
our champagne. "Sip it slowly."

"So here's the second part." Rand traced the items on
his list with his finger. "Ginger and Cliff Grable."

I held up my hand. "Wait a minute. Let me set this up in
my head. Was Ginger working at the station while she was
with Kas?"

"Oh no. She had the accident, left the station, then she
met Kas and later they moved into the condo. She got some
kind of insurance settlement after the accident, so that explains where some of her income came from, that and any
money she got up front on her cookbook. She started working on the book while she recovered."

I wished I had known about Kas when I cornered
Carol Ann Riley, but most likely Carol Ann's association
with Ginger had ended while Ginger and Kas were still
lovey-dovey.

"Okay. Now, Ginger and Cliff," I said. "On the telephone
you mentioned something about his first wife committing
suicide?"

"It was kind of a big deal, that's the only reason I know.
She was on some kind of antidepressant, and afterwards
Cliff sued the drug manufacturer and maybe even her doctor. He claimed the antidepressant made her kill herself.
There were some studies the manufacturer hadn't been
completely up front about, that kind of thing. The story
was in the papers for weeks because the manufacturer has
offices here, and the first round of legal stuff happened in

local courts. If the lawsuit went anywhere, though, I never heard. They stopped covering it after awhile. I don't know if Grable had any kind of case, but I think he was trying to call attention to the problem. That sort of thing."

"So then, in the throes of grief, he met Ginger. Maybe while he was here giving testimony or something." Now I felt even sorrier for poor Cliff.

"Here's what I know. You're right, Ginger met Grable when he was here for one of the hearings, and she latched onto him right after she got the restraining order on Novy."

"How soon after his first wife's death?" Lucy asked Rand.

"I don't know. A while. At least a couple of years, since it takes time for something like that lawsuit to get moving. I still remembered who he was when I heard he and Ginger were together, but it wasn't like his name was in the paper every day at that point."

"There's probably something on the Internet about the lawsuit. I'll look it up when we get back." Lucy could say this. Her computer isn't haunted.

"Do I hear you right?" I asked. "You think Ginger latched onto Cliff just to get away from Kas? Or do you think she latched on because she needed money to pay Kas off?"

Rand sat back with a smile. "Don't you just love the way one question opens up a bunch more?"

No, at the moment I just wanted easy answers. Something on the order of: Kas wanted Ginger to pay him what she owed for the condo. He drove to Emerald Springs on Christmas Eve, confronted her, then killed her when she told him she'd run out of checks.

On arrival I had noted that Lucy and I were almost a decade older than most of the clientele. Apparently this is a hot spot for twenty-somethings. Now a guy in his midtwenties came over to the table and asked Lucy to dance. She glanced at me, and I nodded.

On the way out to the main floor she leaned over and said. "I'm going to see if Baby Snookums or his drinking buddies know where Kas Novy is tonight."

She left me alone with Rand, so I used the time well. "You said Ginger got an insurance settlement? Is there a way to find out how much she got?"

"Our floor manager thinks it was pretty much a token. Apparently both drivers were at fault, only Ginger was less so, if you know what I mean? The roads were slick, she was going too fast for weather conditions, but the other guy slid through a stop sign. She didn't have much of a case, so she took what the other guy's insurance company offered because she didn't want to go to court and lose everything."

"I'm putting two and two together here. First, I doubt Ginger's publisher paid a whole lot up front for her cookbook. Second, she only got a small insurance settlement. But she moves into a luxury condo, lives the high life here at the club. I know for a fact there was no family money to squander. So either she was living off Kas Novy's largesse, or she was doing something to make money under the table."

"Ooh, like what?" Rand's eyes were shining.

Unfortunately I could think of a lot of possibilities, not a one of them pretty. "When I talked to Mabyn she told me that some people think Technotes has gone downhill. Some people aren't as comfortable here as they were, that there have been prostitutes in the vicinity, rumors of illegal gambling. Have you heard anything like that?"

"I really love being here with you. But this isn't the kind of club where I usually hang out, if you catch my drift?" The eyebrows did a mini-stampede. "So I don't hear every little thing."

No, although I'd seen guys dancing together in the other room, I was pretty sure Rand hung out in places where that was more the norm. As if to present evidence, a huge bald guy wearing black leather pants and a purple muscle shirt came over and tapped Rand on the shoulder. Rand turned around, gasped, and stood, and they gave each other a back-pounding hug.

Rand turned to me when it was over. "Aggie, you gotta meet Bruiser."

"You're kidding, right?" I held out my hand.

"Bruce to you," He shook with care, as if he knew what those sausage fingers could do if he wasn't paying attention.

"Come on," Bruiser motioned toward the music. "Let's catch up."

Rand petitioned me with his eyes. I had no problem sitting alone. I had a lot to figure out while my partners in solving crime had their fun. I waved him off.

I swirled the champagne that was left in my glass and considered everything I'd learned so far and everything I still needed to.

"I've been looking for you."

My head jerked up, and I saw the bouncer or doorman or whatever title he went by. I hadn't realized I had company. "Me?"

"Yeah. Want to dance?"

I didn't. No, no, no, in a big way. I shook my head. "Who's minding the store?"

He took what had been Lucy's seat. "Out front? We take turns when it's cold."

"So what do you do when you're not deciding who's dazzling enough to make it inside?"

He had one of those smiles that money can't buy, white teeth against olive skin, humor flashing in his eyes. "I pick up pretty women."

Okay, I was flattered, all thirty-five years of me. I was also sure there was more to it than that. "And keep your eye on things inside, right?"

"Sometimes it's the same job."

"What was it about me that worried you?"

"You? I figured this might be a onetime visit for you, correct? So I thought I ought to make your acquaintance while I can."

"I don't look like a clubber?"

"Not so much."

I smiled, too. "How'd you know? Other than my being old enough to have babysat most of your regulars?"

"You looked like you were swallowing the whole set up, you know? Like you were inhaling it. And now you don't look bored enough. Even people who aren't bored try to look bored."

"All that when I was just trying to get inside and warm up?"

"So, you just sightseeing? Checking us out before you go back to wherever you came from?"

I decided there was nothing to be lost by telling the truth. After all, if we were kicked out just because I'd known Ginger, that would be interesting enough to make this trip worth it.

I considered how best to put it. "I'm looking for a murderer."

He didn't even blink. "Now that's more than I expected. I thought maybe you were looking for a good time, you know, away from hubby and the kids?"

"No, I like hubby and the kids a lot. Sorry."

The smile still lit his eyes. "So what makes you think you'll find a murderer here?"

He was sitting directly across from me. I hoped he didn't think I was playing footsie with me, just because I couldn't bend my legs.

"Did you know Ginger Grable? She used to be Ginger Newton."

His expression didn't change. "Yeah, I heard she died."

"Somebody killed her. I'd like to know who."

"Why?"

"Other than the fact that murder's not a good thing? Because I grew up with her. And somebody I love is under suspicion."

"Tough break, huh?"

"You didn't answer my question."

"We all knew her. She practically lived here when Kas opened the place. She liked to tell us how to do our jobs, especially the cooks. If they'd listened, we'd be out of business by now."

"She and Kas were an item, I guess?"

"You might say that."

"I know they lived together. On the river somewhere."

"Kas still lives there."

This was news. I pondered what this meant. At the end had Ginger simply given the condo to Kas to pay off whatever she owed him? If so, there went that motive for murder.

"When he's, shall we say, not living elsewhere?" he added.

I'd been lost in thought. I almost missed this. "I'm sorry . . . What did you say your name was?"

"Ilya."

"I'm Aggie. Ilya, what do you mean about Kas living elsewhere?"

"I mean our man Kasimir is in jail."

For one wild moment I thought perhaps Kas Novy had admitted to killing Ginger, that Sid was off the hook, and I could change back into jeans that didn't cut off my circulation. Then I realized how unlikely this was.

"I'm guessing not for Ginger's murder," I said.

"She died on Christmas Eve?"

I nodded.

"That's always a big night here. A couple of private parties. Kas never left, not until early Christmas morning."

"Then why was he arrested? And when?"

"The cops stopped him on the way home two nights ago."

"For what?"

He smiled again, and didn't answer.

"You know, I hear he's something of a celebrity in town. If he was arrested, why isn't it all over the news?"

"Why do you think?"

I considered. "He paid the right folks to keep quiet?"

He laughed. "Nobody has that much money."

I screwed up my face in thought. Kas had been arrested, and the news hadn't leaked out, at least not to the general public, or Rand would know.

"The cops must have wanted to keep his arrest a secret because"—I looked up—"because they weren't done making arrests?"

"You're doing pretty good."

"Why are you telling *me*, then?"

"Because I've got nothing to lose. Besides, it'll be all over the papers tomorrow morning."

"What will?"

"They searched his condo and found a fortune in drugs. Business hasn't been so good lately. Maybe Kas was paying the bills and maybe paying some of the backers in L.A. who helped him start this place, by doing a different kind of business on the side."

"Here?"

He turned up his hands. "Me? I never saw a thing."

"Right." I leaned closer. "Why is this place still open then?"

"I'd guess there were no drugs on the premises. Kas was going on vacation so he probably took everything back to his condo to make sure it was safe, or to sell wherever he was going. And like you said, I think they had other people they were interested in and didn't want to alert them Kas was in custody. So this place has been crawling with undercover cops. I could point some out to you. That's how I first figured something was up. Then everybody who works here found out what that something was before we opened tonight. Me, I'm looking for another job."

"How long, do you know? I mean how long was he selling drugs?"

"Probably long enough that your pal Ginger was in on it."

I stared at him. "Ginger was selling drugs?"

He had mastered an elegant shrug. "I don't know if she was selling anything except herself, and that, only to Kas as far as I know. But judging from the way she acted, she used. She used and for all I know, he supplied."

"What kind of drugs?"

"Oh, I'd guess they found a little of everything in the condo. Just a guess, of course."

"You mean heroin? Coke and crack?"

"Maybe, but Kas specialized in the things your local pharmacist keeps under lock and key." The smile again. "Or so they say."

Ginger had told us she was still in constant pain from an injury to her back. Had she linked up with Kas as a way to get drugs to ease the pain? Or had she become drug dependent during recovery and refused to wean herself off them?

"Who are they looking at for Ginger's murder?" Ilya asked.

"My sister, for one."

"Bad news."

Had Ginger broken up with Kas over money? Had there been more than a loan on the condo at stake, or had Ginger owed Kas for the drugs she was using, too? It was unlikely Ilya would know, but there was one question he might be able to answer.

"So if Ginger needed drugs, who supplied them after she broke up with Kas?"

"If I were you I wouldn't be too quick to paint Kas out of that picture," Ilya said.

"What do you mean?"

"I watch and I listen. I have to do something to stay awake."

Like striking up a conversation with little Dorothy on her trip to the shocking pink Land of Oz. I nodded to encourage him.

"What I saw wasn't at the job," he continued. "I saw Ginger and Kas together, not all that long ago. At a bar over by the university."

I whistled softly. "I heard she got a restraining order against him, but I guess that was a long time ago," I said.

"Well, they weren't exactly holding hands. But they were sitting at a table talking."

"And you never saw her at the club again?"

"Not on my watch." That last word seemed to strike a chord with him. He looked at his, what I guessed was a Rolex knockoff, then got to his feet. "Back to work."

"You've been a big help."

"Like I said, none of it's a secret now." He held out his hand and I took it. I'd expected it to feel soft and pampered, but his palm was rock hard.

I had a sudden inspiration. "Ilya, had Kas been in trouble before? I mean, before he opened this place?"

His eyes shone, but he didn't answer.

I went on. "Because if he had been, and he was setting up a nightclub in my town and say, I was in charge of vice or whatever it's called by the local police force, I'd want to put somebody undercover right from the beginning. You know, somebody who could be all over the place, watching and talking to people. Just to keep tabs. Somebody like a doorman."

"Maybe they ought to put you in charge." He squeezed my hand, then lifted it to his lips and kissed it before he disappeared out to the dance floor.

14

I can function on five hours of sleep. Barely. Unfortunately, after I finished explaining to Ed why I had been forced to spend hours in a Cincinnati dance club, *and* after I'd showered and washed the smell of smoke out of my hair so both of us could sleep, I only got four and a half. Four and a half means I have no sense of humor, and I'm too foggy-brained to get the punch lines anyway.

At eight the next morning I dragged myself out of bed and crept downstairs where Sid and Ed were eating breakfast and chewing far too loudly. I could hear Saturday morning cartoons from the den, but I couldn't summon the energy to drag myself that far to say hello to my daughters. I hoped someday they would find me.

"Lucy called." Sid got up from the table to get more milk and slammed the refrigerator door. I was too tired to yell at her.

"Tell me she's not perky," I said.

"Sounded perky to me." Sid didn't sound perky. She

sounded like she was mumbling underwater, although possibly the pounding in my head caused the distortion.

"I hate perky people." I rummaged for aspirin and took two. I hadn't had nearly enough alcohol for a hangover, and at the very least, this seemed unfair.

"Lucy's coming over in awhile to check something on your computer."

I made a mental note to fashion a garlic necklace before she arrived. It was the least I could do for Luce. I poured coffee and plopped into a chair. The coffee didn't taste like Vel's. I missed her already.

Ed knew better than to try a conversation. He got up and rinsed his dishes, then he kissed my head on his way out. Gently. He is nothing if not thoughtful.

My words stopped him at the door. "You'll be at church, right? Where else would you be?" This sounded remarkably like an accusation.

"And you'll be spending the day poking around where you shouldn't, right? What else would you do?" Funny, but that accusation thing had persisted.

"I found out some good stuff last night!"

"Aggie, stay out of this investigation, okay? Sid, talk some sense into her."

I don't know if Ed slammed the door, but it was a definite possibility that this time the bang wasn't in my head.

"So you guys went out without me," Sid said. "To a club!"

"You are treading where few have trod before," I warned her. "Watch your step."

"You could have invited me along."

"What, with Roussos as chaperone?"

After half a cup of coffee I felt a mite better. Enough to apologize. "I didn't mean to throw that in your face."

"I feel like I'm in jail."

There was a significant pause as her words sank in. "I

hate this!" Sid got up and began to unload the dishwasher. She had figured out how far to push me, though. She didn't slam cabinet doors or rattle dishes any more than she had to.

By now I could see the bottom of my mug. On a normal morning this means I'm half human. This morning it just meant I needed more coffee. I got up to get it.

"What you need is something to do," I said. "Why don't you come with me today and strip wallpaper. I thought I'd bring the girls. Junie can come, too. She can check out the house."

"She's seen it."

So Lucy *had* taken Junie by on their outing. Lucy was a good friend, even if she could be perky on almost no sleep.

"Junie can still come." I found my way back to a chair. I was glad no one had rearranged the furniture.

"She's going shopping. She's looking for fabric."

"Good luck there. I think the closest fabric store is about twenty miles down the road."

"She'll be gone a lot of the day then."

"You'll come?"

"You're babysitting me?"

"Sid, humor me, okay? Pretend you care how I feel."

Sid sat down at the table and rested her face in her hands. "I guess it's better than staying around waiting for my boss to call and fire me."

Before I could try to reassure her, Teddy came into the kitchen and crawled up into my lap without greeting or invitation. "Moonpie's gone."

Moonpie is for the most part an indoor cat. He'll wander outside when we get the paper or the mail, or even stay there if we're working in the yard. But he never goes far.

I gave her a good morning squeeze. "He's probably just hiding."

"He ran outside when Daddy opened the door this morning, and he didn't come back in."

"Did you look in the trees? Behind the lilacs?"

"He's gone."

Our street is busy enough this worried me. Moonpie's a cagey guy, but maybe not that cagey. And this is a typical Ohio winter.

"I think he'll come back when he gets tired of playing hide-and-go-seek, but we'll go look for him as soon as I get dressed."

"Maybe he's jealous."

My brain was working slowly, but I realized she was talking about Cinnamon. "Maybe he is," I agreed.

Sid patted Teddy's shoulder. "I ran away once when Gi— when somebody else was staying with us, and she was getting all the attention. But I came back when it was time for supper."

I'd forgotten that. Sid had been maybe eight. And Ginger had come for another of her long visits. I think that one had lasted almost a year. "Aunt Sid didn't go very far," I told Teddy. "And Moonpie won't, either."

"How do you know I didn't go very far?" Sid said, after Teddy went back to finish her program.

"You spent the day in the toolshed. Vel saw you go inside. We knew where you were the whole time."

"There's no drama when you have older sisters."

But of course, older sisters or not, now there was too much drama in Sid's life to suit either of us.

By the time I'd showered—this time to wake up— changed into my work clothes, and hunted unsuccessfully for our cat, Lucy had arrived. I found her at Ed's computer in his home office.

"Has it levitated yet?" I asked, rolling the sleeves of my buffalo plaid shirt over my elbows. "I can brandish a crucifix. Or maybe a Star of David."

"*You* are the problem. There's nothing wrong with the computer. And you won't believe what I've found."

Gone was my party girlfriend. Lucy was wearing realtor clothes, so I assumed she was going off to earn big bucks when she was done here. She looked professional in conservative camel herringbone slacks and a turtleneck sweater of a slightly darker hue with a multicolored fuzzy scarf draped over her shoulders.

I rubbed the scarf between thumb and forefinger. "That looks like a Junie scarf. Everybody got one for Christmas. Mine's green."

"She gave it to me as a thank you for taking her around town the other day."

"Apparently you took her to the Victorian?"

"She thinks we're amazing."

"I have a nice mother."

"Your mother is a keeper. Okay, are you ready for excitement?"

Clearly I wasn't, but that wasn't going to matter.

"Cliff Grable may look staid and boring, but his life is anything but. Everything Rand told us about the lawsuit stemming from his first wife's suicide is true. But here's the thing. It's not the only suit he's taking part in."

I screamed for my enthusiasm to show itself. It slogged toward the light. "Oh"—Even in my sleepless state I knew more was called for—"interesting."

"Remind me not to let you stay out past midnight again. I'll print this out for you before I leave, but here's the story in a nutshell. There's a whole interview from a magazine for inventors, so it's legit—"

"How do you find this stuff? You come in here, turn on the computer, and it purrs like a kitten. Then it spits out useful information."

Lucy ignored me. "The interview is kind of a cautionary tale. Apparently Cliff is something of a whiz kid but a lousy businessman."

"He's one of those guys who can't read people."

"Right out of college he went to work for some firm, had a great idea—something that makes no sense to me—and basically just gave it away to his employer. They realized what they had and managed to cut him out of any subsequent profits by claiming he came up with this idea while he was on salary. And the contract he'd signed said as much."

"Wow, strike one."

"The only good thing that came out of it was that everyone wanted to hire him. So several years later and somewhat smarter, Cliff got a great job and came up with an idea for a new hot water heater valve that significantly cut energy consumption. This time he made money, but once again, the idea was so successful he only made a fraction of what it was worth. When he tried to negotiate better terms, he lost his job, rumors circulated about his instability, and no one else would hire him."

"For a smart guy, he's a slow learner."

"No, it's more like this time he did protect himself, but the company's a lot richer and has a fleet of lawyers. They hoped he'd cave and accept a payoff, particularly if his financial situation got desperate. They underestimated him, though. He sued and the lawsuit is pending. If he wins, he'll be worth a fortune."

"And the lawsuit against the drug company?"

"Could go on for years. It's a class action suit, but if they win he'll be better off for it."

"So he's a rich man in waiting. Maybe. How long has this lawsuit against his old company been in process?"

"The papers were filed a little less than a year ago."

"After he was already married to Ginger. I bet she loved that." I sank to the love seat beside the computer desk. "Every penny he has must be tied up."

"His attorney might work on contingency fees, but I think there would still be a lot of other expenses, court costs, consultants, etc. And if he's not getting a salary, then where's the money coming from?"

That was the big question. "What else does the interview say?"

"The rest is advice to other inventors on how to keep the

same thing from happening to them." She swivelled in the chair and her eyes were sad. "At the end he said the best advice he could offer was to find somebody to stand beside you when you're going through this kind of turmoil. Cliff said he was so grateful to have his wife's support."

✦ ✦ ✦

With the holidays almost over, Lucy and I had to get busy and find a handy person to help us with the harder repairs. But the wallpaper in the upstairs bedroom where Cliff and I had worked on Christmas Eve was history now. We had been pleasantly surprised to discover that whoever had installed it had stripped previous layers and primed the walls. So one layer down, and we were ready to patch and choose a color buyers could live with until they put their own stamp on the house.

Normally I would suggest one of a million shades of off-white, but since anyone buying the Victorian would expect a certain level of frou-frou, we had decided on lavender, a shade pale enough that painting over it would be a cinch if our new owners weren't purple people. Since a house sells better furnished, we would move the single bed that had graced the room back inside, put a fuzzy white rug from the church rummage sale on the floor and a flowered comforter and various throw pillows from the same sale on the bed. The dresser had gone with most of the other furniture, but I would move a bookshelf against the opposite wall and a vanity catty corner to that. This gave the feeling that the house was occupied but uncluttered.

I explained all this to Sid as I showed her what we'd done. At the last minute the girls had been invited to spend the day shopping with Junie. She had promised new dresses for their American Girl dolls, and they were going to pick out the fabric. We had the Victorian to ourselves.

"This wallpaper came off pretty easily," I said. "I thought we'd start across the hall today."

"Uh huh." She was less than enthused.

"Pep up there. If you don't, I might fall asleep on my feet. I'm counting on you to keep me dizzy with excitement."

"I don't really love my little condo. I'd like an extra bedroom, and a view. Plus the drive to work can be really awful sometimes. And Ludwig, the guy who manages our dining room, is such a creep, I read the newspaper classified section every Sunday looking for a new job for him. I circle promising ads and leave them in his box."

I wasn't sure I understood. "And?"

She faced me. "And I want to be there! I actually found myself wondering how Ludwig's Christmas went. I listen to audio books in my car, and I was halfway through this great novel by Elizabeth George, and I want to be stuck in traffic again so I can find out how it ends."

"I'm sorry."

She let out a long breath. Not a sigh exactly, more like a leaky tire. "I know. And I love you and the family and being with you."

"It's not having any say in where you are."

"And wondering if I'm going to jail."

We walked into the hall and I opened the door of the room we would be working in. It was the master bedroom with a small attached bath. This wallpaper was a black and white grid splattered with dinner plate-sized dahlias in colors nature purposely avoids. Like the paper in the room we had finished, this wasn't in good condition. And luckily it, too, appeared to be only one layer deep. If the walls had been properly primed, we were in business.

I walked through the doorway and the lights came on. "Well, will you look at that. Cliff 's been here."

"They come on during the day?"

"Just when it's gloomy like today, I think." After that first night, the lights had behaved. Of course I made a point of not touching the switches.

"This is his next great invention," I said. "Maybe this

one will finally make him a millionaire. Apparently the most advanced version of these switches does everything except walk the family dog."

"Isn't it a shame that somebody so brilliant has been slapped in the face so many times?" In the van on the way over I'd told Sid what Lucy discovered online.

The stepladder was already in the room. I dragged it to the wall nearest two double-hung windows. "The thing about Cliff is that he doesn't seem to notice. I wonder if he'll ever realize Ginger was using him?"

"Maybe in her own weird way she loved him." Sid caught my eye, and we both shook our heads at the same moment. "Nah."

Now I filled Sid in on what I'd learned last night. By the time I finished, I was at the top of the ladder with the clothes steamer heating on the shelf and my spray bottle of fabric softener and water beside it. While I talked I had picked at the edge of a roll and found, to my delight, that it was loose enough to peel a good distance. She stripped off a rose-colored cardigan that Junie had knit for her and put it in the closet out of harm's way, donning an old flannel shirt of mine to cover her turtleneck.

"So you think Ginger married Cliff to get money to pay off this Kas person?" Sid buttoned my shirt to the top.

"That's what it sounds like. If she was really into drugs, she might have owed him for a lot more than her portion of the down payment on the condo."

"Remember that last night she was . . . alive? At dinner? She kept staring off into space. I assumed she was plotting evil deeds. But she did seem unfocused, you know?"

I had thought of that, too. "Her mother had serious addiction problems. Ginger grew up watching her. Maybe Ginger got addicted after the accident, and she just couldn't shake loose."

"Or maybe she realized she was working a gold mine. Beautiful woman with decent acting skills. Verifiable car accident and injury. Back pain, which is impossible to quantify. A market for pain pills and a boyfriend who sells them."

Put that way it did seem likely. I started steaming the paper, moving down the ladder steps as I went. I showed Sid how to use one of the scoring tools, and she climbed the ladder and began at the top where I had steamed.

"I'm not sure I understand the draw. Who wants to be zonked out all the time?" I asked.

"I heard something on a talk show about some of these drugs. They come in time release tablets, designed that way so the user can't get high, but if you crunch the tablets, then you can shoot or snort them."

"Ick!"

"It produces a big rush. I guess for some people that's worth it."

I heard the downstairs door open, then footsteps in the downstairs hall. At first I thought it might be Lucy, but the steps were too heavy.

"That might be Cliff," I said softly, to cut off further speculation. I knew he had been at the house several times doing some simple electrical repairs. He'd asked my permission, and I suspected this was therapy, a way to stay busy.

Sid lowered her voice, too, and descended the ladder so we were both on the ground. "I'm surprised he's hanging around town."

"I think he's waiting for the cops to make an arrest."

I saw Sid wince. "Or maybe he doesn't want to go back to their house or on to his family's, where everybody will fuss. Maybe that'll make it all seem too real."

The footsteps started up the stairs. I went out to make sure it was Cliff. It was, and he waved from the landing, toolbox under one arm.

"Sid and I are stripping paper," I said. "What are you up to?"

"I thought I'd replace the plugs in the bathrooms. But I don't have to do it today."

The inspector had noted that the plugs next to the sinks needed to be replaced with ground fault circuit interrupters to protect against shock. Apparently Cliff had noticed this, as well. He was all set to work, wearing his too-short jeans and what looked like a brand-new work shirt.

I wanted him to feel included. "Why don't you start in this bathroom and leave the door open. Then we can talk."

He looked so grateful I really wished there was more I could do for the guy. "I'll have to turn off the power," he warned.

"We'll have enough light for what we're doing."

He left and I steamed while I could. In a few minutes the power went off. Luckily this room had enough windows that we were okay, although I was glad we had started nearby. Sid and I used the scoring tools, then the bottle of fabric softener and water and scrapers. When Cliff returned he left the door open between rooms and set to work.

I'll have to confess, although I wanted to make Cliff feel better, I also wanted to send Sid back to Atlanta where she could circle ads for Ludwig and sit in traffic jams to her heart's content. I tried to figure out how to ease into a long list of questions. Like whether Ginger had been an addict. And how they lived so well when she had no visible income and his was probably providing Tahitian getaways for a gaggle of lawyers.

"You know, Cliff," Sid said, beating me to choosing a subject, "I never heard details of the way you and Ginger met."

"At a party in Cincinnati. I thought she was the most beautiful woman I'd ever seen. I didn't see any point in introducing myself, but about halfway through the night, she introduced herself to me. We were inseparable after that. I couldn't imagine she'd want to marry me, but she was the one who insisted."

I thought of Officer Jim and the stranger danger puppet

show. Cliff needed a front-row seat. Ginger had enticed Cliff to marry her just the way a kidnapper entices a child into his car. Flattery, promises of rewards, lies. And he was as naive as a first grader, at least when it came to Ginger.

"I met Bix at a party," Sid said, surprising me since the Bix word had rarely issued from her throat since the night he left town. "Same thing. He sought me out at the country club where I work, and I felt like a million dollars. Here was this really cool guy and I was the one he wanted. After that he was my date for every event."

"Did Bix leave town?" Cliff asked. "I haven't seen him since . . ." His voice trailed off.

"He left on the twenty-third. He went to spend the holiday with his parents in New York."

"Really? I thought I saw him in town on Christmas Eve. But everything's a jumble in my head."

"He's gone for good. I don't think he's the guy for me," Sid said.

Cliff's voice sounded strained. "There were some rocky moments with Ginger, too. She wasn't always easy to be around. Love isn't all it's cracked up to be."

I leapt in, aware that the questions I wanted Cliff to answer were too many, too personal, and too soon after Ginger's death. But my opportunities were limited.

"I think you know I've been doing some checking around," I said. "I want to find out who murdered Ginger, and I want Sid off the hook."

"I can't imagine they're really serious about Sid being the killer," Cliff said. "The last time I spoke to Detective Roussos he said they think it had to be somebody strong enough to move the . . . to move Ginger after, you know."

Sid looked at me, hope leaping in her eyes. "Don't count on anything," I cautioned her. "They haven't said you can go."

"I know, but still!"

I went back to my questions. "Along the way I've come

across a few things about Ginger I don't understand. I need some help figuring them out. I think we all need answers."

"What kind of things?"

I knew this was all the encouragement I was going to get. He sounded wary, and we hadn't even really begun.

"Well, I've been talking to people who knew her in Cincinnati. This is a little touchy, I know, but I think she wasn't telling the truth about that second cookbook."

There was a heavy silence. It stretched so long I wondered if he was packing his tools.

"I just found out myself," he said at last. "Yesterday I called the publisher to talk about paying back the advance, and somebody in the accounting department told me there was no advance, and there was no book in the works with them."

"I'm sorry." The words seemed inadequate.

"Ginger hated to admit defeat."

"Don't we all," Sid said sympathetically.

Cliff stepped out of the bathroom and leaned in the doorway. "She was confident on the outside, but inside she was still a little girl."

"I can relate to that," Sid said. "I feel that way sometimes."

The moment was historic. Sid was comparing herself to Ginger, admitting they had shared emotions, just to make Cliff feel better. I was so proud of her.

"It must have been confusing," I said. "Because, well, the money she said she got as an advance must have come from some place else."

"I know where," he said, as if I hadn't just introduced the most indelicate of subjects. "She owned a condo in Cincinnati. I guess she didn't want me to know she sold it. She and an old boyfriend bought it together. I guess she didn't want to remind me."

Since I knew Kas had been living in the condo until his arrest, this seemed like wishful thinking. True, if Ginger and Kas had owned it together, maybe she had sold her share to him. But judging from what I had heard already, Ginger had been in debt to Kas, and even if she'd turned over her share of the condo, it would only have been to pay him off. Would she have come out with enough extra to help Cliff? Of course I didn't yet know just how much help he'd needed.

"I guess Cincinnati real estate is a good investment," I said.

"Most of my assets are tied up. Ginger's more or less supported us for the past few months."

I suspected that when Cliff got home and started looking through papers, he had a big surprise in store. There weren't going to be any records of a property sale. There weren't going to be any records, period. I was afraid no one would be issuing tax forms in Ginger's name this year. The food on Cliff's table had probably been bought with drug money.

"I've got one more question," I said. "It's not a good one, so I'll apologize in advance. But Cliff, I've been told that Ginger had a drug problem."

"Who told you that?"

"Somebody who knew her before you were married."

"Well, it's not true." He turned and went back into the bathroom. Sid looked up from scraping the wall and raised a brow. I shrugged. I certainly wasn't going to argue with him.

"Thanks," I said. "If it had been true, it might explain some things and the police ought to know."

"Well, it's not. When she was in a lot of pain she might take a pill to ease it, but that was rare. I would certainly know."

I wondered. There was so much about Ginger he had been blind to.

"You should have seen her when she was little," Sid said. "One time she fell off a bike and scraped both knees and elbows, nasty scrapes, too. I would have screamed my head off. Not Ginger. She got back on the bike and rode it all the way home without a tear."

Cliff gave a strangled laugh, but I could almost feel the tension ease. I blessed Sid for not recounting the whole story. The bike had been Sid's, and she'd been towing Ginger on the back when they both hit the pavement. Yes, Ginger had gotten back on and ridden the bike home, but in doing so she had left poor Sid to walk home alone through a thunderstorm.

"Aggie, do we have more rags?" Sid asked. "The scraper keeps getting gummed up."

I was ready for a break anyway. "I've got some downstairs."

"I can do it, I'm ready to turn on the power so you can use the steamer before I do the next bathroom," Cliff said.

"I'll get the rags, you get the power."

"I'll come with you. I need water," Sid said.

They followed me downstairs, and Cliff went to restore the power while I dug under the sink for rags. I found them in a heap in the corner, not the way I'd left them. When I started to pull them out I saw why.

"Remember when Bix refused to come inside because we might have mice?" I stood and made a mental note to call the exterminator. "Well, I'm afraid we do. Or maybe rats."

"How do you know?"

"Because the rags are now a nest." I'd seen what looked like seed hulls and shredded paper, too.

"I should have figured right then that he was worthless," Sid said.

Cliff joined us in the kitchen. "Who's worthless?"

"Bix. He's afraid of mice."

"You've got mice?" Cliff made a face.

I gestured to the cabinet. "You want to help me set traps?"

He shook his head. "Not that I'm afraid of them or anything."

Sid and I started to laugh and Cliff smiled, the first real smile I'd seen since Ginger's death. Sid was gazing fondly at him. I couldn't imagine there was any hope for the future there, but I was glad that for even a moment, we had forgotten to worry and simply enjoyed this new friendship.

15

I still hadn't swept the cobwebs out of my brain, and by the time Sid and I finished removing the majority of the bedroom wallpaper, I knew I had two choices. I could go home and try to nap with the telephone ringing and people trooping in and out. Or I could walk home and hope that fresh air and exercise did the trick. In an early winter surprise the day had turned warm, nearly fifty degrees, and morning gloom had been preempted by afternoon sunshine.

Sid agreed to take the van back home for me, and I promised to stop on the way and buy homemade pierogies from a woman who made and sold them out of her house near the Oval every Saturday afternoon. Sauteed in butter with onions, drowned in sour cream with sauerkraut on the side, pierogies are an Emerald Springs treasure. I rarely miss waiting my turn in Mrs. Kowalczyk's kitchen.

The snow of Christmas Eve night was a memory, and what was left of it was running across sidewalks and into the street. The unseasonable warmth had sent dads out a few days early to pack up the Christmas lights for another year. Children plunged arms into rapidly melting snowmen to fashion snowballs that flew in a million directions the moment they were launched.

I took unfamiliar side streets and lingered on corners watching the sun glint off slate roofs. I made friends with a dalmatian and kept my eyes open for a silver tabby who might have strayed too far. I was surprised when I wound my way to Robin Street to find DiBenedetto's Grocery at the end of the block.

Although I had been able to form a fuzzy picture of the store Vel had fallen in love with, I hadn't been sure where it was located. But here it was tucked into a short block in the midst of a residential neighborhood, with a barber shop on one side and a video rental on the other. I decided to stop in and see what the fuss was about.

As I had remembered, the store was dark and unattractive on the outside. Once inside, however, it was the epitome of Old World charm. The meat case had a small selection, but everything looked particularly fresh and delectable. The vegetable section—which was supposed to interest me more—was filled with things that were in season or stored well. Winter squashes and bushels of apples, sweet potatoes, and carrots with lacy green tops.

"Can I help you?"

I turned to face one of the most gorgeous men I have ever seen. I guessed he was closing in on forty, with black hair just beginning to turn gray and liquid brown eyes. I was reminded of the Roman gods in Florence's Uffizi Gallery. He was probably six feet tall, broad shouldered and narrow hipped. And although he was dressed casually, he knew how to wear clothes.

"I've never shopped here before," I confessed. "But my sister has been raving about this place." Now, I thought I understood why—and not because the red cabbage looked firm and succulent.

"Thank her for us."

"Unfortunately she's gone home. A pretty blonde about my age? A little taller? Vel?"

It's not possible to teach a man to smile like this. It's a talent he's born with. A slow ignition that lights the eyes one watt at a time. A smile that heats a room, even when it's not aimed precisely at you.

"Vel understands food," he said. "My father fell in love with her."

"I think it's mutual."

"Are you Aggie or Sid?"

This acquaintance had clearly gone further than I'd imagined. Names were involved. Memory was involved. I wondered if they had exchanged phone numbers or e-mail addresses. I wondered if they had discussed where to go on their honeymoon.

"Aggie," I said, holding out my hand. "Aggie Sloan-Wilcox."

"I'm Marco DiBenedetto." My hand disappeared into his.

"The store's really not very far from my house. Now that I know where you are, I'll be back."

"Let me show you what we have that's particularly good this afternoon."

Fifteen minutes later I stood in the checkout line with one of those firm, succulent red cabbages, a bunch of carrots, a pound of fresh spinach fettuccine, and an ounce of dried porcini mushrooms. Marco carried my bag to the door while a pretty teenager came out from the back to help a couple of other customers.

"You'll be inviting Vel back to visit?" he asked.

"She flies in whenever she can." And I suspected a sudden upswing in flights booked.

"She likes Manhattan. I lived in Brooklyn for awhile. The city certainly draws you in. But I wanted to raise my children here with family."

"You have children?"

"Three boys."

My fantasies spiraled into a nosedive. In my mind I had moved Vel to Emerald Springs and renovated the right house for her and Marco. I knew one in a good neighborhood that had been on the market for too long, and I knew just what needed to be done to polish it into a jewel.

No house now.

I don't know if Marco read my mind, my expression, or just heard his own answer. His smile smoldered once more. "Unfortunately my wife moved to California when I moved here with our sons. Or I should say my ex-wife."

That was a sad thing, but I had trouble working up the appropriate amount of regret. "Single parenting must be tough."

"It's better than having two parents who don't agree on much of anything."

We said goodbye, and I thought how much fun it would be to go home and tell Sid what I'd discovered. This might even take her mind off her problems for a full minute.

After another unfamiliar block I planned to cut over to the Oval to get the pierogies, but as I crossed the street I noticed a sign in the yard of a green-shingled house on the far corner. Since I was in discovery mode, I wandered that way to see what other local establishments I'd missed. In a moment I was standing in front of a sign for Peter Schaefer, MD, Pain Management.

I was glad the house wasn't ringed with picketers.

Immediately I saw the value of having the office here on this quiet block surrounded by older, modest homes in good repair. Even in winter the yard, with its expert landscaping and wide brick walkway, was a serene invitation. If I was suffering from unbearable pain, I would choose this comfortable home over a sterile office building as a place to find release.

"Mrs. Wilcox?"

I turned to find Peter Schaefer coming up the sidewalk toward me. I'd heard a car pull into the small lot that faced the side street, but I had paid little attention. Now I noticed a sleek white sedan parked in one of the spots.

"Hello." I held out my hand. "I was walking home and saw your office. I didn't realize you were right here."

"I wanted a place that feels like home for my patients."

"You succeeded. Do you serve chicken soup?"

"If that's all I did, life would be simpler."

"I know you've had a few problems."

He didn't seem in a hurry. He was wearing jeans—good jeans—and an Irish fisherman's sweater under a casual winter parka. A bag from the garden supply store was tucked under one arm.

"When I moved here I hoped the community would accept what I'm trying to do. I guess I thought if I helped enough patients, the word would go out that I was doing good work and no one would bother me."

"In a small town it's the hare and the tortoise all over again. The hare being the bad news."

"But the tortoise eventually wins?"

"If he keeps putting one foot in front of the other." I puzzled over that image for a moment. Did a tortoise move one foot at a time? My analogy might need work.

"That's optimistic," he said. "They may tar and feather me while I'm plodding toward the finish line."

"Why did you choose Emerald Springs? It's so far off the beaten path."

"I was practicing in Chicago, and I got tired of the rat race. My partner in the practice died, and I thought it was time to pull up stakes and try a quieter lifestyle. There was a need in this area for what I do, and when I saw Emerald Springs I knew this was the place for me."

I know that looks can be deceiving, but Peter Schaefer has a quiet dignity and warmth that makes it difficult to imagine him initiating or feeding addictions. I decided to take advantage of it.

"Dr. Schaefer—"

"Peter."

I nodded. "Peter, I have a couple of questions you might be able to help with."

Warmth changed to wariness. I suspected he, like most doctors, was asked to diagnose everything from athlete's foot to terminal cancer on sidewalks like this one.

I held up both hands and broke out my most disarming smile. "It's not what you think. I don't need medical advice. It's about pain relief and what you do."

The wariness didn't abate. "It's a big subject."

"Well, it's general stuff. Since the topic keeps coming up, I'd like to be armed with facts."

He nodded slowly. "Okay, but I was about to treat my pond. I've been away for the holidays, and I came back to a mess. If you don't mind maybe we can talk while I mix these chemicals."

We walked along the sidewalk, then across grass that crunched under our feet. The backyard was surrounded by a wooden fence that also blocked out the parking lot, and once he unhooked the gate and we walked through, I understood why. The front yard had been welcoming but the backyard was an oasis. Graceful evergreens, specimen shrubs, beds that were probably filled with flowers three seasons of the year. And best of all, a small waterfall cascading over boulders into a pond about ten feet in diameter. Benches were strategically placed at angles to enjoy the view.

"Oh, it's lovely. Did you design it?"

He looked pleased. "Yes, and I did all the work the front-end loader didn't."

"I am so impressed."

"I've got a problem with string algae. Not something I would expect this time of year, but it's been warm enough that I've had minimal ice."

"The pump keeps the water circulating fast enough to keep it from freezing?"

"Until the temperature stays low for a good while. But I should have taken care of this in the fall. I just expected the problem to go away on its own." He gestured to a bench. "Take a seat. I'm just going to mix this with a little water and pour it in." He held up a bottle.

I watched as he fetched a large white plastic bucket, dipped it in the pond to get water, then set it on the edge. I waited until he had measured the chemical and added it to the bucket. Then he dumped the concoction in.

"I hope this doesn't kill my goldfish. It's not supposed to." He picked up a long-handled fishnet and scooped out some leaves.

I figured our time together was limited, so I began. "I guess my biggest question is how a doctor can measure pain. How do you know who to help and who to avoid?"

He rinsed the bucket in the pond, then he turned it over to drain. "You mean, who's lying and who isn't?"

"Yes."

"There aren't any reliable tests, if that's what you mean. No instruments can detect degree of suffering. Everyone's pain threshold is different. Discernment takes a lot of training and a lot of listening. Of course medical records are important, X-rays, blood work, the usual. Thorough examinations. I require my patients to document everything, every symptom, their response, what helps, what doesn't."

"Do you see certain kinds of problems more than others?"

"We see a lot of conditions repeatedly. Headaches, joint pain, neck and back pain. There's something called trigeminal neuralgia that causes severe facial pain, almost like being struck by lightning. It's so severe suicide sometimes seems like the best option."

"And you can help?"

"Not always."

"How do you help?"

"Well, this garden is a start. I offer meditation classes to my patients. Sometimes they practice here, or I just send them out to relax while they're waiting to see me. I refer them to other practitioners when I think it will help. But it often comes down to drugs."

He put the net on a rock. "Four billion workdays are missed every year due to pain. If we can manage it early and well, we can save lives, reduce suffering, keep people out of the hospital, and even decrease the burden on our healthcare systems."

I was in sympathy, but I decided to ask the hard question. "Someone told me you prescribe hundreds of pills per day for some patients."

"In the same way that pain thresholds are different, so are tolerance levels. A small dose that works for one patient won't work for another. And patients build up a tolerance to some of the drugs we use, opioids in particular, and need more to obtain relief. We start with small doses of the short-acting opioids, and increase amounts or switch to long-acting. Sometimes we add other drugs to the mix while keeping careful records, until we achieve our goal. So yes, it sometimes looks as if we're prescribing a ridiculous number of pills. But sometimes, that's what it takes."

I wondered about Ginger. Had she really needed this kind of help? Had she been forced to turn to Kas to get it because someone like Peter Schaefer hadn't been available to her? Or had the extent of her pain been exaggerated so she could obtain drugs to sell?

"Clearly you're wondering about something," he said.

I guess I had been silent too long. "I'm wondering how many of those drugs end up on the street."

"You and too many other people," he said.

I heard the bitterness. If he was a good man trying to end suffering—and that was my best guess—the bitterness was understandable. "But how good are your safeguards, Peter? Can you weed out the addicts from the patients who really need help?"

"Addicts need help, too."

"Well, not that kind of help."

"I've had addicts come to me with unbearable pain completely unrelated to their addiction. Try figuring out how to deal with that."

His was not a job I wanted. Ending suffering was noble. Contributing to the illegal drug trade, which promoted excruciating suffering, was despicable.

"I won't keep you any longer." I rose. "It's clear there aren't any easy answers here."

"This is about more than questions from the community, isn't it?"

I should have known he'd see through me. I hoped he was this insightful with his patients. "I've just learned someone I know may have been procuring and selling prescription painkillers. I just wanted to understand more about it."

He didn't look surprised, but he didn't look pleased, either. "Don't ever make the mistake of believing that everyone who writes a prescription does it with the same care and concern. This is my specialty. I'm trained, and I'm competent. But there are a lot of clueless doctors, and more than a few who are dishonest. They hurt all of us because legitimate specialists are coming under increasing fire. Pretty soon people who suffer won't have anywhere to turn for help. Doctors will be too frightened of going to jail or losing their licenses."

"Good luck with your algae problem."

He smiled a little. "It's one of the simpler problems I have to deal with."

+ + +

Hours later I was melting butter in a large skillet when Sid wandered down from her long winter's nap. The pierogies were plump and perfect, some filled with potatoes, some with cheese. I told myself they wouldn't be even better if I fried up a little kielbasa to go with them.

"What's that smell?" Sid sniffed the air.

"Red cabbage to go with the pierogies. I found a sweet-and-sour recipe that looks good. I miss Vel's cooking."

She filled the kettle with water and put it on the stove for tea. "I got a call when I walked in the door. You'll never guess from whom."

I was guessing it hadn't been Roussos telling her she could return to Atlanta with no fears.

"I'm clueless," I said. "Who?"

"Hertz. Seems Bix never returned the rental car, and he's not answering his cell phone. Unfortunately they had my number, too."

"Whose name's on the rental agreement?"

"His, but I signed on as an authorized driver. They have my credit card information, too."

I wished Bix was sitting right here. Sid could pry open his jaws, and I would stuff him full of every single food in my kitchen that wasn't organic or imported—which includes pretty much everything. Death by processed cheese slices and grape Jell-O. It was too good for him.

"What are you going to do?" I asked when I had calmed a little.

"Lest you think it ends there, I'll sweeten the pot. I called directory assistance for Sag Harbor. That's where his parents are supposed to live."

"Supposed to?"

"There are no Minards in Sag Harbor."

"Maybe he has a stepfather with a different name."

"Not that he's ever mentioned."

"And you tried his cell?"

"Repeatedly. I left three messages. And, of course, I called his number in Atlanta."

"I'm so sorry."

"Yeah, me, too. Sorry I picked such a loser."

While we both thought about that I dumped chopped onions in the skillet and stirred them until they were soft, then turned off the burner. The rest could be done right before we ate.

The back door opened, and Teddy stomped in with Junie behind her. Today Junie was clearly paying homage to Eskimos. Her parka was lined with thick faux fur and fastened with something akin to walrus tusks. Her down gloves were thick enough for building igloos. Junie moves from north to south like a migratory bird, and she always winters where the weather is warm. Emerald Springs is a shock to her system.

"Is Moonpie home yet?" Teddy asked.

"No, I'm sorry." I had conducted another search of our yard and the immediate neighborhood this afternoon, but still to no avail. I even called the animal shelter.

"Were you and Junie looking for him, too?" I asked. There had been a note on the table when I returned home from my walk explaining that Deena was shoveling stalls at a local horse farm, and Junie and Teddy were spending the afternoon together.

"No, we were looking for angels." Teddy left to hang up her coat, but Junie stripped off hers beside the door.

"Where were you two?" I asked my mother as the layers came off.

"After we got back from the fabric store she asked me to help her with her story for school."

That surprised me. Teddy had refused to let me see it the last time I asked.

"And?"

"And, she's not getting anywhere with it. Not because she doesn't have an imagination, but because she's still wrestling with angels."

"She has a lifetime of that ahead of her, I'm afraid."

"When you found out Santa Claus was just a concept, you spent most of your time trying to figure out who came up with the whole idea in the first place and whether we ought to report them. You always wanted to get to the bottom of things. Sid, you said as long as the Christmas presents kept coming, you didn't care who brought them. My little Material Girl."

Sid made a noise deep in her throat, something between a laugh and a groan.

"Teddy's more like her dad," I said. "She wants to understand all the universal implications."

"I thought she ought to see some real angels, so I took her to the food bank and we put together bags of food for families in need. I told her all those people were angels in action."

"How did you know about the food bank?"

"Lucy told me about it when she was giving me the grand tour. I called and they told us to come over."

I put my arms around her and squeezed. "Extra pierogies for you, Grandma. That was a wonderful idea. No wonder I turned out so well."

She patted my cheek. Stripped of outerwear she was resplendent in white stretch lace, a plump, perceptive snowflake. "Teddy's thinking it over."

"She can always do with a little Junie magic."

"I need to see more of her. And Deena. They're growing up too fast." She sobered. "It seems like only yesterday you were all still with me. Ginger, too. And now there's nothing left of that part of my life but memories."

There was no self-pity in her voice, but the fact that she would express her sorrow over Ginger, in any form, was telling.

"You know," I said, "I cleared all Ginger's things out of the hotel. I have them in my closet. There was some lovely jewelry, and Cliff didn't want it. I thought maybe you would."

Wisely Junie didn't refuse or say she wanted Sid and me to take it. "Yes, I'd like that."

"I'll get the suitcase after dinner. You can go through the jewelry yourself."

The back door slammed and Deena came in, followed a minute later by her dad. Hugs were exchanged, the table was set, and I sauteed the pierogies with the butter and onions. Not a one was left by the time dinner was over.

Ed is reading our girls *Black Beauty*, and after we cleaned up the kitchen, Sid and Junie stayed downstairs to listen. Since I had heard last night's chapter, I knew that Black Beauty had just met the pony Merrylegs as well as a snappy chestnut mare who scared little children and regularly bit the hand that fed her. Ironically the mare's name was Ginger. I was hoping for a happy ending to that particular plot thread.

I used the opportunity to go upstairs and take Ginger's suitcase out of my closet. Lying open on my bed it was a sad reminder. I doubted Junie would want Ginger's clothes, but she often surprises me. I took out the things I had carefully folded and laid them on the bed with the jewelry in its satin case. I checked the two inside pockets to be sure nothing else was there, then closed it. There were two pockets on the front, as well, which I hadn't checked on Christmas afternoon, since I hadn't needed the room. Now I unzipped them to see if there was anything else for Junie to go through.

The first pocket held the sort of things I always leave in a suitcase for the next trip. Packets of tissues, a container of Tylenol and some cough drops, some extra underwear, an old issue of *InStyle*. I threw everything away and unzipped the second pocket, which appeared to be empty. I swept my hand through it to be sure there was nothing hiding in the corners. Surprised, I felt a bump, and when I opened the flap wider and peered inside, I saw a zipper that opened to an inside pouch. It wasn't exactly a secret pocket, but close enough. I unzipped it and reached inside.

The bump was a notebook, about five by seven inches, bound with tape and thread like the composition books I used in high school for serious essays. Since I'm basically an optimist, my first thought was that I'd discovered a diary, and with it, perhaps, the key to Sid's freedom. I opened the notebook and leafed through the pages, not sure at first what I was reading. Then as I started again and read more closely, I understood.

Sid wouldn't be calling the airlines tonight, but I still hoped that very soon she would be winging her way back to Atlanta.

16

Talking to Ed on Saturday nights is like talking to an astronaut as he's suiting up to orbit the earth. I've learned to wait until Sunday services have ended before I broach anything more important than "I took your blue suit to the cleaners so you'll have to wear the black one." I wanted to tell him what I'd found, but instead I decided to call Carol Ann Riley in Kentucky and ask her a few more questions. We'd left on a cordial enough note. I hadn't made a citizen's arrest.

I tried twice before I got her, marching outside in the interval to shout "Here kitty, kitty, kitty," until I was hoarse. By then it was nearly ten, and everyone had gone to bed except Sid and Junie, who were watching the Bette Davis classic *Dark Victory*, and sniffing audibly. I used the telephone in the kitchen and kept my voice down—although they were both so entranced I could have taken the phone to the sofa and carried on my conversation right between them.

I greeted Carol Ann like an old friend, and she was polite. This is the wonderful thing about people from Kentucky.

They are politer to strangers than the national average and less likely to hold little things against you—like suspecting them of murder. I didn't push that theory far, though, and knew better than to engage in chitchat. Carol Ann has lived in other places, too. There's no telling what she's learned.

"I'm going to get right down to business," I said, "because it's late and I'm sure you've had a long day. I have reason to believe Ginger was using and maybe selling drugs, and I wonder if you can confirm it. Remember, she's gone now and you can't hurt her by telling the truth. And she can't retaliate."

She didn't hesitate. "That was one of the reasons I left."

I hoisted myself up to the counter and leaned against a cabinet, something I tell my girls not to do. "You didn't mention this when we were having coffee."

"I know. I considered it. But I didn't want to speak ill of the dead. Well, any more ill than I already did that day."

I guess Kentucky kindness is extended to the recently murdered, too. Now, however, Carol Ann made up for lost time.

"It all started after her accident. She probably *was* in pain. She certainly complained enough. She'd try one doctor, then she'd try another. I just figured she couldn't find the right help and was shopping around. Then I started to notice she was seeing more than one doctor at a time. She'd have an appointment with this one, then a few days later with that one. The next week there would be a new one."

"Not just different types of specialists?"

"Mostly? No. I didn't keep her calendar. She did that herself, but she would forget and leave it lying open. So I had a pretty good idea."

"Do you think she behaved like somebody on drugs?"

"Sometimes she would fall asleep in the middle of a sentence, or wobble when she walked. We were working on the cookbook, and we would finish a recipe, and by the next morning she would forget we had even started it. But not all the time. In fact not even most of the time."

"Was she with Kas Novy when you worked for her?"

"So you know about him?"

"I know he's in jail on drug charges. Did you?"

"I saw something in the Cincinnati paper, but it was no surprise. Charming? With that accent and those fakey manners? But you couldn't trust Kas as far as you could drive a semi on a nickel's worth of gas. He gave me the creeps."

"So you were working for Ginger when she got involved with him?"

"Yes, and I was still with her when they moved into that place on the river. Ginger was better for a while, like she was happy for a change and didn't need to be angry at everybody in the room. I almost liked working for her. Then they started fighting, and I can tell you things went straight to hell after that."

"I'm just asking for an opinion here. But do you think Kas Novy had anything to do with Ginger being on drugs?"

"Being on drugs? No. I think that started with the accident." I could almost hear her thinking. "But he was involved in it all right."

"Was she getting drugs and giving them to him to sell?"

"How did you know that?"

"You have proof?"

"Not a bit. But I'd hear snatches of their fights. They were always fighting about money. They bought that condo—"

"Together? Both names on the title?"

"No, and that was funny. Only Ginger's name was on the title, although I think most of the money that went into it was his. It was something about his taxes and not wanting to list it as an asset, like maybe he was afraid the IRS would wonder where he got the money to buy it. I never got all the details."

"He must have been madly in love with her to trust her that way."

"Oh, I'm not so sure. He used to make a lot of jokes about all the friends he had and how nobody ever double-crossed him. He'd say that like it was funny, but she never laughed."

"Do you think she was getting drugs for her pain and letting him sell them at the club as a way to pay her share of the expenses?"

"Where else was the money coming from? Oh, I think he supported her at first, but he was the kind of man who expected a lot in return. A man with a wandering eye, if you want the truth. In my opinion, Kas started to get tired of Ginger right after they moved in together. So he started asking for more than her warm body in bed. She could have moved out and let him sell the condo, but she liked living there. So I guess she made her choice."

I thanked her and hung up.

I was still sitting on the counter when Ed came downstairs. "You look pretty silly," he said. "Don't let the kids catch you up there."

"This is what mothers do to get even. I can't track in mud or have a food fight with myself, because I'm the one who has to clean it up."

"How much longer is the movie?" He hiked his thumb toward the den.

"Most of an hour."

"The girls are asleep, and after I make one more poignant plea for Moonpie to come home, we could go to bed."

"You finished your sermon?"

"Uh huh."

"The order of service, the readings, the prayers, what to say in social hour when Fern asks if my sister is going to be arrested?"

"I'm going to say that my wife is working on it, and if

history is any clue, she'll nearly get herself killed trying to solve the case."

I slid to the floor. "That will do nicely. Go call Moonpie and I'll slip into something warm and toasty."

He raised a brow.

"Our bed," I said. Then I kissed him.

+ + +

Sundays are predictable. Church, social hour, Ed staying afterwards to meet with prospective brides and grooms, to do counseling or meeting with newcomers. Dinner when he finally gets home, then a quiet afternoon when the girls either visit friends or have them here. Junie and Sid went through the motions with us, although Sid didn't attend church. She was too embarrassed and way too old for me to insist. Junie, resplendent in a hat with an entire little town circling the brim and the church steeple rising from the crown, regaled the congregation's needleworkers with tales of her trip to the fabric shop.

Late in the afternoon Ed closed himself up in his study to take a phone call. I was alone in the living room when he emerged.

"You're going to love this," he said.

"I can hardly wait."

"Ida Bere has asked permission to use the social hall on Wednesday night for a meeting to discuss the illegal sale of prescription drugs on our city streets. Of course we know who her focus will be."

"What did you tell her?"

"That she can as long as she pays the customary rental fee. She thought since some of the people organizing it were church members, she could have it for free."

"Would you charge for a group you agreed with?"

"It's policy." He flopped down beside me. "They have a right to meet. And besides, I don't have enough information to know if this is hysteria or grounded in reality."

"I wanted to talk to you about Peter Schaefer."

"It'll be more fun talking to you than it was to her."

I wasn't so sure. I told him about running into Peter on the sidewalk and chatting with him as he worked on his pond. "But that's not all," I said, before he could take me to task for using Peter to get information. "Remember that suitcase I took home from Ginger's hotel? I found something I want you to see. You'll stay right there?"

"I'll spend the time finding a polite way to tell you to leave people in the church out of your search for Ginger's killer."

"He's not a member yet." I took off before he could answer.

I returned with the notebook and settled beside him. "This was zipped into a pocket in the front. I nearly didn't find it. Not hidden, exactly, but not easy to spot, either."

I opened the notebook and handed it to him. "Look at it, then I'll tell you what it is."

He examined the pages, turning them slowly. "So what is it?"

"It's a medication log. That column on the left is the time a drug was administered. The number next to it? PL? I think that's pain level. The ratings go from 1 to 10. Next to that"—I pointed—"I'm guessing the letters are a code for the medication taken. 'O,' maybe in this case for Oxy-Contin or something else. Beside that? That's the number of pills. Then beside that is the pain level after an hour. See this note at the top that says one hour?" I pointed to that, too. "And finally, here's a place to put side effects, which was the real clue to what I was looking at. See, here it says 'dizziness,' and here it says 'headache.' "

"How did you figure this out?"

"When I talked to Peter, he mentioned the importance of record keeping. He said he required his patients to document everything, every symptom, responses, what works, what doesn't."

Ed leafed through again, then he closed it. "What are you telling me?"

"The morning before Ginger died, Vel saw her standing on a sidewalk in town. She said Ginger was looking around like she thought someone might be following her. So, of course, Vel followed her, but she lost her."

"And?"

"And that was when Vel found the Italian grocery store she fell in love with. Or at least she said it was the *store* she loved."

"Aggie . . ."

"Ed, the store is just a block from Peter Schaefer's office. I think Ginger was on her way to see him."

"You think this record is for him?"

"I'm going to find out. Unfortunately it's not dated, but it has days of the week, and you can see it's only a few pages. I've got good reasons to think Ginger was seeing a lot of different doctors and getting prescriptions for pain meds. Then she was selling them. There's a big market. You can put yourself through college doing this."

"Maybe she was seeing somebody at home and making notes to take back."

"Yes, but don't you get it? We've wondered all along why Ginger came to this reunion. Not because she wanted to catch up with our lives. And not even to make trouble in the family. Sid thought Ginger wanted to get her hands on the money Junie made from her quilt, but that was such a long shot. I think Ginger checked around before she said yes and discovered that we have a resident pain specialist here, a man who speaks out for the right to give large doses of opioids when someone really needs them. She probably made an appointment the moment she realized what an opportunity this could be, and then she told Junie she would come."

"You're going to accuse Peter of giving Ginger drugs? A man who wants to join our church?"

"No. I want to ask him if Ginger was his patient, that's all."

"And what does this have to do with her murder?"

"What if he was prescribing large amounts of a drug with high street value? And what if she was carrying those meds the night she was killed? Maybe somebody saw her fill the prescription or even watched her come out of his office and figured there was a good chance she had drugs with her. Maybe she resisted."

"Then tell Roussos. Have him do the asking."

I sat back. "He doesn't listen to me. I talk to him and he nods like I'm some kind of looney tune. Then he ignores me."

"You don't know that. He likes you. He may even admire you. He just can't tell you what he's doing on his end. He can't compromise his investigation, and you can't be Watson to his Holmes."

"I just want to talk to Peter again. If he tells me Ginger had been to see him, then I will tell Roussos. Maybe that'll be enough information to interest him."

"What about patient confidentiality?"

"She's dead!"

He closed his eyes and leaned his head against the back of the sofa. Sundays are hard on Ed, and so am I.

I tried to make it more palatable. "You can come with me tomorrow, if you like. It's your day off."

"I told you a few days ago, I'm taking New Year's Day off instead so I can take the girls to the concert in Columbus—if Deena ever figures out who's going. Tomorrow I have to be at a prayer breakfast in the morning, a luncheon program at the food bank on world hunger, and in my office for appointments all afternoon."

"Then I'll go alone."

"Please don't."

"I could take Lucy."

"Please don't!"

I considered. "How about Jack?"

He was silent so long I thought he'd given up hope I would ever say another sensible word. But then he nodded. "Okay. Call Jack."

"I'm telling you this as a courtesy. I'm not asking permission."

"As if I hadn't figured that out."

"You love me anyway, don't you?"

"I wish you'd take up mountain climbing or skydiving. Anything but this."

"It's not a hobby, Ed. It's life or death."

"That's the problem."

+ + +

Every young, single attorney wants to spend New Year's Eve with the wife of his minister. I figured by the time Peter's office hours ended on Monday, Jack would be on his way to a party. Instead when I phoned, I asked Jack to meet me at Schaefer's office at 8:30 the next morning. From his sign I knew office hours began at 9:00, and I guessed Peter would be in a little earlier to prepare for the day and check the pond. Maybe his receptionist would be helpful while we waited.

Jack was agreeable. I think almost anything that gets him out of the office sounds like fun.

New Year's Eve morning was also unseasonably warm. I had promised the girls they could each have a friend over. Teddy invited Hillary Frankel to spend the day, but Deena shrugged at my offer. Judging from the constant ringing of our phone over the holiday, she is getting more calls than a registered Independent in an election year. Everyone wants to be Deena's best friend. I think she's afraid that anything she does will be interpreted as a sign she's already made choices about whom to invite to the concert tomorrow. I'm glad she has family to keep her busy, since friends have been noticeably absent.

Teddy and Hillary planned a house-by-house search for Moonpie, and Junie promised to accompany them. I'd extended my inquiries to every vet in the area. I suggested that Deena make a poster to put on telephone poles with Moonpie's photo and promise of a reward. Sid offered to take her to the copy shop in my van once it was finished.

With the medication log in my purse I walked over to meet Jack at Dr. Schaefer's office. The streets were clogged with the Emerald Springs version of rush hour, which means there were a few extra cars per block in the downtown area, and I actually had to pay attention to traffic. I waved to a couple of people who looked familiar, and a block from the office I pretended not to see Ida Bere, who was hunched over the steering wheel of a boxy sedan, as if she was hoping to ram it into the first pedestrian who got in her way.

Jack had parked across from the doctor's office, and he crossed the street when he saw me. I guess New Year's Eve isn't a big client day because he was dressed in khakis, a shirt with no tie, and a leather jacket. I was sorry Sid wasn't with me to see how good Jack looks in a bomber jacket.

I had given him the rundown on the telephone. Now we gave each other a friendly hug.

"Thanks for doing this," I said.

"It's on my way to work anyway."

"If we can just prove Ginger was here the evening she was killed, that has to be worth something."

"You know it still won't prove Sid didn't kill her."

"If Ginger was killed right here, do you think Sid could have moved her to the manger scene?"

"How far is it?"

"If you cross this street, cut through the yards across the way, cross Cardinal Street that way, you're at the driveway into the Catholic church lot where the manger scene was set up."

"It could have happened that way. It was dark, and there probably weren't many people around. Stores were closed, church services were in session."

"Or people were at home eating dinner. And it was snowing. Sid doesn't remember seeing anyone else outside when she went for her walk that night."

"Well, if you can convince Detective Roussos this might be the scene of the crime, he'll send a team to look for evidence. But it's been a full week now. We've had snow and runoff and lots of people have probably come through here."

"If Ginger was selling prescription drugs, that opens up a whole new avenue of inquiry, even if she wasn't killed here." I pointed to the white sedan in the doctor's parking lot. "I think that's Peter's car. Shall we try knocking on the front door first?"

"What's the alternative?"

"We could try the pond." As we walked up the front sidewalk, I explained about Peter's meditation garden. I rang the bell, and when that didn't bring anyone, Jack rapped sharply on the door.

"It's possible they won't answer until they're open," Jack said when nobody came.

"I think it's worth checking the backyard since we know Peter's already here. The gate wasn't locked yesterday. It has a high latch. From the inside it looked like one of those childproof varieties."

"It's trespassing, more or less."

"I think under the circumstances it's worth it. We'll just take a peek. If he's not there, we'll leave and wait on the front steps."

He didn't hesitate long. He followed me to the other side and around to the gate. I rapped on it, but when that didn't bring an answer, I reached over the top and felt for the latch. From the direction of the pond I could hear the pump grinding and water cascading over boulders. If Peter was there, he wouldn't hear us over the noise. We'd had a similar latch at our last house, and I opened it without a problem. I swung the gate toward us and ushered Jack through.

Tall evergreens screened off this side of the yard, and it wasn't until we were past them that I saw Peter. Jack saw him just a split second after I did.

Peter Schaefer was lying facedown on the ground, one hand trailing into the pond, the fish net with its aluminum pole floating just beside him. Two goldfish were floating belly up beside the net. I started toward him, but Jack grabbed me.

"Don't touch him."

"He needs help. Maybe he had a heart attack."

"Get inside and turn off the power. Stay far away from the pond though. Do whatever it takes. I'll call the rescue squad."

I realized then what Jack had realized first. Peter Schaefer had been electrocuted in the pond he had lovingly created as an oasis for his patients to enjoy. And until we turned off the power, electricity was probably still coursing through the water.

17

Peter's nurse-receptionist was a woman named Wilda whose grandmotherly appearance completed the image of home and comfort that Peter had tried to create for his office. When Wilda wasn't choking back sobs, she was praising us for finding Peter and calling the rescue squad. I was a particular favorite since I had gone inside and flipped the circuit breakers.

"He's going to be all right. I just know he will be," Wilda said again. "But what if you hadn't found him in time?"

I wasn't so sure Peter was going to be okay. The rescue squad hadn't made any guarantees since he'd been in both respiratory and cardiac distress. Jack had followed them to explain the details to the emergency room staff.

The police had come and gone, and I had made a request that they call Roussos, only to find that he wasn't on duty until later in the morning. Besides, they were treating the incident as an accident. The extension cord to the pump was frayed and wiring exposed, the ground under it was wet from melting snow, and the ground fault interrupter plug, which should have been disabled at the first unusual surge, hadn't worked properly. Although the circuit breaker should have tripped, the whole system had needed updating and just hadn't been up to the task.

There was a lot of evidence to support this. Wilda remembered there had been a problem with the pump previously, but Peter, something of an amateur electrician, had fixed it. One of the cops had pointed out that "amateur" was the right word. The extension cord wasn't even the type meant to be used outdoors, which explained all too well why it had frayed under harsh weather conditions.

The paramedics had told me that with prolonged shocks of this nature—of a voltage lower than if an electric heater or hair dryer had fallen into his bath water—the length of time Peter remained in a coma would tell all. More than one day was bad news.

I handed Wilda another tissue and patted her shoulder. "We did find him. And the hospital has skilled staff who know what to do."

"If he hadn't insisted on doing everything himself. That pond is like his therapy. His job takes so much out of him. All that suffering. All those people who need him, then the ones who just pretend they do." She shook her head.

I had told myself Wilda was too upset to question, but here she had provided me with the perfect opening. Heaven help me, I took it.

"You know, that's why Jack and I were here in the first place. We wanted to ask him about somebody who might have been trying to use him."

"Well, it's a good thing you came this morning." She blew her nose. "I'll need to cancel the afternoon appointments, won't I? He didn't have anyone coming in this morning. He had two cancellations yesterday."

"I guess you'd better."

We were sitting in the reception area on a comfortable sofa. Wilda sat back and squared her shoulders. "You were here because of one of his patients?"

"It's possible she was a patient." I decided to explain, since this would be my best chance to get information. I finished by telling her about the medication log, then I pulled it out to show her.

Wilda nodded after one glance. "Yes, that's one of ours." She took it and opened it, scanning the first page. "And yes, Ginger Grable was a patient here." She snapped the book shut. "But not for long."

If I ever win the lottery, I know this is exactly how it will feel. "Can you tell me the details?"

"She called about a month ago and made the appointment. Dr. Schaefer requires all medical records first, of course. Sometimes it takes awhile to get everything."

A month ago, just about the time Junie had dreamed up this reunion.

"Is Dr. Schaefer well known in the field, Wilda? I mean, do people come from other places to see him?"

"Oh, a lot of people make the trip here for his help."

"But how does that work? How can he follow them?"

"After the initial workup and treatment, patients travel here periodically, and in between they're required to fill out monthly reports. He reads every one, makes phone calls. He's extremely conscientious."

"So someone like Ginger might have heard of him as far away as Indianapolis and made the appointment to get relief?"

She was silent a moment. "I really shouldn't be talking about this, should I?"

"Ginger's dead, and we need to find out who killed her. Whatever you can tell me might help."

That seemed to reassure her. "His patients come from as far way as California. Mrs. Grable's records arrived in bits and pieces because she moved from Cincinnati, where the accident occurred, to Indianapolis. So several doctors were involved. I had to call a number of times to get everything. Dr. Schaefer went through them, of course, before her first appointment. We see a lot of patients with the same history. An accident, back or neck pain. Reams of paperwork, X-rays, you name it. Some of them are at the end of their rope. It's a sad thing when people suffer."

"But he took her as a patient?"

"Yes, he did a complete workup when she came in, and he didn't see any reason not to take her on. At least not anything he could put his finger on. Not at first."

"I'm not sure what you mean."

"There was something going on, or he was afraid there was. I guess he's developed a sixth sense. He gave her a log and asked her to start filling it out, and he gave her a prescription for a very limited supply of a form of oxycodone. That's what he does at first. He prescribes for a few days, sometimes just a day. That way he can change medications, increase them slowly, whatever he decides to do. But with Mrs. Grable, he just wasn't sure he trusted her."

"And something happened to make him think he'd been right to be cautious?"

"She came in on Christmas Eve morning with a man. She showed Dr. Schaefer this log, and he went over it with her while the man stayed in the waiting room."

"Can you describe him? I'm curious. A tall guy, kind of gangly, wire-rimmed glasses?"

She chewed her lower lip. "No, I don't think that's right. He was blond, a little soft in the middle, if you know what I mean. One of those noses you don't forget, kind of prominent, pointy." She demonstrated by making a V with her fingers and putting her fingertips on each side of her nose.

Bix Minard. It was a perfect description. But what had Bix been doing here with Ginger the morning after Sid kicked him back to Sag Harbor? Or thought she did. And how long had he remained? Long enough to murder her?

Wilda continued. "I guess she was pushy with Dr. Schaefer, asking for more drugs. He wasn't increasing her dose fast enough and she was leaving town on Christmas

Day. She had depended on him not to let her suffer, that kind of thing. I guess something about the whole appointment set off his alarm, because after Mrs. Grable left, he said he was going to go back over her chart. A little later he asked me to get a doctor in Dayton on the phone, and I caught him just as he was leaving for the holidays. Anyway, they spoke for a few minutes, then Dr. Schaefer came out and told me to call Mrs. Grable and get her in again for the last appointment of the day."

"Did he say why?"

"I'm the only person he confides in. I just want you to understand that. He's not loose-lipped."

"Doctors often confide in nurses."

"He found a notation in Mrs. Grable's chart from her Cincinnati physician, just a scribble at the bottom of a page. He'd missed it the first time because the records had come in so late and he'd had to read through them quickly. It was a referral to this other pain specialist in Dayton, somebody Dr. Schaefer knew from conferences. During the call the doctor confirmed that Mrs. Grable was still his patient, currently on medication he was prescribing."

"In other words she was trying to get more than she could possibly use herself."

"She was on a very large dose. Or I should say she was getting a lot of medication. That's all I know."

I wondered how many doctors were prescribing for Ginger Grable. If she wasn't asking an insurance company to pay for the prescriptions, then who would know she was doubling up, or worse?

"That's all I know," Wilda said. "And more than I should have told you, I guess."

"No, this was the right thing to do. But did Ginger come in later in the afternoon?"

"His last appointment was at 5:20. See, he was going away for the holidays, so he wanted to see everybody who needed him on Christmas Eve, so he could head out of town with a clear conscience. He asked me to make her appointment for 5:45. But I left before she got here, so I don't know if she came in. I've been out of town at my sister's. Today was our first day back at work. I wish we hadn't come in at all."

"Is there any way you could find out?"

"I could check her chart."

"Would you? Please?"

Wilda got up, tossed her tissue in the trash beside her desk, and went to an extensive filing system. After a minute, she pulled a chart and leafed through it. Then she put it back. I stood by her desk and waited.

"She was here."

Ginger had been in this office right before she died.

"You know she died right after that appointment," I said.

Wilda looked surprised. "No. On Christmas Eve? I've been away. I didn't know. I mean, I knew she was killed, but I didn't know when or really, how."

And Peter Schaefer had been away. Maybe he had discovered the time of Ginger's death and talked to the police when he returned—or maybe he hadn't. It was possible Roussos didn't know that Ginger had been here at all. Probable, I thought.

I wondered if Bix had been here for that second appointment, too. Clearly some sort of infatuation had developed between Ginger and Bix, but how long had it lasted? And had it ended in a lover's quarrel that turned to murder? Had Ginger confided her plan for procuring drugs? Had Bix, disappointed when they didn't materialize, become violent?

And where was Bix now? Running as far and fast as possible in a Hertz rental car, before his involvement was discovered?

Another thought occurred to me. I didn't want to make Wilda's burden heavier, but I had one more question.

"I know Dr. Schaefer's been catching a lot of flack. Has he been getting threats? Has it reached that point?"

"We turn off our voice mail at night now. Every morning when I came in there were dozens of angry calls, like somebody had gotten a lot of people organized to make them. We had to give our patients a special private number to leave messages. During office hours I still get a few, but it was the nighttime calls that were shameful."

I wondered if Ida Bere had organized this particular phone campaign, Ida Bere, who I had seen just a block away on my walk to the office. So many suspicious people, so little time to investigate.

"You don't think somebody did this to him?" Wilda asked.

I didn't. But it would be one more thing to tell Roussos.

✦ ✦ ✦

I stopped by the church first to tell Ed what had happened. As I'd hoped I caught him between the prayer breakfast and hunger luncheon. I wish *my* job came with hot meals.

I gave a quick wave, then sailed past Norma without giving her a chance to engage me in conversation. I shut Ed's office door, just in case she followed, and used my body to bar entrance.

Ed was on the telephone, which Norma would have explained had I given her the opportunity. I waited until he was off, then told him why I had barged in and taken him prisoner.

He listened, frowning. "The poor guy. What an awful thing." He pulled me away from the door and hugged me. "And what if Jack hadn't warned you?"

"I hope I would have figured it out myself before I did something stupid. But it wasn't like poor Peter was hanging on to a power line. The voltage was a lot lower. And lucky for him the fishnet slipped out of his hand. Metal, water, electricity . . ." I shuddered.

"I'll go over to the hospital and tell them I'm Peter's minister. I'll see how he's doing."

"His receptionist told me everything I wanted to know about Ginger." I gave Ed the synopsis.

"And now you're going straight to Roussos, right?"

"I'm on my way."

He looked relieved. I took advantage. "Would you mind if I crawled out your window?"

"It will look just a tad too odd, Ag."

I took a deep breath. "Then you'll stall you-know-who so I can get out?"

"You ask a lot, don't you?"

Ed left first, and I heard him ask Norma how she was coming on typing his board report. I gave another fast, friendly wave and made it outside without incident.

My minivan was parked in the driveway, and I went inside to tell Sid I would need it for awhile. I found her in the kitchen making tea. The girls were nowhere in sight.

"It's quiet in here," I said.

"Deena's upstairs designing the poster, in between fawning phone calls from her friends. Maddie's with her."

Apparently Deena had made at least one choice. "Are Teddy and Hillary casing the neighborhood with Junie?"

"Just this street. For all the good it will do."

"They might find something."

Sid poured hot water in a mug and held up the kettle in invitation. I shook my head. "Well, I found out something of my own," she said. "But not about Moonpie. About Bix."

I wondered if I should tell her what I had learned. I decided to hear her revelation first, in case I could be spared having to report Ginger's final crime against my sister.

Sid jiggled her tea bag. "I called the club and talked to Tanya, you know, my assistant who's taking over for me on the party tonight?"

"Right."

"I told her about Bix and the rental car. Actually I told her the whole sordid story. And do you know what she said?"

I was in my nothing-could-surprise-me mode. I shook my head.

"She said Bix is nothing more than an Ivy League gigolo, and she thinks he's been using me to get into functions at the club and find a rich woman to take care of him. He tried her, first, but somebody warned her. I guess a lot of people are on to him. She didn't know he'd latched onto me until Bix and I had been together for awhile. Then she was afraid to tell me. She said she was afraid I would think she was jealous, and it would affect her job."

"Oh, Sid." I grimaced. "Ouch."

"Why am I so stupid about men?"

I held up my hands in a "don't shoot me" pose. "The men you choose are like that collection of toothpick holders over your head. Pretty enough to look at, valuable just because some book or register says they are, and completely useless."

"I didn't really want an answer."

I dropped my hands. "Did she have any thoughts on where old Bix might be these days?"

"She gave me a couple of names. Women he was seen with before me. I guess I'll start calling."

I decided not to hit her any harder. But at some point I had to examine the probability that Bix had seen Ginger as a better catch than my sister. Most probably after Ginger's glowing report of her own success at our dinner table.

"I'm going to talk to Detective Roussos," I said.

"Oh?"

I filled her in on the events of the morning, minus the part about Bix at the doctor's office. Her eyes widened. "And some people say Atlanta's a dangerous place to live."

"I promise this is unusual."

She didn't look convinced, and for that matter, neither was I.

The trip to the police station was a quick one. Unfortunately, the municipal parking lot was a sea of melting slush. This is the only lot in town where we are forced to feed meters day and night, as if to point out that the city's work is never done. Adding insult to wet feet, I chose a meter that swallowed my quarters and gave nothing in return. I had to scribble a note to put on my windshield with the time and facts, and hope that whoever checked these things believed me.

Our police station is in flux. By early summer a brand-new station and jail will open at the service center on the edge of town, something fairly state of the art. In the meantime the cops make do in a dilapidated relic covered with gray asbestos shingles. Indoors the duct tape repairing the carpet is itself repaired by duct tape. Since the last time I was here, someone had scraped off the peeling paint, but nothing had been done to cover the bare spots.

The man in uniform sitting at a beat-up metal desk behind a grilled window told me to have a seat and he'd see if Roussos wanted to talk to me. If wanting to talk to me was key, I was sorry I hadn't brought *War and Peace* for company.

Surprisingly the detective arrived quickly.

"You want coffee?" he asked in greeting.

"Not if it's made on the premises."

"Let's go over to McDonald's."

I wasn't sorry to leave. On the way out I showed him my van and my note. He scrawled his name at the bottom. I love having friends in high places.

McDonald's was on the next block. I try to avoid fast-food restaurants because the smell of hamburgers cooking, lots and lots of hamburgers, pretty well reduces my scruples to useless abstractions. After crisply fried bacon, the thing I pine for most is a Big Mac.

I settled for a cup of coffee and slid across a plastic bench in the corner while Roussos served us. Just me and Roussos on a fast-food date. As excitement goes in my life, it was downright titillating.

"So, what's up?" he asked after he'd set it in front of me and seated himself. "You solved the crime yet?"

"You know, Roussos, you can be so condescending."

"I'm just an Emerald Springs cop, remember? I don't do four-syllable words."

"You know how important it is to get this investigation right."

"And for some reason you insist I'm trying to get it wrong."

I took the top off mine and added packets of cream. He watched, as if this was a behavior he had never seen in person.

"You heard about Peter Schaefer?" I asked.

"Uh huh. And I heard Little Mary Minister's Wife was the first one to find him."

"You know, if you hadn't shot a man on my account a few months ago, I'd think you were something of a jerk. As it is, I know you've made it your personal mission to keep me out of trouble. So I discount the sarcasm."

"This coffee's not going to last very long."

I smiled at him. He nearly smiled back. I was just as glad it was almost. Roussos has a lethal smile, and even married hormones jiggle in response.

I started at the beginning and told him everything I knew so far. And no, the coffee did not last that long. By the end he was frowning.

"You do get around." He crumpled his cup in his fist.

"This is my sister."

"We are not partners in this."

"I got that message."

"So this Minard character stayed in town and was at the doctor's with Ginger on Christmas Eve?"

"For her morning appointment. I don't know about the evening." I realized something. "You don't seem surprised about Ginger being a patient of Peter Schaefer's."

He didn't answer.

"You suspected she might be, didn't you?"

Again, no answer.

"And did you suspect she was killed after she came out of his office? Maybe for drugs?"

Strike three.

"I'm doing all the talking," I pointed out.

He seemed to consider. "I'll tell you two things. But on one condition."

"Uh oh."

"You stop snooping. And don't let me see that dimple of yours. I mean it. You've done a lot more than you should have already. Now stay out of this."

I chewed the inside of my cheek to keep the dimple in check. I really wanted to know what he had to tell me, and what would I do next anyway? I was fresh out of places to go.

I had to bargain a little. He expected it. "If I get an idea, will you listen so I don't have to check it out myself?"

"Listen, yeah. Follow orders, no."

That seemed fair. "Okay."

"Okay? As in okay, I will let the police department do the job they're paid to do?"

"Uh huh. Unless it looks like you're trying to pin this on my sister. Then all bets are off."

"We aren't trying to pin it on her. In fact we aren't going to."

I sat forward. "Can she go home?"

"Unless something comes up between now and late afternoon. I'll call her myself."

"What changed your mind?"

"One of the two things I mentioned. We think Mrs. Grable was killed near the doctor's office. And there was no way your sister could have gotten her body over to the Catholic church. Someone bigger and stronger did. Miss Kane couldn't even have gotten her in and out of a car by herself."

"Plus she didn't have a car. Her boyfriend took off with their rental."

"We know that, too. I didn't know he was still here on Christmas Eve."

I was delighted Sid was as good as off the hook. But I was also curious. "And number two?"

"We have a team over at Schaefer's looking at the setup in his back yard."

This time I sat back. Changing positions is the only way to make a body-language statement in a McDonald's booth.

"You don't think this was an accident?" I asked.

"I don't think anything. They teach us not to jump to conclusions."

"A murder and an attempted murder, in practically the same place."

"We don't know that. And remember, you made an agreement. Leave this to us."

"Yeah. Okay." I smiled at him, dimple and all. "But you're going to keep me in the loop, right? In case I have any final thoughts?"

He closed his eyes and shook his head.

"I keep your job interesting. You can't say I don't."

He opened his eyes and checked his watch. He began the slide to freedom. "Then I won't, on your say so. And I'm heading the other way." He hiked his thumb away from the station.

"Thanks for telling me what you could."

This time he did smile. Briefly. I watched him thread his way between toddlers clutching Happy Meals and an employee mopping up a spill. I realized I was alone, with no one watching what I did. I could have that Big Mac and no one would be the wiser.

I managed to hurl my body out the door just in time.

18

Junie made her wonderful Polish tomato soup for dinner, but Sid, ecstatic that she could finally go home, didn't even wait for the first luscious slurp to make her announcement.

"I booked a flight out of Columbus for early tomorrow morning. It was the only seat left on the plane and the only flight that wasn't filled."

"I can get you there." I passed a basket of day-old whole grain rolls from the bakery. "You're sure you're ready to leave?"

Sid's eyes lit up as she smiled. I hadn't seen a genuine smile since the moments just before Ginger walked through our front door. This visit had been hard on her in a number of ways.

"Can I go to the airport with you?" Deena asked.

"You're already going to Columbus tomorrow, remember? Your dad's taking you to the concert tomorrow night."

"Not anymore."

I looked up from my soup. The agreement had been that

Deena could only see the Botoxins if her father or I accompanied her. "You know that was the deal," I said.

"Chill, Mom. Daddy doesn't have to go. Nobody's going."

I caught Ed's expression. Rarely have I seen such unadulterated joy.

"Since when?" I asked.

"I sold the tickets to some high school girls. Yours, too. And I got enough money for mine that I can throw a party. A Friday night sleepover with all my friends. We can have pizza and rent movies and stay up. Maddie and I worked on it today."

And nobody had to be excluded.

I beamed at my daughter, who had wrestled with this weighty challenge and come up with a solution that in the end, would bring her pleasure without hurting anyone else. Whether it had been intended that way or not, Ginger's gift had helped her clarify her values.

Ed's joy visibly dimmed. The reality of a sleepover with at last a dozen fifth-grade girls was seeping in. But good guy that he is, he reached over and ruffled his daughter's hair in appreciation.

"I'm proud of you," he said. "That was a great way to handle things."

"And I'm going to buy Botoxins' CDs with whatever money's left so we can dance all night."

"I'm pretty sure I'm supposed to be in Hong Kong that weekend," I said. "But I know your father'll be here. Whenever it is."

Only Teddy still looked unhappy, and I knew why. Every telephone pole in a four-block radius had a likeness of Moonpie stapled to it, but so far nobody had called with a sighting. Junie caught my eye. I nodded toward Teddy.

"Teddy, I want to make brownies tonight," she said. "Will you help?"

Teddy picked up spoonfuls of soup and let them dribble back into her bowl. "I have to write my story."

"You have all day tomorrow," I told her. "We could use some brownies around here. It's New Year's Eve, and we're going to be staying up late. You can, too."

She didn't say no, but she didn't look happy about it.

After dinner I went upstairs to help my sister pack. Never has anyone enjoyed packing more. She was positively radiant.

In typical Sid style she was folding each item of clothing carefully. "Have you seen my rose sweater? It's the only thing I can't find."

I remembered Sid wearing the cardigan the day she had helped me strip wallpaper. She had replaced it with one of my old flannels. "Did you bring it back from the Victorian?"

"Darn."

"Easy to do. I left a shirt there last week."

"Can you mail it to me? It's one of my favorites."

"I'll do you one better. I'll go and get it."

Sid clutched a nightgown to her chest and tried to look thoughtful. "It's New Year's Eve. I know you want to stay home and celebrate."

I didn't tell her, but I wanted to run by the hospital first and see if anyone would give me news about Peter. Repeated phone calls hadn't gotten me anywhere, but I might be able to sweet-talk somebody in person. When Ed had visited, Peter hadn't yet come to.

I handed her the last pair of jeans hanging neatly in the closet. "I don't mind a bit. Then we can spend our last evening together."

She looked relieved. "That'll be great."

I was on my way out the door when the telephone rang. I grabbed it as I slipped into my winter jacket.

Lucy was on the other end. "Aggie, I'm stuck at the office

waiting for a buyer who's supposed to come over and write a contract on a house."

I leaned against the wall since there were too many people around for me to sit on the counter. "You disappoint me again. I depend on you to have a life for both of us. You're supposed to be off dancing and drinking champagne. Hopefully some place where the proprietor wasn't recently arrested, but still."

"Well, if this guy ever shows up, we're supposed to go out for drinks to celebrate. But he's close to seventy."

"You can come over here and play Clue with us."

"I've been playing my own version. I thought I'd check out some more stuff about Cliff and the lawsuit while I was waiting. It's more interesting than I expected."

I could almost hear Roussos whispering in my ear, and silently, I whispered back. Yes, Detective, I *am* done investigating. But you never said a word about Lucy.

I lowered my voice. "So, what did you find? Are his inventions worth even more than it sounded like the first time?"

"Not *that* lawsuit. The wrongful death suit for his first wife. I found an article about it in the Internet archives of a newspaper in Schaumburg, Illinois. Apparently that's where Cliff and his wife Marilyn were living at the time. She owned a travel agency and went by her maiden name, which was Matthews. Anyway, it seems she had some neurological condition that causes pain in the cranial nerve. Something called *tic douloureux.* Have you heard of it?"

"I don't think so. And it caused her death?"

"In a way. I guess even though there are treatments, nothing really helped her. So she saved up pills, and when she got enough, she ended her life. The antidepressant may have sped her along the road to suicide, which is what Cliff's lawsuit was about. But he also sued the practice. The doctor who prescribed it for her, a man named James Lawson, had been accused of not taking enough precautions once before; in fact he lost his license due to medical misconduct in regards to a different case, but that charge was dropped and he got it back."

"So Cliff's lawsuit against this guy is still pending?"

"Against his estate. He died just about a year after Cliff's wife. A three-alarm house fire. The article said there was another doctor in the practice but he couldn't be held accountable because he'd never prescribed for her."

I wondered if this was just another story of a doctor who had been blamed for a death he'd had no part in. Or had Lawson carelessly refused to take the time that was needed to be certain the drugs he prescribed were safe and being used with care, the way Peter Schaefer claimed that he did?

"Anything else?" I asked.

"Just that Marilyn Matthews was loved by a lot of people. There was a big turnout at her funeral. The story quotes old friends, that sort of thing."

I heard what Lucy didn't say. What a contrast to Ginger.

Lucy promised to drop by later if nothing better came up.

This time I made it out the door. I drove to the hospital first, and did manage to find a sympathetic nurse who "couldn't tell me anything," but did let me know through a series of hand signals and throat clearings that although Peter hadn't regained consciousness, his vital signs were stable.

The outside light was shining brightly at the Victorian, and I parked in the driveway. On the porch I fumbled with the key, but eventually I opened the door. Since it was dark and somewhat spooky, once I was inside, I locked it behind me.

The house still smelled like violet potpourri, although we had cleared away every trace of it weeks ago. Tonight it seemed more cloying than usual. I flicked on the stairwell light and went up to the master bedroom. The switch was off, but I flipped it and the light came on. Sid's sweater was in the closet where I'd seen her neatly fold and store it.

"Gotcha, troublemaker," I said, tucking it under my arm. I knew I was talking to the sweater because the Victorian seems eerily empty at night, almost depressed. Houses have personalities. This one wants to be filled with light and life, and it's waiting for a better day. Lucy and I are like beauty consultants supervising a makeover, but the house is hoping for somebody to love it.

I might need to change professions if I start giving our houses names and asking them to dinner.

I left the switch turned on, and as if someone else had crossed the threshold—someone with less propensity for technology disasters—the bedroom light went off as soon as I exited. Downstairs with just the light from the porch bathing the room, I tiptoed into the kitchen and listened for the sounds of mice rustling in the cabinets. But either our mice were underachievers or running elsewhere tonight.

I was halfway across the living room when the master bedroom light came on and light poured into the upstairs hallway. I stopped and waited, reminded of the last time this had happened. Cliff said he had replaced the defective switch, but now it was malfunctioning again.

"Turn yourself off," I shouted up the stairs, but of course, nothing electrical listens to me.

When I was halfway up, the light went off again. I waited, the room stayed dark, and I turned back, making a mental note to tell Cliff. When I reached the bottom, the bedroom light flicked on again.

"Okay, okay." I marched back up, resigned to flipping the switch. If I was lucky, it would do the trick until Cliff replaced it.

I stood on the threshold and reached for it. Something furry and considerably larger than a mouse ran across the room and disappeared into the closet where I'd retrieved Sid's sweater.

And the light went off.

"Eek" seemed too tame. Profanity wasn't called for—I try to use it sparingly and only when blood or leaping flames are involved. I strongly considered vacating the house until I could come back with reinforcements.

I heard rustling at the same moment the light flicked back on. This time the furball was coming straight for me. I leaped to one side, and as I did, I realized what kind of furball it was.

"Whoa there, fellow." I stepped forward, and the little animal didn't run away. I squatted and reached for it, and it still didn't run. Guinea pigs are tame creatures when they've been handled frequently at pet stores. This one was black and white with shorter fur than Cinnamon's. It was probably starving, and it probably missed having a friend.

I stood, holding the little warm body against my chest, and went farther into the room where the light was better to examine it more closely. Why hadn't Cliff told me that one of the *two* guineas Ginger had bought for Teddy had gotten loose in the house? Had he been embarrassed that one had slipped out of the cage on Christmas Eve while he was here working? As if, with Ginger's death on our minds, any of us would care?

Then, with a sickening thud, I understood. Why the guinea pig had been out of its cage in the first place. Why Cliff still hadn't mentioned its presence when I told him I found a rodent's nest downstairs. Why Cliff had continued to work on the house. Why Cliff had stayed in Emerald Springs, even burying Ginger here where she'd had no connections except me.

"Yikes."

I whirled and started toward the bedroom doorway. Unfortunately it was now occupied.

I stood very still, trying to figure out in a split second how to salvage this. I tried smiling brightly. "Cliff, good grief, you scared me to death! How long have you been there?"

He still looked like his lovable nerdy self. A little sheepish. A little befuddled. "You found the other guinea pig."

I rued the day I had ever given him a house key, but

clearly something as simple as a lock would never stop Cliff Grable.

I babbled. "Isn't he cute? And you really should have told us. I wouldn't have been upset he got loose. Now Teddy can have two, like Ginger planned."

"I know I'm not very good at figuring out people," he said in a conversational tone, like two old friends passing the time. "Even as a kid I never really understood what made my classmates or teachers tick, although I got a little better as I got older. Marilyn, she was my first wife, used to interpret for me. She said it was like trying to teach me Swahili. You would have liked Marilyn. Everybody did."

"You've had a hard time." I stroked the guinea pig, to keep my hands from shaking.

"But even *I* know you're pretending, Aggie."

"I'm not pretending. I'm not mad about the guinea pig. I—"

"You *know* why it was running loose, and you know I've been trying to find it. The lights were going on and off, weren't they? When you came up? Or maybe after you came in? The way they went on and off Christmas Eve."

Pretending never seems to work for me. I guess I need acting lessons. I edged toward the wall so I could position myself for a run for the doorway.

"My family knows where I am," I said, "and people know you're the only person besides Lucy who has a key."

"I don't know what to do with you." He sounded as if he meant it.

I sized him up. He was bigger and stronger, but I was trained in self-defense. Of course for all I knew, so was Cliff. Lesson One. Never underestimate your opponent.

I played for time. "Tell me why. Why you used the guinea pig and the motion detectors to set up an alibi so you could kill Ginger. Why murder, Cliff? If you didn't want to be married to her, why didn't you just divorce her? That's what people normally do."

"You think I set out to kill *Ginger*?"

It was the slight emphasis on that last word that put it all in perspective.

"It was Schaefer, wasn't it? You went to kill him." And at last the reasons clicked into place, as well. Lucy had given me the final clue; I just hadn't yet put it all together. Peter Schaefer had told me his last practice was in Chicago, and that his partner had died. Schaumburg was a suburb of the city, Schaumburg, where Cliff Grable and Marilyn Matthews had been living when Marilyn committed suicide. The same Marilyn who had suffered from a condition that sounded like the one Peter had mentioned to me when he was explaining the theories of pain relief, a condition so painful that she had killed herself to escape it.

Lucy had said that the partner of Marilyn's doctor avoided prosecution. But if I was right, he had *not* avoided Cliff Grable's wrath.

"He killed my Marilyn," Cliff said.

"But her doctor had a different name . . ." I couldn't remember. I edged a little closer to the wall.

"Lawson. James Lawson. Yes, but Peter Schaefer was his partner."

"Did he ever prescribe for her? I thought the courts found him innocent."

"You know a lot."

"And so do other people who will put two and two together if I disappear."

"Schaefer didn't prescribe for Marilyn, no. At first I wasn't going to kill *him*. Then I came here and I met him at your open house. There he was, in the flesh. It almost seemed like a sign when he and that other character Sid was with, what was his name?"

"Bix."

"Yes, Bix noticed my fraternity ring. What an idiot. He'd already discovered somehow that Schaefer was a Delta Xi, so he introduced me, and that's when I realized who he was."

"You'd never seen him?"

"No, everything he did for Marilyn was by phone. I never saw him in court. He was exonerated before it came to that."

"I guess he didn't recognize your name."

"Marilyn went by her maiden name. The suit was in her name, and besides, I'm not even sure Bix used my last name when he introduced me."

"So you thought seeing him at the party was a sign you should kill him?"

"Don't make me sound like some kind of fruitcake. I don't act on signs. I'm a scientist. No, even at that point I was going to let it all go. Then I discovered that my wife"—he cleared his throat, but the rage couldn't be cleared away so easily—"My second wife was seeing him. He was giving her drugs. Just the way his partner gave Marilyn drugs. So damned many drugs! And they made it so easy for her . . ."

"Oh, Cliff . . ." Despite everything, I felt sorry for him. In his mind, Ginger had been a victim, just like Marilyn. He couldn't see that Peter's mission was to help patients, not to hook them on drugs or give them the means to kill themselves. And maybe there was some grain of truth to his suspicions. The jury was still out on whether the kind of medicine Peter practiced harmed or helped.

He was pacing now, unfortunately right in front of the door. Back and forth, but blocking my exit still and watching me as he went.

"Cliff "—I cleared *my* throat—"a moment ago you said you weren't going to kill *him*. You sort of emphasized that last word."

"There's a lot you can do with wiring."

The three-alarm house fire that had killed Peter's partner. I moved away from that subject rapidly, even as I moved closer to the wall and the door. "I know you didn't mean to kill Ginger. What happened?"

"I heard a phone call she made to the doctor's office. I was beginning to get suspicious that something was going on because she kept disappearing. I knew she wasn't with your family, and Emerald Springs is no shopping mecca. So I picked up the extension in the kitchen. Good thing we took a suite, huh? Then when she left the room I found an appointment card in her nightstand, and I knew. I realized I had been wrong to let Schaefer off the hook. So the night after we had dinner here I went to his office. I did some scouting, and I found the pond. I figured it would be easy to rig things so it looked like a simple accident."

"What if somebody else had gotten there first?"

"What's the first thing a homeowner does when he sees fish floating in his pond? He scoops them out so nobody else will see them. I figured that wasn't something Schaefer would leave to his staff or that they would agree to do for him. I was going to set it up while everybody was off at the Christmas Eve service, then whenever he came back? I figured the first thing he would do was check the pond. I planned to disconnect the ground fault interrupter. It's not hard. Make a few adjustments to his extension cord, get inside and do a little work on the circuit breakers. His pump had enough juice, which was thoughtful, wasn't it?"

He was describing Peter's accident perfectly, except the date and victim were wrong. "So what happened on Christmas Eve instead?"

"I didn't really think I'd need an alibi. I had no idea when Schaefer would return and find the fish, and I doubted anyone would suspect it was sabotage. But I figured an alibi wouldn't hurt. Ginger said she was going to the church service, so I dropped her off in town a little early, like she asked, to do some last-minute shopping. When I got here I saw the woman next door gazing at me and the house through her window. I had the guinea pigs to give to your girls that night at dinner. I came in and set the black and white one loose. I had treats, and I scattered food through the rooms that had my switches, so it would come and go. Then the moment it got dark, I left by the back door."

He seemed happy to talk about this, as if he was explaining how he had gotten Ed's train running after decades.

"I guess something went wrong though," I prompted.

"I had a long black overcoat I keep in our car for emergencies. I put it on to cover what I was wearing in case anyone noticed me, then I made my way to Schaefer's. It took a little longer than I'd expected. I was afraid I wasn't going to have time to do everything. But it didn't matter because he was still there. He was just closing the front door. It was Christmas Eve, and he had stayed late to give his patients enough drugs to destroy their lives. On Christmas Eve! I watched him drive away, and I knew killing him was the right thing to do, even if I had to wait for a better time."

He stopped pacing. "And then I realized who his last patient had been."

"Ginger."

"She was coming down the sidewalk when she saw me."

I waited, because what else could I do? Cliff looked like he was far away, most likely reliving the next events. But he was still between me and the door.

He finally glanced at me. "I told her I knew what she was doing and why, and I wanted to help her. She looked at me like I was dirt under her feet. You know that look?"

I was afraid I did. "She wasn't the woman you thought she was, Cliff. But she fooled a lot of people in her time."

"I told her I loved her, that I wanted to help. She said she was sick of my help, that I was nothing but a loser, and it was my fault she had to score drugs from people like Peter Schaefer to sell, that if I had just taken what I'd been offered by my last company, we could have lived in luxury."

"Cliff, she owed money to someone. She was trying to pay it back."

He stepped toward me, his eyes blazing. He pointed a finger at me and jabbed it at my chest. "Does that matter?

Does why she was doing it matter? She was putting those drugs out on the street! I guess she thought I realized that, too, that *that's* what I had meant when I said I knew what she was doing. But until that moment I thought she was just trying to get relief. Then all I could think about was the fact that this woman had used me! She had married me because I was an easy target, and when she didn't get what she wanted, she found a way to find drugs and sell them. Drugs like the ones that killed my Marilyn!"

I stood perfectly still as I scrambled for a way to get around him or disable him badly enough that I could escape. But anything I tried might push him over the edge. And where would that leave me? Free to have another heart-to-heart with Roussos? Or sitting somewhere in the great beyond listening to Ginger describe more bad ideas for another cookbook.

Before I could act I heard steps on the staircase, and a voice.

"Aggie? Who are you talking to?"

It was Sid. Cliff hadn't locked the front door after he came in. Sid had let herself in, and was on her way upstairs.

She appeared before I could shout a warning.

"Hey, Cliff, it's you." Sid smiled at him. "Putting in more switches?"

He stared at her. She cocked her head. "I just came over to see if Aggie realized my sweater's in the closet. I forgot to tell her, and she was taking so long. I thought maybe she was searching the house."

She glanced at me. "Aggie, I finally got in touch with Bix. He's in Pennsylvania with some woman he used to date. He's been there since . . ." Her voice trailed off, and she turned back to Cliff. "Cliff, what's going on?"

He didn't speak.

This time when she looked at me, she was frowning. "Is that another guinea pig? You got Teddy another one after all? Why, to cheer her up because of Moonpie?"

When no one answered she fell silent.

I addressed Cliff. "There are two of us now, Cliff. Are you going to kill two innocent women? Isn't it time to end this a better way?"

"Kill?" Sid squeaked. "What are you talking about? Cliff's a good guy."

A good guy who had never stopped grieving for the first woman he loved, a woman who had been able to explain the world to him. A good guy who had seen a way to avenge her and taken justice into his own hands. How quickly a good guy becomes a bad one.

Sid didn't move away from Cliff. In fact she moved closer. She stretched out her arm and touched his. Just one brief, light touch. "Ginger?"

He gave a sorrowful nod.

She sighed. "Oh, Cliff, she hurt so many people. She just never learned not to. I guess when you're hurting yourself, it's like leveling the playing field."

My little sister. The Material Girl. The princess. And yet here she was, facing a murderer and showing a compassion so genuine, it broke my heart.

Why wasn't she making for the door!

There were more footsteps, and this time the body in the doorway was Detective Roussos, followed by a woman in uniform. Their guns were drawn.

"Step away from him, Miss Kane," Roussos said calmly.

"I was never going to hurt them," Cliff said. "Not Aggie, and not Sid. Just so you know."

Sid backed away and Roussos filled the space where she had been. He holstered his weapon, then he pulled Cliff's arms behind him and snapped handcuffs in place. "Cliff Grable, you're under arrest for the murder of Ginger Grable and the attempted murder of Peter Schaefer. You have the right to remain silent."

19

Life seems to be improving for me. After all, the last time I faced a murderer, I got a concussion. This time I was only badly shaken.

"I'll stop trembling next year," I promised Ed. "That gives me, what, another two and a half hours?"

Junie sat on the sofa, one arm around me, one around Sid, who had been sniffing suspiciously for the past fifteen minutes. "My precious girls. What were you thinking?"

"Well, I wasn't thinking Cliff Grable was a murderer," I admitted. "At least not in time to do anything about it."

Ed had Teddy on one hip and Deena clutched against his side. "Would this be a good time to point out that I told you not to pursue this?"

Ed could be forgiven. His face had drained completely of color as Sid and I gave the abbreviated version of our evening's adventure. Now Deena's sturdy little body was probably keeping him upright. Besides, he wasn't the first man to say "I told you so" tonight.

I managed to get to my feet and put my arms around all

of them. Ed kissed my forehead. Teddy hooked a hand around my neck. Even Deena forgot she's supposed to be breaking away and wrapped her arms around my waist.

"Girls, you come with me." Junie got to her feet and held out her arms for Teddy. "We're going to see if the brownies are ready. Then we're going to fix something good to go with them. That's what this family needs."

They went, although Deena gave one long, searching look before she left the room, just to make sure Sid and I were really okay.

"Let's hear it all." Ed took Junie's place on the sofa and dragged me down beside him.

After Cliff was arrested, Sid and I had driven to the station to give brief statements, but not a lot of detail was needed. Apparently Cliff started talking in the police car and continued in what passed for an interrogation room. For his sake I was sorry the station hadn't settled into nicer quarters. But I guess Cliff wasn't going to be in nicer quarters for a very long time.

So far I'd only said that Cliff killed Ginger by accident, and he was telling me the story when the police showed up. I wasn't going to lie to my daughters, but I needed a little time to sort out how to present it to them.

Now I explained how Cliff had planned to kill Peter and killed Ginger instead when she came out of Peter's office that night. "I guess for the first time he realized what a fool he'd been. And it hit him hard."

"What happened then?" Ed asked.

In an unusual attempt to assuage my curiosity, Roussos had told me the rest of the story as I was leaving the station. Sid was already waiting in the car.

Roussos's lips had drawn down in a grim line, and his eyes had not warmed. "You couldn't stay out of it," he added when he finished. "Even after you promised me."

I couldn't dredge up a dimple to save my life. Instead I turned up my trembling hands in defeat. "What was I supposed to do? Tell Cliff I promised you I wouldn't interfere and ask him to please go somewhere else and confess?"

"Aggie"—and when Roussos uses my first name, I know he's upset—"the guy could have killed you or your sister. We could have gotten there too late. Your luck's going to run out some time. Tell me you're all done with this stuff."

"I don't have any *plans* to do it again."

But Roussos is on to me. He did not looked convinced.

"Somebody's got to keep you on your toes," I said.

He left me in the parking lot at the same defective meter where I had parked before, but good guy that he is, he did take my brand-new parking ticket inside. I hope he gets me off the hook with the meter maid, but I'm afraid in ten days, somebody's going to show up to arrest me. Roussos may want me where he can keep an eye on me.

"So what happened then?" Ed repeated, prodding me back to the moment.

"Apparently when Cliff saw Ginger leaving the office, he was so furious he followed her a little way, and they argued. When he finally realized what was going on, he shoved her. She fell, and when she tried to get up, he shoved her again, and that time her head bounced off a rock. When she went limp he realized what he'd done. It was dark by then. Not a soul was around, and his car was parked at the Victorian. He picked her up in his arms and ran across the street, through yards, hoping he would find somebody to help. She stopped breathing when he was cutting through the Catholic church parking lot. He put her on the ground by the nativity and tried CPR, but she was dead. There wasn't anything he could do."

"So he just left her there?"

"I guess at that point, he figured the only person he could save was himself. So he ran back to the Victorian. On the way he stuffed his old overcoat in a Dumpster behind some business or other, then he let himself into the house through the back. He didn't see the guinea pig, and there was no time to look. He was flipping off the switches upstairs to eliminate the motion detectors when he heard the neighbor at the front door and let her in. The timing was sheer luck, and of course she'd been watching the house and wondering why the lights were going on and off, like he hoped. He sat her at the table to chat, and that's where he was when you and Roussos came to find him. Maybe he was afraid there was blood on his hands, just like there was blood on that coat. Remember, he was washing his hands when you and Roussos arrived, like he was cleaning up after work?"

"And he's been at the house, ever since," Ed said. "Pretending to help you. Pretending that burying Ginger in Emerald Springs was the right thing to do. All because he still wanted to murder poor Peter Schaefer and find the other guinea pig."

"Because if he didn't find the guinea pig, somebody might figure out that he murdered Ginger," Sid said.

"He's gone over there every night to search. But guinea pigs aren't nocturnal, so it was probably sound asleep somewhere. I just lucked out. He tried to keep the motion detector lights switched off at night, just in case. But I flipped the one in the bedroom and left it on when I went downstairs. So the motion detector was on and working when the guinea pig came through after me, probably looking for food."

Ed tightened his arm around me. "How did Roussos figure it out and get there tonight?"

"Roussos knew a lot already. He told me Cliff was always his best suspect. But he couldn't find anything to tie him to the murder, including a motive, and Cliff's alibi, although not perfect, was pretty good. When Roussos started to dig, there were so many people who might have wanted Ginger dead, he got tied up following all the leads. Someday I'd like to sit down and compare notes. He may have found suspects I didn't even know about."

"Remind me not to be a fly on that wall," Ed said. "But what got Roussos there?"

"Cliff thought he had staged the scene at the pond so well that no one would suspect it was a setup. He planned to go back late tonight after he did another search for the guinea pig and fix the plug. He had dismantled the ground fault interrupter, and he wanted to fix it. Only Roussos was already suspicious, so he got a team out right away, and checking the plug was one of the first things they did. Tonight he got confirmation that it had been tampered with, plus a neighbor identified a photo of Cliff and said she had seen him on the street last night. Then she said she thought maybe she'd seen him there before. Maybe on Christmas Eve when she was on her way to church."

"How did Roussos know Cliff was at the Victorian?"

"He didn't. He tried the hotel first. But the Victorian was an obvious possibility, since that's where he'd found Cliff on Christmas Eve. He would have tried our house next."

"I'm glad he thought of the Victorian," Sid said. "But Cliff wasn't going to hurt us."

I leaned over Ed to look at her. "Sid, Cliff killed two people. Ginger and a doctor in Chicago." I told them that story. "And poor Peter Schaefer may not survive."

"No, Peter's going to be okay," Ed said. "I called the hospital right after you called me from the station. He's awake. I talked to his doctor briefly. They're confident he's going to make it."

So Cliff was not quite the evil genius he had believed he was. And for once, scientific miscalculation had definitely been for the best.

"I didn't know what to think when I walked in on you," Sid said.

"What were you saying about Bix? I was a little preoccupied."

"I finally got him on his cell phone. He's with some woman in Pennsylvania, an old girlfriend. He has use of her Porsche, so he finally dropped off the rental. He even paid the fines."

"A man of great integrity."

"Do you know he left Emerald Springs on the *afternoon* of Christmas Eve and drove to her house for the holidays? I asked him point-blank why he stayed in town that extra night, and you know what he told me? He didn't even have the decency to lie. He stayed because of Ginger."

I winced. I was sorry that had come out.

"What a jerk," she said. "But apparently he caught on fast and took off the next afternoon. Maybe he realized Ginger wasn't all the things she claimed to be."

That was my guess, too. Or maybe Ginger had realized that Bix wasn't going to help her solve her money problems. Two users. In a way they'd been perfect for each other.

"I'm going to call Jack," Sid said. "He deserves to hear this from me. I'll leave you two alone."

After she left, Ed and I moved apart just a little so I could look at him. I could hear laughter from the kitchen. We wouldn't be alone for long.

"You know I can't live through too many more of these moments, don't you?" he asked.

"It's not like I want solving murders to be my life's work, Ed. But when they get dumped at our doorstep, what can I do?"

"Next time look the other way. I'm not kidding. Gaze off into the distance. Wear blinders. Step over the body and go on to the grocery store or the library like nobody was lying there."

The doorbell rang and I sprang up to get it.

"Don't think we're done with this conversation," Ed said.

A pretty blonde teenager stood at the front door with a familiar silver tabby in her arms.

"Teddy," I shrieked. "Deena! Look who's here."

The girls came into the hallway, and when Teddy saw Moonpie, she leaped forward and held out her arms.

"Then he *is* your cat," the young woman said. "The one on the poster."

"Where did you find him?" I asked. "We've missed him so much."

The young woman made the transfer into Teddy's arms. Moonpie hung there like a sack of rice, but I thought there was something of a smile on his feline face.

"My aunt lives behind you on the next street," the young woman said. "She found him in her tool shed a couple of days ago. I think he was trapped when she was getting her garbage can. She's been keeping him inside her house and feeding him. But she wasn't sure what to do. She hated to take him to the pound. He's such a nice cat, but she already has three. Then I saw your notice on the telephone pole."

I sniffed. "Just like Sid."

"I'm sorry?"

At least when Sid had run away to our tool shed, we had known where she was. I held out my hand. "I'm Aggie Sloan-Wilcox."

"Angela Grant. My friends call me Angel."

Teddy looked up from crooning to the limp Moonpie. "You're an angel?"

"No, but they call me Angel."

Teddy's eyes got huge behind her glasses.

Angel smiled. "He'll be okay then?"

I looked down at Teddy. "They both will. Please, can I give you a little something for your trouble?"

Angel shook her head and turned away. "Absolutely not. I'm thrilled to bring him home." At the bottom of the porch steps she gave a quick wave. Then she was gone.

Deena and Teddy started to fight over who was going to hold Moonpie. I hadn't introduced the subject of the other guinea pig yet. The second little guy was still at the station chowing down on lettuce and carrots and whatever else the female cop had found for him in the fridge. We could bring him home tomorrow when he was no longer evidence.

We would have more pets than children.

Ed took Moonpie away from the girls and led them all to the sofa. But the excitement wasn't over yet.

"Come get your brownies," Junie called from the kitchen.

Sid came downstairs at a gallop, taking them two at a time. "Jack and I are going out for a drink to celebrate."

I linked arms with her and dragged her into the kitchen. The fragrance of warm chocolate greeted us. "Have a brownie first so Teddy won't be disappointed."

"Ta da!" Junie said.

On the table was a crystal punch bowl, and truly, as punch bowls go, it was spectacular. Light twinkled in every facet, and rainbows sparkled on the wall. The bowl was filled with an exotic mixture of fruit juices with multicolored scoops of sherbet floating on top.

"Junie!"

"I told you my old friend in Tampa would come through." She clapped her hands. "Will it do?"

"The Women's Society will love it. Quick, bar the doors. Don't let the kids near it." I glanced at Sid. "Most especially don't let Sid—"

"You cut it out," Sid said.

The doorbell rang one more time and I started down the hall. I expected to see Jack, but Lucy opened the door and let herself in before I could. "I hear there's a hot game of Clue in progress."

"Hotter than you know." I put my arm around her. "Come have punch, come have brownies. Come hear my story."

"I have a little business to transact first. Where's your mom?"

I guided her into the kitchen. Everybody else was there, too. Apparently Teddy had gotten custody of Moonpie, and she clutched him tightly in her arms. I hoped he was breathing.

"Aggie, we have an offer on the Victorian."

This took me a minute, but I had an excuse for slow reflexes tonight. "It's not even for sale yet."

"Technicalities. We have a buyer, and now we can renovate it for her, just the way she wants it."

"What are you talking about." I realized Lucy was wiggling her eyebrows at Junie, and Junie's face was wreathed in smiles.

"No . . ." I shook my head. "Junie?"

"I'm going to open a quilt shop, precious. You need one in Emerald Springs, and I need a place to settle down. Where better than right here, where I can watch Deena and Teddy grow up?"

"A quilt shop?"

"I've seen every nook and cranny of this country and I don't need to see one bit more. I've been talking to your needleworkers, and they assure me there's a need here. We're going to fix up a little apartment on the second floor and I'll conduct business on the first. Lucy's checked out everything with the city. We've been sneaking around all week to surprise you. But once I saw that house, I just knew. And now we're all set."

"We'll take down the old garage and put in some parking spaces," Lucy said. "Since it's a walkout basement, it looks like a few alterations will bring it up to code so we can finish it for classrooms."

"It won't be huge," Junie said, "but it will be big enough for this town and me."

I looked at Ed. Ed was looking at me, one eyebrow cocked. Junie was coming to town to stay. And what about Vel, who might well have a fondness for Marco DiBenedetto? And Sid, who was going out for drinks with Jack, the best guy she'd dated in forever? Men rooted firmly in our fair town.

Just moments ago Ed had been worried about a little thing like me solving more murders. Now he had to prepare for an invasion.

He stepped forward and put his arms around Junie. "Nobody could be happier," he said. "Welcome to Emerald Springs, Junie. Welcome home."

I sniffed. See, the thing about being married to a minister? As a species they aren't perfect, and the good ones don't claim to be. But I know that my husband doesn't lie.

What a guy.

"Tomorrow I'm going to write a story about an angel," Teddy said. "Will you help me, Junie?"

Junie was teary-eyed, too. "You know I will."

"And a cat and a guinea pig."

"That sounds like a book," I said, hugging Teddy and Moonpie together.

I guess Moonpie got tired of all the togetherness. He wiggled down and took off. Teddy started after him, and Moonpie, who knows how to dodge, ran under the table. She dove for him and banged the table leg, then she tried to stand while she was still underneath. The punch bowl slid forward, sloshing punch as it went.

Ed grabbed it just as it slid off the edge. He stood there with the bowl in his arms, waves of punch and glaciers of sherbet spilling over the edges onto his clothes.

"Next year will be quieter," I said, as Teddy exited, rubbing her head, and Ed carefully set the punch bowl in the middle of the table. "We'll all behave like we were born to this job. Immediately from the stroke of midnight on. I promise, Ed."

I really don't think he believes me.

Don't miss the next Ministry Is Murder Mystery
featuring Aggie Sloan-Wilcox

Beware False Profits

Coming soon from Berkley Prime Crime!

For a minister's wife I spend too much time in bars.

Okay, maybe "bars" isn't exactly the right word. Sure, Don't Go There, in my hometown of Emerald Springs, Ohio, is a working class, slugfest, "Daddy won't you please come home," semibiker bar. And yes, despite the inherent warning in the name, I've "been" there a few times too many. Just asking questions, of course.

Technotes, farther afield, isn't really a bar. It's a dance club with enough blinking lights to trigger seizures and enough taut, gleaming skin to make me sadly aware that my vegetarian diet is not a diet at all. I've had reason to go there, as well.

But the Pussycat Club in Manhattan's West Village? This one is new to my radar, and trust me, it's going to be hard to top. No pun intended, but judging from some of the photographs in the glass case at the entrance, Saturday at the Pussycat is a drag queen review with ladies who are far weightier on "top" than I. And I'm often forced to resort to Frederick's of Hollywood for a bra that fits.

I'm getting ahead of myself, of course. Ed and I did not come to Manhattan to inspect, spectate, or even speculate at the Pussycat Club. We came for a much needed romantic weekend, something that hasn't happened in years.

This all began when my mother Junie decided to call Emerald Springs her home, too. After decades on the road between one craft or renaissance fair and another, Junie decided that hanging her hat, not to mention her quilts, in one place was a treat she deserved. She bought an old Victorian house I was flipping with my friend Lucy Jacobs, and moved in, lock stock and barrel.

With us.

The problem is that the Victorian still needs work, and Junie can't live there yet, much less turn the bottom floor into the quilt shop she envisions. Although we're working on it full tilt now, Lucy and I had more or less been taking our time until Junie signed the contract. Lucy works full time as a realtor, and I, well, I work full time at being a mother to two daughters, a wife to Ed, and inoffensive to the congregation.

This last role is the hardest.

I was not born to be a minister's partner. I'm not sure anyone is, of course, but truly some people seem more inclined toward this job than others. I was raised to be as bohemian and free thinking as my mother. My two sisters and I traveled coast to coast with Junie, attending school here and there, calling new members of Junie's Husband-of-the-Year Club "Daddy" until the next meeting of Junie's Divorced-but-Still-Dear Club. Junie has been married five times, and Sid, Vel, and I each have a different father. Despite our upbringing or because of it, no sisters are closer.

But back to bohemian. On the religion scale Junie's friends ranged from shamans to charlatans, Spiritualists to skeptics. When we went to church as a family, we only went to churches with names that intrigued my mother.

The Holy Raiders Revival Church. The Sect of Secrets and Signs. The House of Heavenly Harmony.

Normally we breezed in and out. As a teenager my personal theology grew to include the following: There may or may not be a God. He or She may look like Lord Ganesh, the Hindu elephant god, or perhaps some amalgam of an elephant as described by three mythical blind men who are respectively touching a leg, a trunk, or a tail.

Then I met Ed Wilcox, seminary student and devoted attendee of the Unitarian Universalist Church. They were certainly more orthodox than I was, but I did feel at home immediately.

Cut to the twenty-first century and the Consolidated Community Church of Emerald Springs, Ohio, where I update the archives, throw rip-roaring holiday open houses, and find naked bodies on the parsonage porch.

You have to remember, I came to this job without a résumé.

Now that Ed has served three churches, one of the things I've learned is that congregations take up most waking hours, and sleeping hours aren't sacred, either. Ed and I have learned to steal moments for conversation and intimacy whenever we can find them. Unfortunately sneaking around can get wearing. When Junie moved into the parsonage and we had one more person in the house to contend with, things began to deteriorate.

So when a Harvard classmate of Ed's suggested we come to the Big Apple and stay in his apartment some weekend while he was off on sabbatical, we bought tickets on the first cheap flight out. And here we are. Standing at the entrance of the Pussycat Club in the West Village on a chilly spring evening, looking at the line-up for the night's entertainment.

"We wouldn't be here if you hadn't given your cell phone number to Norma," I reminded Ed yet again. "What were you *thinking*?"

"I was thinking there might be an emergency." Ed had not come to New York with the appropriate Pussycat clothes. He was wearing a pinstripe dress shirt and pleated khaki pants. He'd planned to ward off the chill with a wool crewneck his mother gave him for Christmas, but I'd reminded him we were not having tea after a cricket match and made him leave it at the apartment.

"For pity's sake, Ed, you knew Norma would give out your number if a parishioner's dog got fleas. You might as well have published it in the *Flow*." Norma: our garrulous church secretary. The *Flow*: our Emerald Springs daily.

"In this case Norma gave it out because we have a missing person," he reminded me. Yet again.

I watched Ed shiver and felt a smidgen of regret that I'd denied him the crewneck. Had it only been black. Or fraying at the cuffs.

I stepped aside so that two guys in their sixties, one with a parochial school uniform skirt over dark trousers, could get through the door. "I really can't believe Joe Wagner is missing. And I really can't believe he was ever *here*."

The Wagner saga had started this morning. Just as Ed and I were getting out of bed after a spectacular marital booty call, Ed's cell phone had chirped Beethoven's Fifth. We'd been planning to find a local deli where we could buy lox and real bagels, spread the *New York Times* from one end of the table to the other, and drink quarts of strong coffee. The rest of the day had been filled with glorious possibilities. But the call had changed everything.

I'd only heard Ed's end, which had gone something like: "Uh huh. No. Of course you're upset. I can't imagine."

I had nearly fallen back asleep, but when Ed put down the phone, I recognized the look on his face. The sweet afterglow of sex, untarnished by the soundtrack of Saturday morning cartoons and Junie's morning mantra was no longer reflected there. This was unmistakably the look of a minister with another problem to worry about.

"Don't tell me," I'd said. "Oh, please don't tell me we have to go home before tomorrow night."

"That was Maura Wagner."

Maura, husband, Joe, and son, Tyler, are members of our church, although of the three Wagners, Maura is least often on the Tri-C scene. Joe's a big, handsome guy, the director of our tri-county food bank and everybody's friend. Need tables set up for a potluck supper? Joe will come early to help. Need somebody to count the dollar bills in the collection plate after church? Joe's the man. Need a chairman for the annual pledge drive? You get the picture. Joe is one of those people who keeps churches healthy. He shakes hands and gives out orders of service. He gives laughing toddlers rides on his strong shoulders and reminds teenage girls that the male of the species does eventually grow up and clean up well.

Maura Wagner is Joe's opposite. She is small and fragile, with Easter-egg blue eyes and a halo of curly blond hair. If Maura stubs her toe, she calls Joe and asks him what profanity she can use. She is weak to his strong, unfocused where he is forceful.

The roles seem to suit them both because from the outside their marriage looks happy. Seemingly the only real bump on their road to marital bliss was the discovery that Tyler, now fourteen, was diabetic. But even this was a bump, not a mountain they couldn't scale. Between Joe's attention to proper doses of insulin and Tyler's resilient spirit, Tyler's life seems normal and happy.

Maura Wagner was one of the last people I expected to bother Ed when we were off on a holiday. I wasn't even sure she knew how to dial a telephone.

"Did somebody die?" I asked, afraid I already knew the answer.

"No, but it's not much further down the list." Ed ran his hand over his chin. For months there's been a beard there, not a very successful one. Last week he disposed of it, leaving chin pallor and a small scar on one cheek. He still forgets it's gone.

"Please don't make me guess." I could envision all manner of crises. I've had too much experience with crisis lately, and was not longing for more.

"Joe's disappeared."

"Disappeared is a big word. Is he late coming home from the grocery store? Sitting through a twelve inning game at Jacob's Field? Or, did he make off with their entire bank account last week and she's only just noticed?"

"No, he was here, in the city, for a meeting. And he didn't come home."

"Joe in New York?"

"Supposed to be." Ed rubbed his hand over his hair, which was still, fortunately, intact. It seemed to calm him. He dropped down to the bed beside me. "He was supposed to be home last night, but he didn't show. At first Maura thought maybe his plane was just late."

"Then she knew what flight he was on?"

Ed looked at me as if my IQ had suddenly dropped into an unacceptable range. "Aggie . . ."

"So okay, Maura is not a detail person. But knowing Joe, he left all the information. He probably laminated copies and posted them all over the house. He probably made Tyler memorize arrival times and airline phone numbers to repeat back to Maura at hourly intervals."

"Maura says Joe goes to the same meeting in Manhattan every month and has for over a year. He leaves on the first flight out of Columbus on the third Thursday and comes home at the same time on the third Friday evening. And that's all she knows."

"Only this time he didn't come home? And he didn't call her?"

"That's the strange part. Apparently she did get a call. She has caller ID, so she knows it came from Joe's cell. But the call was garbled, the way they are when the tower's too far away, or the caller's inside a building. She thinks it was Joe on the other end, but she's not even sure of that. And she couldn't understand a word."

I could just imagine how frustrating this had been. But Joe *had* called home. Maura knew he was alive and probably just held up in New York. Why had she bothered Ed?

"Did she call his hotel?" Ed gave me the "look" again and I narrowed my eyes. "You're telling me she doesn't know where Joe stays when he's here?"

"Apparently he moves around. She says he shops for the best deal every time. She doesn't keep up."

"This doesn't sound believable. Joe knows Tyler could have a problem while he's away. He would never leave without telling Maura where he's staying."

"That's why he carries the cell phone."

"So, has she tried to call him back?"

"She's not that helpless. Repeatedly, apparently. Through the night and all morning until she called here. The whole church knows we're in New York this weekend, even Maura."

"What does she expect you to do?" I looked at him and saw the answer. "No, Ed . . . We aren't going to spend our only Saturday in Manhattan looking for Joe, are we? Please tell me we aren't."

But of course we did.

Now, after a day of following clues, here we were at the Pussycat Club on a borderline seedy West Village street. There had been compensations. I've done a lot of detective work on my own this year, and this was the first time I hadn't been forced to shield my activities from my husband's suspicious gaze. Today Ed and I had been a team, albeit a reluctant one. And even if our activities hadn't been as much fun as a leisurely stroll down Fifth Avenue, at least we'd been together.

"Let's go over what we know one more time," I said now, "and maybe we'll have a great idea, which will include hopping in a cab and going somewhere else. Like out to a great restaurant for dinner."

"Repeating the facts won't change them."

I repeated them anyway. "Joe was supposed to be in the city at a meeting of an organization called Funds for Food. He told Maura he came here to attend a similar meeting every month."

"And now we know there is no organization in New York called Funds for Food, and that nobody at any of the local food banks has heard of an organization by that name." Ed glanced at his watch.

Behind us, the perpetual serenade of police sirens and honking horns was crescendoing. I spoke louder. "Our repeated calls to Joe's cell phone have gone unanswered."

Three guys pushed past us. One was dressed as a cowboy, the second a cop, and the third was unmistakably an Indian chief. His headdress nearly didn't clear the doorframe. They were three guys short of the Village People. I stifled the impulse to raise my arms and make the letters *YMCA* in salute.

Apparently Ed didn't even consider this, because he was still listing facts. "Unfortunately just as we were about to give up and tell Maura we'd hit a brick wall, you had to try one more time."

I wrinkled my nose in apology. "Sorry, I get going and I just forget to stop."

"Whoever picked it up—"

"A guy with a gravelly voice—" I reminded him.

"Said there was nobody named Joe Wagner there."

"But just before Gravel Voice spoke, I heard—"

Ed sang the finale: "Pussycat, pussycat, I love you. Yes, I do."

"Welcome to the West Village's own Pussycat Club," I finished on an exhale.

"See any good reason to hail a cab?" Ed glanced at his watch again.

I opened my mouth to say no, that it looked like we were stuck with paying the cover charge, and trooping inside to see what we could discover. But as I avoided eye contact with my significant other, my gaze fell on the photos displayed in the case just in front of us.

"Ed . . ."

"You know, we could be in and out of there in minutes, Aggie. But first we have to go *in*."

"Ed . . ." I took his arm. "I, well . . ." I turned him a little. "Look at these photos and tell me what you see."

I didn't want to influence him, so I averted my eyes and watched as three heavily made up women in sequins and fishnet stockings sauntered into the club.

Ed sounded tired. It had been that kind of a day. "I see what I'd expect to. The Pussycat Club's a no-holds-barred kind of place. Old fashioned burlesque on Mondays and Tuesday, Vaudeville on Wednesdays and Sundays, Female impersonators on Thursdays and Saturdays. Something for every . . ."

He stopped. I let my eyes drift back into focus. "That's some coat, isn't it?" I said.

Ed leaned closer. But I didn't have to watch to know exactly where his eyes were riveted. He was staring at the gorgeous dame, third from the left, posed in a stunning full-length fur coat with just enough shapely leg peeking out the opening. How many animals had gone to the happy hunting ground to provide enough pelts for that number? Because the gorgeous dame had to be six-foot-three in her bare feet and broad shouldered to boot. She had straight black hair and thick bangs, like a young Cher, and the toothy, flirty smile was Cher's as well.

But the face was not. Nope, under the false eyelashes, the layers of foundation, the close, close shave, the face was even more familiar.

"Maybe we've been working on this so many hours we're just seeing him everywhere," Ed said at last.

"Or maybe we're looking at the real reason Joe Wagner comes to New York once a month."

We both stared at the photo a minute longer. Then Ed sighed. "Exactly what are we going to say to Joe if we find him in there dressed like that?"

I took Ed's arm and pulled him toward the door. "I Got You, Babe?"